IT WAS VERY DARK WHEN I WOKE.

I knew with absolute certainty, just as I had known earlier, that someone else was in the room with me. Fumbling in the darkness, my hand touched something soft and unfamiliar. My heart almost stopped beating as I realized what it was: human hair, long and thick, on a level with the edge of the bed.

I screamed loudly and tore my hand away. My mind was not working at all. I was in a blind, animal panic, utterly terrified by that single, repulsive touch. I lay in the darkness like someone stunned, unable to think or act.

On the other side of the bed there now began a singularly unpleasant rustling sound. It is impossible to describe it adequately. Dry, insect-like, powdery, as though something long dead were alive and moving. It seemed to be creeping closer. . . .

Also by Jonathan Aycliffe

Naomi's Room

By the same author (writing as Daniel Easterman)

The Ninth Buddha
Brotherhood of the Tomb
Night of the Seventh Darkness

Published by HarperPaperbacks

WHISPERS IN THE DARK

IN THE DARK

JONATHAN AYCLIFFE

HarperPaperbacks
A Division of HarperCollinsPublishers

HarperPaperbacks   *A Division of* HarperCollins*Publishers*
10 East 53rd Street, New York, N.Y. 10022

Cover illustration by Edwin Herder

First printing: May 1993

Printed in the United States of America

HarperPaperbacks and colophon are trademarks of HarperCollins*Publishers*

10 9 8 7 6 5 4 3 2 1

For Beth
Who Has Always Haunted Me
And Always Will

ACKNOWLEDGMENTS

Many thanks to everyone who assisted with this second chiller: my editors, Patricia Parkin in London, and Karen Solem and Katie Tso in New York, whose gentle criticisms brought the text to life; my indefatigable agent, Jeffrey Simmons; my wife, Beth, whose sensitivity in these matters is unsurpassed; and Barbara Heathcote, the librarian in charge of local studies at Newcastle Central Library, for giving me direct access to her special collections and making numerous suggestions.

They shall inherit it . . . forever.

Exodus 6:8

St. Botolph's College
Elvet Place
University of Durham
Durham City

4 September 1991

Rev. Norman Savage
The Vicarage
Kirkharle
near Kirkwhelpington
Northumberland

Dear Norman,

Well, here they are: the papers I promised, the ones you wanted so badly. I wish I'd never said a word to you about them. You can make of them what you like, but don't blame me if they give you bad dreams. It's only right that I should put them into your hands, I suppose: they're bound to have a special interest for you as vicar of your parish. And perhaps . . . Perhaps there are things you vicars do in cases like this. I'd like to think so. I'd like to be sure she is at peace. You'll understand. When you've read her journal to the end, you'll understand. If you can read it to the end.

You wanted me to tell you all I know about the journal, how it came into my possession, and so on. Well, there's not a lot to tell, really. Let me be perfectly frank, Norman. By the time you get to the end of this thing—if you get that far—you'll be wondering if it isn't all some sort of elaborate hoax. Of course, you know me better than that, you know I'd never perpetrate such a thing. Apart from anything else, it's hardly in my interest to play fast and loose with things like this. It's enough of an embarrassment that I found them in the first place.

But you may start thinking, poor Simpkins, he's been taken in hook, line, and sinker. He needs to get out in the world more, take a few deep breaths of real air. Maybe I do, but I can assure you this thing is no hoax. Or if it is, it's so damned elaborate, so clever in every verifiable detail, that the hoaxer is a genius. His greatest genius, of course, having been to hide the journal so well that it was only ever discovered by the wildest chance in the first place.

Look, let me tell you straight: I think it is important these matters be believed, that they be treated with respect, with gravity. The pages themselves breathe conviction. You haven't read them yet, you don't know what I'm talking about, but you

will, if you have an ounce of feeling in you. Or awe.
I know I did. Believed them, that is. I'd only read a
few pages, I'd scarcely begun, but I knew, I knew
for a certainty that she was writing from her heart.
Yes, that's what I mean, the heart: she felt every
word she wrote, she wasn't performing some literary exercise. How could it have been otherwise,
under the circumstances? After what she had seen.
And heard.

I've had them checked out, Norman, as much
as I was able: the names, the dates, the addresses,
the workhouse entries, electoral rolls, burial records. Everything fit, Norman. She had a good memory, our Charlotte, and an eye for detail. The point
is, all the facts check out. It's a genuine document,
and I for one believe she saw and heard everything
she says she did.

I found the narrative a month ago among my
father's things. Do you remember, just after the
funeral, I told you there was a lifetime's junk to
clear out? My mother, God bless her, never kept
things very tidy, and he, if anything, was worse.

Most of it consisted of papers directly relating
to his practice, patient records and that sort of
thing, the accumulations of a busy city GP. I've
passed it all on to the man who's taking over the
practice, a young chap by the name of Calvert. No
doubt he'll have thrown out half of it himself by
now.

The present document was in a file he kept in
his safe, along with his bonds and insurance documents. She'd been his patient, of course: I was able
to check that right away from his files. She came to
him in October 1968 suffering from recurrent de-

pression. He gave her the usual nostrums, but they did her little good. Father was the old-fashioned sort of family doctor. Instead of packing her full of more little pills or shunting her on to a so-called specialist, he talked with her. Judging by the entries on her notes, he spent a lot of time with her just talking.

And then, in 1970, he suggested she write down a proper record of what was troubling her. I think it troubled him. He had his breakdown the following year.

Well, Norman, it's in your hands now. You needn't say anything about it if you don't want to. But, knowing you, you will.

Best wishes,
John

CHAPTER 1

June 1970

When I was a little girl, they told me that God was good,
that God was love. They whispered to me in the winter
nights, saying God loved little children. There was a
hymn they made us sing. We sang it in the workhouse.
Every morning when I was a little girl, and twice on
Sundays:

> Little beams of rosy light,
> Who has made you shine so bright?
> Little blossom sweet and rare,
> Who has made you bloom so fair?
> 'Tis our Father, God above,
> He has made us. He is Love.

That was sixty-eight years ago. A lifetime. I know
better now. I have known better since I was fourteen.

God is not good. God is not even wicked. God is just indifferent. I remember praying to Him all that winter, that particular winter, with its endless wind and ice, but He never answered me. Nor has He answered me since. I have not lost my belief in Him. I know He exists. It is just that I know I cannot depend on Him, not in the things that really matter.

Dr. Simpkins says I should put my story down on paper. He says it will do me good to get it out of my system. What does he know, what does anybody know? But I'll do it to humor him. And it will give me something to do of an evening, now the nights are drawing in again. The long nights, when I lie awake for hours listening. Breathing and listening. The way I did all those years ago. That lifetime ago.

What do I listen for? Well, that will have to wait until I have told some of my story. Not even Dr. Simpkins knows, do you, Doctor? But he will soon, I will put it all down on paper as he recommends. The beginning of it all. The end of it all.

I came into this world in December 1887. It was the year of the Royal Jubilee Exhibition in Newcastle, at which my father had a stand. A year of snowstorms and gales and a protracted miners' strike in Northumberland. My brother Arthur was born eighteen months later. He was a sickly child at first and nearly died. My mother came near her own death having him, and the doctor said she was to have no more children. Well, that was not usual for those days, people had large families (and quite a few in the churchyard, as often as not). When I was little, I used to wonder why it was that Arthur and I were the only ones. Nowadays that's quite a normal thing, but then they would look at you strangely if you said there were only two of you. They would pity you, though Arthur and I never felt any need for pity. At least not at first, not when we were very small.

My father, Douglas Metcalf, was a wealthy man, a clever man who had made his money in the Tyneside chemical industry. Those were the days of the big alkali companies around Haverton Hill, and my father set up his own saltworks between Tennant's and Allhusen's. That was four years before I was born. He used the new Solvay process, and in a few years had made enough money to build the house I was born in, Kenton Lodge. We lived in Gosforth, in what was then more or less open country to the north of Newcastle, not so very far from where I live now.

We would go to Bridlington every year for two weeks' holiday. I remember the softness of those nights. An orchestra played in the glass pavilion, popular songs of the day. The music drifted to my window every night, and there was a sound of waves in the distance as the sea fell against the shore. The music and the falling waves lulled me to sleep. Sometimes I would wake in the middle of the night, when the orchestra and its audience had long gone to their beds, and the waves continued to fall in the stillness, and I knew that the sea went on for ever, out into the night. And every year when we came back to the city, the sounds and smells of the seaside would remain with me. They are with me now; very faint, but unmistakable.

I remember a calico nightdress with crocheted work on its neck and sleeves. And the gas lamp burning above my bed, the flame like a golden halo. But ours was one of the first houses to have electricity installed. Not many people now remember that the world's first electric light was lit here in Newcastle. That was exactly nine years before I was born, to the very day. Joseph Swan demonstrated the prototype of his famous lamp before a gathering of the Newcastle Chemical Society. My father was in the audience, was indeed a member of the committee that year.

And I remember the fire in the night nursery, turning to ashes as the winter night went on. And an apple tree that grew right outside the day nursery, where Arthur and I were put to play when we were small, with Hannah, our nurse. When I was older, Hannah would take me for a walk each afternoon, with Arthur in his pram, and then both together, one on either side of her. Sometimes we were allowed to buy sweets in a shop on the High Street run by Mrs. Clutch: Cupid's Whispers and Tom Thumb Drops, Spanish ribbon, everlasting sticks, Red Sugar Cakes, and a stretchy toffee called Wigga Wagga.

The memories never leave me, never so much as fade. Why should that be, when so much else has gone, so much of the past, the precious things, the things I once thought I would never forget and now have? He comes to my thoughts every day without fail. Arthur. Arthur and the others, they are abiding presences even now. I have become an old woman almost without realizing it. This year I shall be eighty-three; my mind is clear enough, but my body has grown to be an encumbrance. For sixty-nine years I have been afraid, I have known daily, blatant, unreasonable fear. And yet what is there truly to be afraid of? Memories? Faces that are always there? Voices that come to me in the early morning, whispering as they used to whisper all those years ago?

It is trite to remark how much has changed since then, how the whole world is different, but nonetheless it is true. The world changes, but we go on, with our memories intact, and our fears, thinking nothing has really changed, that we are the same people we ever were. Sometimes I wake in the mornings, silly old woman that I am, and expect to see my mother standing over my bed, watching as she used to watch, perhaps smiling at me. Or Hannah, dead these sixty years or more.

Or else Arthur. Arthur as I first remember him, a small boy coming to my light-filled room to tell me his dreams. Such dreams. I remember none of them now, but I can still see his face, the expression of fear on it, the uncertainty the night had left there, like a faint scar.

He was such a sweet child. Nowadays that's almost an insult. My daughters find it hard to understand why my grandchildren are such a worry to me. But they dash about so fiercely and watch such violent programs on television. Oh, I know it isn't fashionable to say such things, but when I see them shouting and yelling, even swearing, I cannot believe they are quite children. Arthur was gentle. He took care of things. And people.

And he was such a pretty child. I don't mean that he was a pampered, ringleted thing, a little boy off a chocolate box, in a velvet suit, carrying a hoop. There was nothing simpering about Arthur, my father would never have stood for that. He was not mollycoddled or spoiled in any way, neither of us was. But the gentleness I spoke of, the awareness of others and their feelings, that was something innate in Arthur, something no nurse or teacher inculcated, and it made everyone love him. There were times, when I was small, when I felt quite jealous of Arthur, of the way both men and women doted on him in that rather prim way they had then. But I did not stay jealous long, for I loved Arthur like the rest of them and wanted only the best for him.

He's dead now, of course, he's been dead for a very long time. But sometimes I tell myself secretly that that isn't true, that Arthur is still alive, that he's here now, in the house, watching me. Watching me quite quietly, the way he used to watch me in bed before I woke. Sometimes I think I could speak to him, just turn my head and say, "Hello, Arthur," and he would reply the way he used to, all those years ago: "Hello, Charlotte. It's been a long time."

I live in a different part of Newcastle now, in Jesmond, among strangers, men and women who pass me in the street and nod, but never say good day. When I was young, a man would doff his hat and nod when he passed a woman of his acquaintance; well, a gentleman would do it for a lady if they passed one another. But not now. That's another of the things that have changed. Still, I mustn't grumble. The young man in the post office on Clayton Road is always very friendly.

Jesmond used to be a better place, what some called a "posh" part of town. It was where the well-off lived, Jews and businessmen, solicitors, bankers, that sort of person, the better sort. Many of my parents' friends lived there. I remember there were plenty of big houses, grand houses three and four stories high, with fine gardens in front set off with railings. Though none was as grand as Kenton Lodge. Most of the railings came down during the last war, of course, and have never been replaced.

It's all changed now. When people started having small families, they didn't want houses that size any longer. Most were sold off and divided into flats and bed-sitters, but a few remain. I still live in this house facing the park. John and I bought it after we were married. He died here, in this room.

I live here in a little peace and a little pain. I live from day to day, hoping for nothing. John left me well provided for, I have money of my own, quite a lot of money, I do not fear poverty. What is there to hope for at my age? I live now only to remember. And that is the hardest thing of all. Not the remembering, I don't mean that, remembering is easy; but the enduring of memory, of the sensations memory brings with it.

I was widowed twenty-five years ago. For so much of my life I have been alone. It is not loneliness that frightens me, however; not loneliness, not hopelessness, not weariness. Death will take care of all that soon enough. No, what frightens me is the smell of memories, the sound and taste and feel of them, knowing there is no one else with whom I can share them. Old Simpkins suspects as much. I have hinted at certain things in his presence. That is why he has suggested this therapy. Maybe it will do some good.

I go to St. George's church on Osborne Road, on Sundays, when I have the stamina for God. There are quite a few of us, old ladies and a few old men, refugees from our oversized houses or our little, tidy flats: a silent, gray tribe full of memories. But none of them share my memories. Only I know what lurks in here. The others would not believe me.

CHAPTER 2

IT ALL BEGAN WITH A SPRAINED ANKLE. OR SO I AT ONE TIME, looking for ultimate causes, used to think. When my mother was seventeen, she slipped on some broken paving on the Elizabethan walls of Berwick-upon-Tweed, twisting her ankle. She had gone there with her entire family—her mother, father, two sisters, an aunt and uncle, and three cousins—for their annual holiday by the sea. It was not a severe injury, but bad enough to keep her off her feet for well over a week. There was talk of going home, but they had barely arrived, the weather was glorious, and she insisted they stay. She would remain in her room at the Crown Hotel, well cosseted and supplied with romantic novels, and visited from time to time by her relations, as they came and went from their holiday pursuits.

Those pursuits included a long-planned boat trip to Lindisfarne, or Holy Island, if you prefer, not far off the coast, a few miles to the south of Berwick. It was, I think, the third day of my mother's invalid existence, and already she had grown tired of the four walls of her room and taken up residence on an antique chaise longue in one of the sitting rooms downstairs. She was by now fretting a good deal at her confinement and growing bored of smoldering glances and base betrayals. I believe she came close to insisting that they take her with them after all, but it was out of the question. The trip would involve much climbing up and down steep steps in order to get in and out of the boat, not to mention some very brisk walking once they got to their destination. Reluctantly she agreed to stay behind.

After lunch, she was helped out to the garden for the benefit of the sea air, though she kept herself well within the shade, for in those days (and mine too) a tan was something thought most unbecoming in a lady. As the afternoon wore on, however, her little arbor grew quite chilly. The sun, which had been fat with warmth all morning, had taken itself off behind a bank of clouds, clouds that had, by midafternoon, become a solid mass that filled the sky. The sea breeze that had been so delightful when she first ventured into the garden, was now growing petulant and uncomfortable. In the end, she returned to the sitting room, gloomily watching the weather worsen through a window that was soon streaked by heavy rain.

The squall grew rapidly into a fully blown storm, as it will do in that region. It was dark by teatime, hours before sunset, and my mother was beginning to worry that her family would be obliged to spend the night on Lindisfarne. The hotel manager reassured her, saying there was a comfortable inn on the island where they could put up if need be. She tried to relax, knowing they would never be so foolish as to set out again in weather like that.

Nor did they. For the boatman, seeing what sort of weather was setting in, had made his mind up to stay at the island, come what may. No one knew quite what happened after that. There seems to have been an argument, during which my grandfather, a headstrong man, had angry words with the boatman, all to no good. They never went near the inn. One of them must have suggested returning to the mainland on foot. Holy Island, as you may know, is connected to the shore by a causeway about three miles in length. People still make miscalculations there, and the new causeway road has "refuges" for hapless drivers caught by high tide, but there was none of that then. They took the old pilgrim route over the seabed, seemingly safe when the tide was out, but utterly treacherous to those unfamiliar with its vagaries.

No one could ever guess how far they got. Perhaps they were only yards from the shore when the tide, speeded by the storm, rushed in and swept them out to sea.

The boat returned the next morning and the alarm was raised. Inquiries along the coast drew a succession of blanks, and no one was in any doubt about the outcome. By the evening of the first day it was a foregone conclusion that all had been drowned. The first bodies were found the next afternoon, washed up on the Fenham Flats, not far south of the causeway.

There was another aunt, a spinster by the name of Harriet, who lived in Tynemouth, where she kept a guest house in the summer months. My mother made her way to her, bewildered with grief, and remained with her until she met and married my father. That was three years later. I still remember Harriet, a kindly, silly woman in a high bonnet trimmed with Nottingham lace, eager to please, and a frequent visitor to our home until her death when I was eight.

My mother had other relatives, none of them close, all of them long since gone to Australia or Canada or South Africa. They were notified of the deaths, according to the formalities of the time, and a few replied in due course, in equally formal letters written in haste between sheepshearing and doing the accounts. My mother told me all about them years later, how dreary those duty letters had been, how she could never hope for more than stilted words and clumsy sentences, how there had never been and could never be a "connection." And yet how much grief could have been avoided had even one of those exiles shown a little feeling then or later.

With my grandfather's death, my mother became something of an heiress. And in time her good looks added to whatever allure her fortune gave her, bringing over a dozen proposals of marriage by the time she was nineteen, all of which, under Harriet's tutelage and her own presence of mind, she turned down flat. She was never gay, she would not go to balls, she scarcely went to church; but word of her money and her looks was not slow in spreading, and she was pursued. Pursued, but never captured.

Until my father came on the scene, that is. How often I remember her telling me of their first meeting, and the next, and the next. She was swept off her feet, he made her dizzy. And when he asked her to marry him, she did not hesitate for a moment. She told me all this later, when I was old enough to understand a little. Even then, years later, she was full of him, she could not stop talking about him to anyone who would listen, even to me, his daughter, or to Arthur. It was almost blasphemous, the way she worshiped him.

We worshiped him, too, of course, Arthur and I, for he was everything my mother thought and, I suspect, much more. Fathers in those days were supposed to be grim and distant creatures who left the care of their children in the hands of wives and nannies. But our father was never a man of his time. He spent hours with us, playing games, reading stories, listening to our worries.

Oh, dear. I've made him sound an awful prig, almost as bad as Arthur. What will you think of me, Doctor, describing my father like that? You won't believe me, will you? You'll say I'm making it all up, compensating for my loss of his affections by creating a fairy-tale prince to take his place. But stuff and nonsense I say. He was a wonderful father, he was the most wonderful father in the world, and Arthur and I loved him uncontrollably. I don't suppose children do nowadays, I expect they have much lower expectations and suffer from all sorts of neglect. But we were never neglected.

Father was a busy man, of course, but not like so many of these modern businessmen, always at the office, carrying on with their secretaries, chasing money as though it had just been invented. No, our father worked hard and had a full social life, but he spent time with us whenever he could, which was often. Sundays, in particular, were sacred.

His great love, his truly great love, was to attend the meetings of the Literary and Philosophical Society in Westgate Road. Once a week, from autumn through to summer, he would kiss us good night and set off in his evening clothes for a lecture on the latest scientific discovery or, for that matter, the works of Homer. He was omnivorous, there was nothing he could not find a use for in that vast brain of his. How clever I thought him, most of all on the two occasions when he was invited to deliver lectures himself. My own father, and all those great men listening to him in their bow ties and stiff white shirts. I thought him the cleverest and the hand-somest man among them, a young god. My mother had converted me to her idolatry. Well, he was my god then, and I have never found a better since.

If they could hear me in church, Doctor, what do you think they would make of me? Eh? An old woman crip-pled with blasphemies. Weighed down with her idolatry, her worship of a long-dead mother and father, her deifi-cation of a brother she will very soon join in death. Perhaps you think, too, how heinous of her, how very improper. I don't know your mind, of course, you never talk to me about yourself. Perhaps you don't think it heinous, merely silly or "Victorian," that all-purpose epithet with which your generation is wont to consign mine to the dustbin of all things sugary and sentimental and hypocritical.

Well, it's true, we did suffer from all those things. And worse, much worse. Ours was an age of very proper vices, and I pray we never see another like it. And yet . . . And yet, I was truly happy then. Not merely in retrospect, in the shadow of what happened later, but truly and deliriously happy all of my childhood. I wanted for nothing, I was healthy, I loved and was loved, sum-mer seemed to last for ever, the whole world moved gently and carried me with it, without distress, as though on a sea without waves. And there was Arthur.

He came to me one day when I was about seven, in floods of tears. He'd seen a man outside beating a horse, the way some people did then, quite thoughtlessly. I don't know why, but he always came to me first from about that age, when he had any fears or worries. Father was at work, so we sought out Mother in her sitting room. Hannah was with us, of course, she was never far away, but she had already learned the unwisdom of trying to rein her young master in too far.

That was the thing, you see, the thing I can't get across. Arthur was pretty and gentle and all of that, and I loved him on account of it, who wouldn't have? But that was simply the superficiality of Arthur, it wasn't what I really remember. There was a force about him, something unstoppable, I mean a real force that no one could bottle up.

He stormed into Mother's room that day—barely six years old—opened the door and stormed in, raging, furious, in tears all at once.

"The poor horse," he shouted, "he's beating the poor horse. And when I tried to stop him he only laughed."

I remember the bewilderment in my mother's face. She looked at Arthur, then at me, then Hannah. We did our best to explain, but Arthur was losing patience. There was no time to be wasted. He rushed off suddenly, out of the room, heading for the front door, which was still open, and out into the street, where we found him shouting abuse at the carter.

I cannot remember now quite how that incident ended, for my memory of it is so focused on Arthur and the fury he displayed. Years later my father would still ask my mother to relate the scene, so disappointed was he to have missed the fun.

And there was so much fun. No matter that Arthur was a boy and I a girl in a time when boys and girls grew up in different worlds. We were never separate for more than an hour or so at a time. We slept in separate rooms, but not many nights passed when Arthur would not sneak down to my room for a story or a game. We were caught and spanked for it often enough, but we kept it up with a determination that surprises me now.

Arthur, dear Arthur, exquisite and fearful Arthur, you hate all this, don't you? My reminiscences, my praise. You always hated fluff, didn't you? I can still see you, after tea with the Misses Singleton, screwing up your face and shouting "What a load of fluff and twaddle." Your favorite words. Are you there now, mouthing those old rebukes at me, "fluff and nonsense," "fluff and stuff"?

I can see him so clearly, Doctor, God forgive me if seeing the dead is a sin: his eyes, his hands, his fingernails. Lying in bed, that time he was ill with jaundice, and it was my job to see he stayed there; setting fire to cook's hat, and taking a beating for it, and coming to me afterward, not in tears, but in delight at what he had done, for it had been such a particularly monstrous hat, and he had so hated it, as he must hate all this; sucking sweets in church, and all the while a rapt, angelic look on his face; running like a hare at the seaside, a strand of seaweed in one hand, streaming behind him; rolling colored eggs down the hill on the town moor at Easter, one after another, so they would crack at the bottom.

The best times were at Christmas, a time of year that Arthur loved above all others. It snowed at Christmas every year, or so my memory tells me. We were great believers, Arthur and I, like all children of our creed and class in those days, and everything was jumbled up in a glorious mental confusion: the baby Jesus, the Wise Men bearing gifts, Santa Claus, angelic voices, Donner and Blitzen, the fairy on top of our tree.

The magic has gone now, and not merely because I am so much older. They have taken the heart out of Christmas. I try as best I can to fill all this emptiness with memories, but I don't suppose anyone notices. My great-grandchildren are greedy for loud games and television, they want rooms full of toys, they think Father Christmas is a bit of a joke. I remember sitting in the window of my father's study, overlooking the garden, with Arthur beside me, watching the sky grow radiant with snow and with that strange pearllike light it brought. There was a fire in every room, burning with resinous logs, and candles, and holly we had picked ourselves, and ribbons we had tied, and a tree heavy with lights that flickered in the darkness. All gone now, all vanished, all packed away in the trunks and boxes of memory.

I've never lied to you, Doctor, I'm incapable of it, I could never tell a deliberate untruth. I do admit there are things I have never told you, things I've thought best to hold back; but I'm telling you now, aren't I? When I say we were happy and at peace, I do mean exactly that. There were worries, I know that very well, my parents had more than their share. But I was unaware of them, and I am glad of it. I had a childhood, I had the best brother in the world, nothing can ever take that from me, nothing. Not even the thing I fear most.

I don't mean death, Doctor, pray do not misunderstand me. You think I fear dissolution, but you're wrong. You think I dread the coming of darkness, but it isn't so. I've known a greater darkness than that. I know there are worse things to fear. You'll see, Doctor, I'll show you, I'll tell you everything, you know I will.

CHAPTER 3

WHAT DID YOU MEAN YESTERDAY WHEN YOU SAID I MUST "SET down the bare facts"? Did you think I was pulling your leg, spinning a tale of happy families, covering up some physical or sexual abuse? You've never liked the fact that I can talk back, have you, Doctor? That I'm not like your other old ladies, perfectly happy to be sent home to suck on pills or slip on rubber drawers for incontinence. It unsettles you that I have a degree, that I had a profession, that I can speak up for myself, doesn't it? Well, doesn't it?

You're all the same, you doctors, you think God made you out of different clay. The least show of independence on the part of your patients, and you think you're about to lose control, may have lost it already. Well, in this case, I have no intention of reassuring you. You have lost it. I'll tell my story as I want to tell it, and no more interference from you. If you're carping at this stage, God knows what you'll be like once I get to the bits that matter. So from now on I'm keeping this record to myself. You'll only see it when it's finished, and I'll only talk with you about it then.

But, believe me, I'm telling the truth. About everything. My childhood was happy, and that's all there is to it. If that seems abnormal to you, so much the worse for you and the profession that made you think that way. But if it makes you happy, I'll mention the one cloud that hung over us. A thin, wispy thing it seemed at the time.

It didn't quite make itself clear to me at first, mainly, I think, on account of my mother's lack of family. By the time I was seven or eight, I knew all about that, what had happened to my grandparents. And then, when I was eight, Aunt Harriet died. She had never really got over her sister's death, all their deaths, never got the water out of her dreams. She had a stroke, but I think she drowned in her sleep, beneath seas of her own making.

I remember a great sense of isolation after that, for my father had no family either, or at least very little. I think it may have been what drew him to my mother in the beginning, a sense of affinity. There had been no tragedy in his life to match hers, no tidal change of that angularity or speed, but something had happened and we knew it, even as children. His parents had died sometime before, his mother first of tuberculosis, his father two years after that of a heart attack, a rare enough thing in those days. He had been an only child, and on his father's death already established in business and free to live his own life.

There was talk—we overheard it sometimes, when they thought we weren't listening—about an aunt, cousins, distant relations of whom we had never heard. By the time I was ten, I knew there had been some sort of breach, a rift that went back well before my father's time to that of my grandfather and, for all I knew, even further still. He never talked of it openly, this break, this estrangement, whatever it was. Of his own parents, he spoke freely and often enough, trying to make us love them a little through his stories and the photographs in his album. Or, if not love them exactly, at least know them, form images of them as though seen through his eyes. He had loved them deeply, felt their loss immeasurably.

But one day—I must have been about nine—I asked a foolish question. I had been at a birthday party that day, I remember, a dreary enough affair, all frilly dresses and pink bows and merciless games that ended in tears. Louisa, the little girl in whose honor the party had been held, had introduced me to no fewer than six "cousins," and I had experienced one of my first real pangs of jealousy.

"Do I have any cousins, Papa?"

I remember the question, thinking it and asking it, as though it were moments ago. The stillness that followed, then my father's outburst, quite incomprehensible to me. It was one of the very few times I can remember him losing his temper. He came to me later, when I was in bed, and apologized. I've already told you, he was not a typical Victorian father.

He said he had not been angry with me, but with circumstance. Yes, he told me, there were indeed cousins, but he had never met them. There had been a split in his family a long time ago—he did not say precisely when—and contact between the two sides had never been resumed. It was not his fault, not his cousins' fault either, for that matter; but neither side seemed to have the will or the need to bridge the gap. In another generation, he thought, even the original quarrel would have been forgotten. By then, the very memory of a relationship would have faded, and it would all become a matter of genealogical interest. It was my first long word, "genealogical," and I never forgot it.

I asked him about the original quarrel to which he had referred, but he merely smiled and said it was a grown-up matter, he would tell me later, if I still wanted to know, when I was a young lady and able to understand such things. He never did, of course. But I found out myself in time.

And that, Doctor, is all I can tell you. Very few arguments, other than those built around childhood tantrums. No mysteries, other than that pale question mark concerning my half-cousins. We were a very happy family until . . .

Until my father died. I was eleven and Arthur nine and a half. I still remember . . . I still remember the door of the nursery opening, and Mother sending Hannah away, closing the door after her, her eyes so full she could not have been able to see. And the horrible knowing of something wrong before she ever spoke, and the knowing everything must change from that moment.

Arthur was very quiet afterward, and all that night. We spent the night together in my bed, with a light lit against the darkness, and we scarcely slept. I had cried myself dry. I had listened to my mother weeping, alone in her room. He had died of a heart attack, prematurely, just like his own father. They had brought him home from the factory, when we were out of the way, and men in black had come to lay him out. He was down there now, I knew, laid out in his coffin, wearing his best clothes, to all appearances sleeping.

I must have fallen asleep, as you will even at the

worst of times. I remember waking, a little groggy from unpleasant dreams. The light was still on. But Arthur had disappeared. He was nowhere in the room, nowhere in the passage. I thought he might have gone to be with our mother, but she was asleep at last, and he was not there.

I found him finally in the parlor, where Father's coffin lay across two dark trestles. He was standing, just standing by the open coffin, as though waiting for something, as though expecting Father to open his eyes and get up. I was terrified, I had never been near a dead body before, but I went in and took Arthur by the shoulders and led him out.

He never spoke of it afterward. It had been a private leave-taking, one in which none of the rest of us had a part. At the funeral he never shed so much as a single tear, and I overheard one old woman remark most unkindly how unnatural it was. But I had seen the look on his face that night as I took him from the room where Father lay and led him back to bed. Of all of us, I think it was Arthur who suffered most during those terrible days.

When the funeral was over, our real troubles started. Even before my father's death, things had been growing difficult for us. The United Alkali Company had been set up in 1890, and before long all the other firms had been amalgamated with it. Tennant's and Allhusen's stayed independent for a year or two, but my father's business was soon shut down and dismantled.

He opened a new company manufacturing electric lights, but was never able to compete with his heroes, Edison and Swan; when they moved to Kent soon afterward, so did most of his own orders. I think it was the strain of that time that killed him.

But it was only after his death that we learned the full truth. My father had made a series of incautious investments over the years and had lost a lot of money in speculations abroad. In his will, he had left everything to my mother, Arthur, and me. But after it was read, his solicitor told us not a penny could be paid. Quite the contrary. There were enormous debts. It seemed that father had borrowed heavily against his expectation of an inheritance from an aunt, a wealthy woman then living in Morpeth. Now that he was dead, the anticipated inheritance would never be paid, and his creditors were already demanding full repayment of both capital and interest. My mother's inheritance had already been spent in a last-minute attempt to save the electric light company. What was left of it was tied to my father's estate through some legal misjudgment. Unless someone came to our rescue, we were ruined.

My mother traveled at once to Morpeth, where my father's aunt, the widowed Mrs. Ayrton, refused her admittance. I remember her returning that evening, distraught and soaking. It had been raining heavily, and there had not been money for a covered trap. There were cousins who lived at Barras Hall, a large house in the wilds of Northumberland, near Elsdon. They were a brother and sister, the children of the Ayrtons. My mother wrote to them, but they did not answer, not even a single line, not even a word of consolation on my father's death.

In growing desperation, she applied to other relatives, and then to friends. Most did not bother to reply. Those that did prefaced their letters with the obligatory phrase "I regret." Our house and furniture were sold, but any profit occasioned by the sale was quickly eaten up by debts and legal expenses. Over a period of months, we moved from humbler to yet humbler quarters. My mother's health, already delicate, suffered exceedingly. I watched her turn gray; not only her hair, but her skin.

In November of 1899, we presented ourselves at the gate of the workhouse, in my mother's former parish of Chester-le-Street. There was a bell above the porter's lodge. I can still remember the sound of it, jangling in the cold air. We stood outside for a long time, shivering, before the porter opened the narrow gate and let us in. The coldest of welcomes. And the harshest of separations. They took Arthur away from us, to the men's wing. They had rules, rules to which they made no exception, though my mother cried fit to burst her heart.

CHAPTER 4

THOSE FIRST DAYS IN THE WORKHOUSE BROKE MY HEART. WERE it not for what happened later, I would say they were the worst days of my life. Even now I am taken back to them in dreams and awake to find my pillow wet with tears. An old woman weeping a child's tears. And yet, why not? We all carry the child in us to the grave. And beyond.

A sharp-nosed, sharp-tongued woman whom I soon came to know by the name of Mrs. Moss led my mother and me to a cold, tiled room where we were bustled into cubicles and told to strip. The clothes we had come in—poor enough rags by then—were searched, labeled, and stored away in a tin chest.

My mother had held on to a few scraps from our past, bits and pieces she had bundled into a cheap cloth bag. There were photographs, a lock of my father's hair, the wedding ring she had refused, against all promptings, to sell or pawn, a Bible given to her by her mother, a handful of letters tied with ribbon, letters my father had written to her and that she would never let me read, some dried flowers, a locket with my father's photograph inside. All were snatched from her and piled inside the chest.

Years later, when I came to retrieve our belongings from that chest, the ring and locket both had gone. Mrs. Moss had broken the law in the first place by admitting to the workhouse a pair with such treasures to sell. The very possession of such items meant that we had not yet been dragged down to that very lowest level of poverty, that state of utter indigence that the Poor Law commissioners had decreed to be the necessary condition of any admitted to the palatial comforts of the workhouse.

Our former lives were stripped from us forever, at a single stroke, as though they had never been. I had brought a small rag doll with me, whom I had named Annabel, and who had been my constant companion from an early age. In spite of my loud protests, Annabel was torn from me and tossed with everything else into the smelly chest.

A cold bath with carbolic soap followed. Then we were made to sit on hard stools while our hair was cropped. Does this seem harsh? It was harsh. You must remember that the workhouse was not the forerunner of our modern welfare state. It had not been set up to ease the misfortunes of the impoverished or save them from starvation. Its purpose was to force the idle poor to seek out work, however mean or hard or dangerous or ill paid. Fear of the workhouse was the goad. And a very effective goad it was.

I had always had the most beautiful copper hair, hair that fell below my shoulders, almost to my waist. It had been washed and brushed every day by Hannah, and I had been promised that when I was older, I might wear it up as a sign that I had become a lady. Now I felt cold shears slicing it from my head, and I wept bitterly to see it fallen on the ground, no longer part of me.

I remember the expression on my mother's face while all this was going on, a look of infinite despair, infinite hopelessness. None of this made the least impression on Mrs. Moss, not my tears, not my mother's despair. She had seen all that before, all that and worse. What were a few more tears, a few more looks of anguish to her? From the day I entered that terrible place to the day I left, I never heard her address a kind or cheering word to me or to anyone else.

We were given coarse woolen frocks to wear, and hobnailed boots with iron tips in which I found it hard to walk. You could always tell a workhouse child by the way she walked, they said, because of the boots. The frocks were dingy white in color, with long blue stripes running from top to bottom. They were waistless, shapeless bags that came down to our ankles, and looked as though they had been cut and sewn by the handless victim of some terrible accident.

Nothing was bright or pretty or soft in that place, there was nothing to lift a fallen heart. No pictures on the bare, whitewashed walls, no flowers on the high windowsills, no smells but those of boiled cabbage, carbolic, and disinfectant. And our hearts had fallen so far, so very far, we could not imagine them ever being raised again. I have been married, I have had children and grandchildren, I have lived a life of reasonable comfort; but my heart has never really lifted since that moment. That moment and what followed.

I thought of my brother Arthur, all alone in the men's wing, my gentle brother with his fair hair shorn. The thought chilled and wounded me. If his terrible dreams should come, I thought—and what other dreams could a child hope to have in a place like this?—where would he go, who would he turn to? Even now I shudder to think of it, what dreams he may have had in that place. The awful thing . . . The awful thing is that I think I know.

My mother and I were parted for the rest of that day. I learned later that they took her directly to a large, cold room full of other women in the same drab dresses, all sitting on hard benches picking oakum. That was still a common occupation in many workhouses, and one that went on in a few, I think, until they shut the places down for good in 1930. Later I spent some time in that room myself, though I was spared at first on account of my age.

She told me afterward how hard it had been and showed me her hands, what had become of them, all callused, raw, and bleeding. They made no allowances for those who were unaccustomed to physical labor or whose hands had not already been hardened by what it pleased them to call honest toil. They gave my mother a bundle of old ropes cut into lengths, most of them hardened with tar. Her quota for that day was a full three pounds, and even by supper she had not half finished. The idea was to unpick the ropes, turning them back into loose fibers that would then be used for jobs like caulking ships. What work it was. What mind-numbing, senseless, unending labor. How my mother hated it. How it destroyed her.

They sent me directly to the workhouse school, a separate place hard by the main building. By that time, most workhouses sent their children outside to the state schools, but ours was one of the exceptions, so I had to buckle down and learn to be a schoolgirl under conditions far from ideal. Until then, my education had been a wholly private affair. Both Arthur and I had been tutored at home by a tribe of day governesses, not a few of whom were of dubious merit. They did not last long, coming and going as the season drove them, or the state of their pockets, or the availability of interesting men. My mother did not think it necessary or economical to engage a live-in governess, so near were we to the city and a constant supply of half-educated young women in search of genteel employment.

The schoolhouse had been divided into two quite distinct halves, one for boys, the other for girls, with a high wall between. Not even at playtime were we allowed to mix. Of all things during those years, it was what I most longed for, to see that rule broken or suspended, that I might see Arthur once more, perhaps even exchange a few quick words with him, so I could tell mother how he looked, how he was growing.

The girls' section—I imagine the boys' was much the same—consisted of a large room about ten feet high and twenty feet long, with small square windows painted over with whitewash. They painted them like that to stop us looking into the adult yard, which was directly underneath. It was stuffy, winter and summer both, for the windows were always kept tightly shut, and the only ventilation we had came through little holes under the ceiling and rows of zinc tubes with small perforations in them, running from wall to wall.

As I was brought in, the teacher looked up with a scowl on her face. I shall never forget her. Miss Golightly was her name, and she used to make a pun of it: "My name's Golightly, but I'll not go lightly with you." And the punning would be followed by a beating with the short leather rod she carried in her pocket.

I was hurried to the front of the class, where I stood, shivering, struggling to hold back my tears.

"Who are you, girl? What's your name?"

I could say nothing, I was frightened to death by the teacher and the eyes of the other children all fixed on me, as at some Roman spectacle, scenting blood.

"Stop sniveling, child. Sniveling won't get you anywhere. You're not here to snivel, you're here to work."

"I . . ." I began, but I could get no further.

The teacher reached out for me with a long, practiced hand and grabbed me by one ear, pulling me hard toward her.

"My name's Golightly, but I go lightly with no one, d'you hear? You'll speak when you're spoken to, jump when you're told to jump, sit when I say sit, and move your bowels when I say it's time and not before. If I catch you talking or laughing or playing behind my back, you'll regret it for a long time afterward. Ask these other girls, they'll tell you all about me. They've known me long enough, they've known the back of my hand and the little stick I carry."

She took the truncheon from her pocket and waved it menacingly in my face.

"I undertake to use Old Martin"—that was her name for the stick, we never could tell why—"a dozen times a day. He's never short of occasions for work, and I'm ever ready to put him to good use. If you're a second late to class, it's Old Martin you'll answer to. If you get your sums wrong, you'll find it easy enough to count his strokes on the palm of your hand. Now stop that infernal sniveling, take that empty place by Annie Greenup, and keep your arms folded. We've wasted time enough."

And the lesson continued. I took in none of it, nor of that afternoon's, nor the next day's, and I received a few whacks from Old Martin in payment for my inattention. There was no one to sympathize with my plight, not even my mother, for we were scarcely allowed to meet and had to sleep in different dormitories. And even when we did meet, she was so wearied by her own exertions and so immersed in her own reflections that she had less and less of herself to give me. From the first day I had to start standing on my own feet.

The other girls were no comfort in the beginning. Quite the opposite. My accent betrayed me, that and my soft hands and pale skin. They could tell at once how far I had fallen to be with them. But they had no sympathy for my fate, for it only served to remind them how far above them I had once been, how cosseted a life I had lived when theirs had from the beginning consisted of little but gruel and hard blows. Why would any of them step to my defense or suggest ways in which to ameliorate the conditions under which I was now forced to live?

In time I fell into the cruel routine of that place. All that cold winter, a loud bell woke us at seven, but from March to September we had to rouse ourselves at five or suffer the consequences. We had prayers at half past seven, then breakfasted on gruel and coarse bread. From eight I was in school, and my mother in the shed. Dinner came at twelve: a little bread and cheese on Sundays, Mondays, Wednesdays, and Fridays. On Tuesdays, it was meat and potatoes, the best meal of the week, on Thursdays a thin soup with bread, on Saturdays bacon. Then back to school. Supper was at six: more bread and cheese. And everything washed down with plain water, summer and winter.

I remember once that an old woman—a woman older than I am now, I think, or so she seemed to me then—managed to get a friend from outside to bring her a pot in which to brew a little tea from time to time. But Mrs. Moss discovered it and broke it into tiny pieces, scolding the poor old woman for this outrageous breach of regulations. Since then, I have never forgotten how important are the small comforts of life.

After supper we had more prayers—and how we all would have preferred a cup of tea to any of that—and were sent straight to our dormitories, children and adults alike. I can still remember the sound of the key turning in the dormitory lock at eight o'clock sharp, and then the interminably long nights that followed. I had my own dreams, of course, every night without fail. Nightmares preparing me for the nightmare that was yet to come.

Time passed very slowly, but it did pass. The other girls grew to tolerate me by degrees and, in the end, even to like me a little—a few of them anyway. My best friend was Annie Greenup, that same fellow sufferer beside whom I had been made to sit on my first day in the classroom and whose desk I always shared from then. We became allies, Annie and I, against Go-Hard Go-lightly and Old Martin, covering for one another's errors where possible, exchanging knowing looks behind the teacher's sturdy back. Annie taught me more than any of my governesses or the righteous Miss Golightly ever could have done. She had always been poor, she knew she always would be, and she knew all the tricks that made poverty bearable.

She was as good as an orphan herself, she told me. Both her parents were alive, or so she thought, but she had no idea where they were. On one occasion, she said her mother had run off with a sailor, leaving her and her brother to fend for themselves. The next time she spoke about it, the sailor became a soldier who had decamped to India, where her mother had followed him. And once—speaking the truth this time perhaps—she said her mother had died of consumption.

Her father was a drunkard whom she scarcely knew. She had spent most of her short life in and out of workhouses, and she dreaded the times her father came to take her out as much as the times he left her in. It was a long time before she told me why. In those days, the sexual abuse of children by their parents was something no one talked about. Annie had been abused for as long as she could remember. The workhouse offered her her only respite. Her eyes were filled with the hurt of it; soft, wounded eyes always on the edge of tears.

Annie and I were roughly the same age. She had no idea when her birthday was, but on an official form she had once been described as "eight years of age," and every year since then she had added another year to her computation. Her brother Bob was a little younger, and it was this similarity in our conditions that brought us together most, though she and Bob were far from as close as Arthur and I had been.

Arthur. I saw him only once during the time I spent in the workhouse. That was about a year after we first went in, in the week before Christmas. The local vicar had arranged a carol service for the workhouse children. He was a new man, fired with zeal to do the Christian thing, and we had seemed to him a worthy enough cause. When we were told of the plan, I knew there might be a chance to see Arthur, even speak to him. I had a lot to tell him, and there was so much I wanted to know. For over a fortnight I scrimped and saved, begged and borrowed in order to have something to give him as a Christmas present. It wasn't much, just a lead soldier one of the girls had smuggled inside and which she sold to me for a high price paid in food from my dinner plate. But it meant the world to me, that soldier, thinking what it would mean to Arthur.

He was there as I had prayed, in the line of boys walking ahead of us to the church. I knew him at once, and every now and then I caught him looking back, searching me out among the girls. They wouldn't let us sit together, that would have been an unthinkable transgression against the Christian spirit, but with Annie's help I managed to seat myself right alongside him when we finally got inside the church. He looked so thin, his eyes stared so, his hair was cropped short, but he was my Arthur all the same, I could not take my eyes off him. And while the others sang "O Little Town of Bethlehem," I managed to whisper to him, across the aisle, a few words. They beat me for that, the worst beating of my life, so I could neither stand nor sit for days afterward; but it was worth a dozen beatings just for those few words.

I told him I was well, that I thought of him every day, that we would soon be together again, he must not lose faith. And I asked him the hardest of questions, if he had been told that our mother was dead. And he said no, he did not know, no one had said.

My mother's destruction had been written on her from the moment she entered the workhouse. That look on her face had said it all. Life held nothing for her now, she was beaten and lost, she had made up her mind to die. And die she did, six months later, at the end of May, on a morning full of sunshine, a morning just like this, with her eyes open and her face turned to the wall. They told me that night, after supper, just after prayers, before we were sent to bed. But they forgot to tell Arthur, or thought it did not matter.

They buried her in a pauper's grave, without a shroud, in a cheap coffin with broken boards. Years later, when I was at last able to have her reinterred in our family plot at Gosforth, it proved impossible to identify her remains among so many unmarked graves, such a mass of nameless coffins, so many broken bones. I still think of her often. Sometimes, when the nights are very dark, my hand still reaches out for her.

CHAPTER 5

WHEN I WAS FOURTEEN, THEY RECKONED I HAD HAD ENOUGH education and put me in the servants' class, the plan being to train me for work as a maid. I could still remember the wretched lives of the undermaids in our house. But after so long in the workhouse, the prospect held no fears for me. Indeed, it seemed the most desirable of things to be out of that place, however hard I might have to slave. In the servants' class, I would work ten hours each day, laboring in the kitchens or the laundry, or cleaning the floors.

I would start in the early morning, right after breakfast, scrubbing the casual ward, where they used to put the vagrants. There were nine cells on a side, and I and another girl would be put to do one side each, as well as the bathrooms and lavatories. All I had for the job were cloths, a bucket, and some soda. I made my own kneeling pad, for that work was murder without one. The job would take all morning, and by the end of it I felt wrung out. But after dinner we would set off again.

There were wooden floors to scrub and long tables to scour, and woe betide the girl who left so much as a spot, whether above or underneath. I had had little enough to do with Mrs. Moss until then, but the work of cleaning and scrubbing and lighting fires was her domain and she spared no pains to make us know it. She was, I suppose, what the doctors now would call a sadist. A lot of them had employment in the workhouses.

By the time I was fourteen, my hair had grown and I was thought ready to enter employment. They let us girls grow our hair out like that, in the year or so before we were due to go into the world. I think it was the only charitable act they ever performed, though it was done less for our comfort than to spare our future employers the sight of our cropped heads. When I see young women nowadays with their heads closely shaved and wearing shapeless bags of clothes, I am reminded of the days I spent with my own hair so ruthlessly cut back and a workhouse dress on my back, and I feel sorry for them. Poor things, no doubt they think me a little soft in the head when they see me looking at them with such a pitying expression.

Mrs. Moss came to me one day early in 1902 with a dour look on her face. It was morning, and I was busy polishing some brass in the room where the guardians took their lunch on their monthly visit to the workhouse. I thought someone had died—that was not uncommon, but I could not think why she should want to notify me personally. Unless . . . A shiver of perfect fear went through me at that moment as Arthur came to my mind.

"You're to pack your things," she said. "There's a place for you outside. They expect you there this dinnertime. It's a doctor's house in Birtley. You're to be the scullery girl. You needn't expect any pay, but they'll feed you and find a place for you to sleep of nights. It's better than you deserve, but no doubt you'll be complaining before you're there a week. Well, then, get going. What are you waiting for?"

My heart had come into my mouth and seemed like to stay there. I could remember almost nothing of the world outside. My mother had been with me all the time before, and now I was to be thrust back out onto the streets alone and expected to fend for myself. The fear I had felt a moment before had not quite passed, and now it changed into a dull sense of dread for myself.

"But I . . ." I stammered, "I don't know the way. How am I to get there?"

"That's none of my concern. You've got two feet, you can walk like other folk. You'd better be there by two o'clock, mind, or you'll find yourself on the street. Mrs. Venables won't put up with that, you'll find that out. She'll have no truck with idle girls."

I stammered again. I could have fallen, my legs were trembling so.

"How do I get there? I've never been anywhere on my own before."

"Didn't they teach you anything in that school? I'll give you the address, you'll find someone outside to show you the way. It's not my business to be coddling those that are too lazy or too stupid to get from A to B by themselves."

Saying which, she grabbed my arm and pulled me to the room where the belongings of inmates were kept. We had an altercation straightaway, as to whether or not I was entitled to take with me the bits and pieces my mother had brought to the workhouse with her. There had been no will, Mrs. Moss said, so my mother's things belonged to the guardians—by which, indeed, she meant herself. And I think she would have kept them, were it not for the fact that she had already stolen the ring and the locket. Such treasures rarely fell to her lot. Sooner than have me make a fuss in a year or two years' time, she let me take all that was in the chest, in the hope I would have forgotten that the stolen items had ever been there. It was pitifully little, but it seemed like untold wealth to me at the time.

"May I see my brother before I go?" I asked, for it was more important to me than anything to have a chance to speak with Arthur again. I would leave him the address for which I was bound, and he would make his way there to fetch me as soon as he was sent outside himself.

"Brother? What brother? Your brother's gone long ago," she said.

Her words hit me like one of the blows she liked to deal out. The blood rushed from my face. I do not know why I did not faint, for the fear I had felt that first moment of her arrival had returned with redoubled force. I was certain for a moment that she meant he was dead.

"Gone?" It was all I could do to force the question out.

"Yes, of course. Did you think he'd stay on here forever, maybe just to wait for his big sister? This isn't a hotel, you know. Our inmates don't pay for their keep like decent folks. Your brother was found a place and sent to it like any other lad his age."

"When? When did he go? How long has he been gone?"

She bent down over me, bringing her ugly face close to mine, her little red eyes gleaming. I could smell gin on her breath, and vinegar. I could smell the sweat of her body, a dark, humid odor. I wanted to be sick.

"I have better things to do, miss," she snarled, "than to stand here all day answering your questions. If you've got any illusions about going back to your old station in life, with maids to wait on you and nurses to wipe your behind, you'd do well to shake them out of your dull head this very moment. If you think it's been hard on you in here, lass, it's been nothing to what you've got waiting for you on the outside."

She straightened up, still leering at me.

"But I have to know. Arthur—"

She struck me hard across the face with the back of her hand. I had suffered her pointless violence often enough in the past, but the particular cruelty of that blow has never left me. Wherever she may be now, I hope she is suffering for that blow. God forgive me, but that is what I truly feel, even now, after all these years, as though my cheek were still stinging from the force of it. For if she had told me then what I wanted to know, if she had made it possible for me to follow Arthur, all that followed might never have happened and he and I, dead or alive, might today be at peace.

I had a long, cold walk to Dr. Lincott's house. Mrs. Moss had sent me in my mother's dress and my mother's shoes, for my own had grown too small. The shoes were too large for me, but I stuffed some scraps of old paper into them and made do like that for a spell. After less than a mile, my feet began to hurt terribly, and in a short while I was limping. I even started to wish for my old hobnailed boots as though they had been the most stylish footwear imaginable. My clothes and other belongings I carried in the little cloth bag in which mother had brought them to Chester-le-Street. An old woman showed me the way.

Dr. Lincott's house was not half so grand as the one in which I had been brought up. But that did not stop me from shaking like a leaf as I came within sight of it. I had seen from a clock that it was very nearly two o'clock, and I was quite certain I would receive a hard welcome, or perhaps even be turned away in spite of everything and forced to make my way back to the workhouse. And all the way I thought of Arthur and that I might never see him again.

I presented myself at the back door, as I had been told to do. Mrs. Venables, the housekeeper, grandly called it the "servants' entrance," but it was no more than a plain back door at the foot of a short flight of steps. I had to knock hard and long before anyone answered. When the door finally opened, I found myself face-to-face with bedlam. A flagged passage ran down to a kitchen, from which came a frightening clatter of dishes and the hubbub of raised voices. The Lincotts kept a small enough establishment—a housekeeper, a cook, an undercook, two maids, and a boy—but between them, they managed to create as much noise as a roomful of costermongers. I was unused to such boisterousness, for it had been all hushed voices and scraping feet in the workhouse.

The boy opened the door wide to discover me on the step shivering and sobbing. For all my fears, it was now my dearest wish to set foot in that house, for I thought I might at least find a little warmth and a bite to eat. Yet I was now mortally sure the door would be slammed in my face. The boy—whose name I later learned was George—called out to someone in the room behind, and moments later Mrs. Venables appeared (though I had not the slightest notion then of who or what she was).

"You'll be the new girl from the workhouse," she snapped, taking a large watch from her dress pocket, opening it, and clicking it shut again. "You're not far off being late. What kept you?"

"Please, ma'am, I—"

"No matter. There's work to do, and it won't get done if you stand there gawping and sniveling. George, see this girl in and tell Lottie to set her about her tasks at once. I'll speak with her later, when I've a minute. Come on, come on, don't dawdle."

She then grabbed me by the neck of my dress and hauled me bodily into the passage. A moment later, she had disappeared.

"Watch out for Venables," George whispered, leaning close. "Cross her, and you'll find yourself back on the street."

He took my bag and tossed it carelessly into a corner. I made to rescue it, but he seized my arm and hauled me down the passage, limping and tripping, into the kitchen. The passage had been freezing cold, but the heat in the kitchen was enough to make me gasp for breath.

A large woman in a floury apron, whom I took—rightly—to be the cook, descended on me like a barge.

"New girl? Got a name?"

"I . . . ."

"Not good enough, girl. Use your tongue. God gave it you for no other purpose. Name?"

"Char-Charlotte."

Her eyes widened.

"Same as myself. But don't go thinking you can be familiar on account of it. You're here to work. And you can start by cleaning those pots and pans. If you'd got here earlier, you'd be halfway through them by now."

And so my day began. No one asked me if I was hungry. I just had to roll up my sleeves and set to work, scrubbing and scouring, with none of the detergents we have nowadays. Because it was a doctor's house, there was an insistence on high standards of cleanliness, which meant that every utensil had to be scrubbed until it shone. After breakfast, after lunch, after tea, and after dinner. Of course, pots and pans and dishes were only a fraction of my work. There were five fires to light every morning before anyone else was out of bed. There were wooden floors to scrub, toilets to clean, bathrooms to wash out twice a week. Laundry and ironing, carpets, brasses, windows, the backs of cupboards, the rear yard—they were all my responsibility.

In return, Mrs. Venables told me I could bed down in the kitchen at night and help myself to whatever scraps were left after the other servants had eaten their share of leftovers from the family table. Some days, I ate little more than a slice of bread and drippings. I never tasted hot tea or butter or jam. George warned me that the last girl had been caught picking morsels of meat from a hambone left on a plate, thrashed, and dismissed on the spot. Mrs. Venables ran her household with a will of steel and a rod of iron.

I was up in the mornings by five o'clock, creeping about in the darkness for fear of waking the others, laying and lighting fires in the kitchen, the drawing room, the doctor's consulting room, the morning room, and the master bathroom. And I would be hard at work from then until late at night, ten or eleven o'clock some-times. If there was a special dinner that went on late, we would all be hard at it in the kitchen until midnight or one. Mrs. Venables would let none of us creep off to bed until every last pan had been cleaned and put away. As for me, I had no choice in the matter, for the kitchen was my bedroom anyway. I still had to be up before dawn to light the fires.

One incident from those days stands out in my mind. Ellen, the maid who normally did the dusting, had been taken ill, and I was sent to the drawing room to dust the furniture before Mrs. Lincott came in for morning tea with her friends from the ladies' committee of the local hospital.

As I was dusting, my heart all the time in my mouth for fear that I would drop and break something delicate, I came to a photograph on the wall near the fireplace. It showed a group of men in evening dress, very formal and starched. It seemed like something from another world, and yet gnawingly familiar. And then I realized that my father had had a photograph very like this one. I glanced at the caption written in copperplate on the mount at the foot of the picture: *Newcastle Literary and Philosophical Society Committee, 1884.*

My heart beating, I looked at the photograph again. My father was standing in the back row, just as I remembered him from his own copy of the photograph, which he had kept in the study, where I had seen it every time I went to visit him there. For it had been his habit to invite me to sit with him for about half an hour every evening and to read to me. I remember *Kitty's Secret Wish* and *Little by Little,* and his soft voice, and the security I felt sitting on his lap while the lamplight fell all round us.

Now, looking at that familiar photograph, I felt my defenses give way and I burst into the most bitter tears. There had scarcely been time to grieve at his death before financial disaster had brought other, equally devastating blows on my head. In the workhouse, my mother's death and Arthur's absence had been all the sorrow I could handle. But now I felt more alone than ever, and nothing could hold back the misery or the tears.

I did not hear the door open or footsteps cross the room toward me.

"What is it, girl? What on earth's the matter?"

I was on my knees, crouching, my head in my hands.

"Come on, child, speak up. What are you crying for?"

When I looked up, I saw a woman standing over me. Not Mrs. Venables, but someone else, a rather younger woman and much better dressed. With a sinking feeling, I realized that this must be Mrs. Lincott, my employer, whom I had not so much as set eyes on before that moment.

It took a long time, but in the end I managed to blurt out something about my father.

"Father? Father? I don't understand. What about your father?"

"He's . . ." I gulped and looked up at her. "He's dead, ma'am."

She looked at me quite softly, with sympathy, I thought.

"I'm sorry to hear that," she said. "Have you just heard?"

I shook my head and tried to explain.

"But if he's been dead all these years, why all this crying now? I don't understand, really I don't."

I pointed to the photograph, to my father, a man in side-whiskers and evening dress.

"He . . . That's my father," I said.

"Your . . . ? Nonsense, girl." Her manner changed, now she could see how I was bamboozling her. "That's one of my husband's friends. Surely you can see that, you stupid girl. Does that look like a common laborer to you?"

I had started to come around a little. I shook my head.

"You don't understand," I said. "My father wasn't a laborer. His name was Mr. Metcalf. Douglas Metcalf. That's his photograph."

For a moment she was quite stupefied, not grasping what I was saying. Then something like the truth began to dawn on her. It was my voice for one thing. In the time I had spent in the workhouse, I had not quite lost my middle-class accent, though often enough I had been made fun of on account of it. And Mrs. Lincott knew the names of her husband's friends.

"Do you mean Metcalf who owned the alkali works?"

I nodded.

Her hand flew to her mouth.

"Good God . . . I'd heard . . ."

She sat down in the nearest chair and stared at me as though I had just fallen down the chimney.

"But good heavens, child, how do you come to be in this condition?"

I did my best to explain, though my understanding of what had happened was then quite rudimentary. Nevertheless she seemed to grasp the essence of what I was saying.

"And you say your mother died in that terrible place?"

I nodded, fresh tears springing to my eyes. It was the first time I had spoken in a civilized fashion with anyone since my mother's death. I imagined this woman—a woman of my own class, a woman who dressed and spoke as my own mother had done—I imagined her rising from her chair and taking me in her arms and tearing me away from my endless scrubbing in order to live with her and her children as one of the family. Like a princess in a fairy tale, restored to her true station after a life of poverty.

For a moment, even now, I truly believe that very thought had passed through Mrs. Lincott's own head. And for a moment, I do not doubt, she was on the verge of acting on that impulse. But with a degree of self-mastery that I can only call heroic, she reined herself in. When she next looked at me, I saw with a fallen heart, she had determined to regard me as the same scullery maid she had taken me for on entering the room.

"Well, I am saddened to hear your tale," she said, rising from the chair. "I shall tell my husband about it. I believe we met your mother once at a dinner held by the Lit. and Phil. To think that she should have died under such circumstances. And so young. How tragic. How very tragic."

The next moment she walked several paces to the door, then turned and glanced at me again.

"Finish up in here quickly, will you?" she said. "I have guests coming in half an hour."

The door opened and closed, and I was alone again.

CHAPTER 6

Nothing improved. Days passed, weeks passed, whole months went by. If Mrs. Lincott ever thought of me, it must have been as something very distant, nearly abstract, an example of how the sins of the fathers are visited upon their children. Or perhaps I was just an embarrassment she preferred to keep hidden away in the scullery. Of me as a person, I am sure she never thought at all. If she did, she never showed it in any concrete fashion. There were no gifts of clothing or bedding, no pieces of extra food. Nothing ever came my way in that house but hard work.

And yet the very expectation I had that I might yet receive some favorable treatment at Mrs. Lincott's hands was based on the wholly irrelevant fact of my having been born into the same class as she, on the coincidence—not such a great one in those days—that my father and Dr. Lincott had been members of a scientific and cultural society. But what else did I have to fend for myself with if not that? I knew no one outside the workhouse, I had not been bred to poverty, there was enough loneliness in me to fill the hearts of a family of beggars.

Spring came and passed, little noticed by me in the shadows of the scullery where most of my work was done. I had no days off. And if I had been given one, how would I have spent it? I had no clothes fit to wear outside, no money, not so much as a penny to buy a slice of pie. There was little for me to look forward to in life: at best I might hope to become a parlor maid and share a cold room under the attic with one or two other girls, and think myself fortunate to have a pair of old shoes and a cheap hat and an evening off once a week. I was old enough for the streets, my body was grown enough to be worth a shilling or two to a sailor in Newcastle or South Shields; but I knew next to nothing of that trade, just the nods and winks I had observed listening to other girls gossiping in the workhouse.

Summer passed. Some days the heat in the kitchen was unendurable. I slipped out into the yard whenever I got a chance, which was seldom enough, and looked over the yard wall and the roofs of the houses round about, up at the blue sky, wondering what it must feel like to be out there, to be as free to come and go as a bird. In its way, summer was worse than winter. I cried more often, alone at night on my scraps of rag. And I thought of Arthur, of the games we had played in our garden at home, where flowers had blossomed and huge trees cast a welcome shadow on soft grass.

Autumn arrived with soft winds, then hard. The days flickered past, one rushing into the next without distinction. One night, very late, I wakened suddenly from a dream to hear the wind kicking and squalling in the streets outside. Something heavy was rolling back and forth in the back alleyway. I could not shake the dream out of my head.

I had seen my brother Arthur. He had been standing alone at a window in a dark house, with a light behind him, the pale light of a candle. He was scratching at the window with his hands, scraping his fingernails against the glass, as though trying to escape from something. I could still hear the scratching, it would not go away. And suddenly, in the dream, I had realized that I myself was standing in the room in the dark house, in the room with the candle, and that Arthur was outside the window, that he was scraping hard with his nails, trying to get in. And I had not wanted him to enter. I had been afraid of his pale face and his long, thin hands.

In October, the first signs of winter appeared. There was a day of hail, and a day so dark the lights were left on from early morning. The next day something wonderful happened. At least, it was wonderful to me. There was a new arrival at the back door, someone—so Lottie said—come from the workhouse to be lady's maid to the oldest daughter of the house, Miss Emily, now turned fifteen. I was in the kitchen when the new girl entered, and I nearly dropped the pan I was scrubbing when I caught sight of her: it was Annie, barely recognizable in a cap and shawl, shivering on the doorstep.

Venables brought her through the kitchen before whisking her away to the maids' room in the attic. As she went by she turned her head and winked at me. I could barely contain my excitement.

That night I lay awake, knowing how close some sort of salvation lay. Every day after that, I waited impatiently for Annie to appear. The longer I waited, the more my hopes fed off her, the more I fantasized about our reunion. But it was over a week before we had our chance. On the second Sunday after her arrival, she sneaked downstairs after lunch.

I shall never forget the look on her face when she clapped eyes on me. She just stood staring at me, up and down, as though I were a freak in a sideshow at the Hoppings. When she finally spoke, her voice was low, as though she were trying to keep it hushed in the presence of the sick.

"What have they been doing to you, Charlotte? You're like a skeleton."

The next moment we were in one another's arms, both of us in tears, then Annie had me at arm's length, clucking and tutting like an old hen.

"You've got to get away from here," she said at last. "You'll kill yourself if you stay on."

"Get away?" The thought terrified me, as much as the idea of spending the rest of my life in the Lincotts' kitchen. "Where to? Where can I go? I've got no money, I've got no one to go to."

Annie shook her head.

"Of course you do, hinnie. You want to find your brother, don't you?"

I looked at her in astonishment.

"Do you know where he is?"

She smiled and raised her eyebrows.

"Maybe I do, hinnie," she said. "Maybe I do."

"Tell me, then, tell me. . . ."

She sat me down at the table.

"Sit still now, and let us tell you. We were took out two weeks ago, Bob and me. He's been given work in Gateshead, I was sent here by that old bitch Moss. We spent a couple of days together first, though, on account of our dad."

"Your dad?"

She nodded.

"They buried him. That's how come we're out."

"I'm sorry."

She smiled.

"Don't be. I hated the old bastard. We'll be better off without him. Anyway, our Bob says he saw your brother before he went out."

"He's still in the workhouse? But I was told—"

"No, before your brother went out, I mean."

"Did Bob find out where they were sending him?"

Annie nodded.

"A place in Gateshead, just like our Bob. Clark's metal foundry. Not the place for a lad like him. Bob didn't think he'd stick it. But he never meant to. He told Bob that first chance he had, he was off."

"Off? But where to? Where could he go?"

"He said he was set to go to relatives of yours in Northumberland. They'd take him in, he said, and then send to have you brought from the workhouse. That was his plan."

"Relatives?" I looked at her blankly, unable to understand whom she could mean. "We have no relatives, Annie. There's no one would take us in."

"Well, your brother told Bob these were folk with a big house in the country, up near Morpeth. He said they were lords and ladies, gentry, and they'd never stand to see him or his sister starve when all they had to do was open their doors and let you in."

My heart shook. Surely he knew, surely he remembered. They had never answered my mother's letter. Not even Arthur could get through those doors.

"Was their name Ayrton? Did Arthur say?" I asked. She frowned, then nodded.

"Yes," she said. "Yes, I think that's what Bob said. Ayrton."

That night I had another dream. I dreamed that Arthur came to me in the night. He had grown older than I remembered him, he was thin and dressed in curious clothes, and his hair had been allowed to grow long. He came to me across the kitchen, stepping through a pool of moonlight that fell across the cold flags, but his feet made no sound. There was no wind outside, not a breath. The house was utterly quiet, huge and brooding all about me. He advanced slowly with his hands outstretched, my little brother, with his mouth open and his eyes wide, like someone wide-awake in sleep. And I heard him speak, but his voice seemed to come from far away, from another place entirely.

"Help me, Charlotte," he whispered. "Please help me."

"What's wrong, Arthur?" I whispered. "Mother's dead, and I can't help you if I don't know what's wrong."

But he only stood there, his white hands stretched out helplessly, the sleeves of a long shirt falling over his wrists, his mouth open, calling in a whisper for help.

I woke with a start. For a moment I thought I had not been asleep at all.

CHAPTER 7

I MADE MY ESCAPE THE FOLLOWING SATURDAY. ANNIE FIXED IT all for me. The Lincotts suffered nothing more than the temporary inconvenience of losing a scullery-maid, someone whom they never even paid for her labors and who could be replaced from the endless stock of the impoverished and desperate.

Annie's father had left her a little money, and out of this she gave me three shillings and sixpence, more money than I had ever had in my life. That's worth seventeen and a half pence nowadays, and it will scarcely buy you a newspaper.

"When can I pay you back?" I asked.

"When you're a fine lady in that big house." She laughed. "You can take me on as a maid."

"No, you'll come and live with us. You'll be my friends, you and your brother."

"You'll forget us when you're rich. Wait and see."

"I'll never forget you, Annie."

And I never have. I remember Annie every day. I've tried to find her so many times, always without success. She slipped away from me without trace, like a boat without a mooring. A long time after that I went to the Lincotts and inquired about her, but they barely remembered her name and could not tell me where she had gone. I did not make myself known to them, nor do I think they would have thanked me if I had.

"I'll write to you," I said. "As soon as I've settled in."

I didn't tell her how unlikely I thought it that any of our dreams would ever materialize. The Ayrtons would turn me back at the door, and that would be the end of the story. My greatest worry was how, after that, I would ever find Arthur.

Annie told me where to go and how to make my way through Gateshead and Newcastle. In addition to money, she gave me something of even greater value: a pair of old but sturdy shoes that fit me properly. As a result, I was able to walk all the way, anxious to save the little money I had. In Gateshead, I found Clark's foundry, a horrid place filled with fumes and noise, where they told me Arthur had stayed a month and then vanished. That was all they knew.

I crossed the river into Newcastle on the High Level Bridge, taking the Ha'penny Lop, the old horse-drawn brake that was still used then and for many years afterward. We all got down at the far end in sight of the castle, and I set off with my three shillings in my pocket, aware of how little I mattered in anybody's course of things. I kept imagining footsteps behind me: Mrs. Moss, coming to reclaim me and the priceless belongings I had stolen from her; Mrs. Venables, indignant, resourceful in her search for revenge; Mrs. Lincott, cold, disdainful, aloofly calling me back to her scullery. At every corner,

I expected to see them waiting. If I saw a policeman, I would shrink aside, as though I were the most sought after of criminals.

I recalled—already a distant memory—trips to town with my mother, when we would go shopping in Fenwick's or Bainbridge's. Afterward she would always take Arthur and me to Tilley's Café in Blackett Street. Everywhere we went, shopkeepers and waitresses would treat us with enormous respect. I thought then that that was just how people were, that they would always treat me so if I smiled and said "please" and "thank you" as I had been taught.

Now, making my way through the city without fine clothes or a carriage waiting to take me home, I saw how things really stood. No one made way for me, no one lifted his hat as I passed by. Once, a stall holder clipped me round the ear as I stood looking at the pies he had for sale, telling me to "get on out of it." I passed the door of Tilley's Café and knew they would not even let me inside.

I spent that first night in a cheap rooming house in Black Boy Yard, off the Groat Market. The room was crowded and dirty, and the thin blanket they gave me was barely adequate against the cold, but I lay there with a growing sense inside me of something I could scarcely name, something I now know must have been freedom, an awareness that I had, in the space of a few hours, taken control of my own destiny.

The next day I devoted to getting free of the city. I followed the instructions Annie had given me, asking directions a piece at a time until I got myself onto Claremont Road. From there I took the long road north through Kenton toward Ponteland. I was tired and hungry, and my feet ached terribly, but I was on my way. The smoke and clamor of Newcastle were behind me now. Before long, I was in open countryside, still heading north—walking, I hoped, along the very road Arthur had taken all those months earlier.

I spent my second night at Woolsington, in a cold shed full of turnips. In return for sixpence, a farmer's wife prepared a meal for me, the first hot food I had eaten since leaving the workhouse.

When I set off the next morning, the weather had taken a turn for the worse. Clouds lay motionless all across the sky. In every direction, the countryside had turned dark, there were shadows behind every hedge and in every thicket. A cold wind moved in from the north, hampering my progress. The wings of blackbirds tangled through the sky. I saw men and women in the fields—old men, old women—but very far away, beyond the reach of my voice, stooped over strange instruments, intent on some dark labor that I could not comprehend.

The farther I walked, the more desolate the landscape grew. Nowadays people make that journey with their children, in large cars, cocooned against the cold and the dark. They drive on smooth, black roads, each one as long as all the roads of my childhood strung together. They carry National Trust cards in their wallets and copies of road maps in the glove compartments of their Volvos. Their worst fear is that they will run out of petrol on the long stretch from Otterburn to Belsay. And what is it they fear? That they may be forced to wait for an hour or two until one of the road clubs sends a man in uniform to their ignominious rescue.

I neither despise nor envy them. They work hard, they are entitled to their weekend outings, their souvenir mugs, their potato crisps. And if the price they have to pay for that is some sort of inner desolation of which they may not even be aware, some loss of self, some unawareness of place and the passion for place, perhaps it is not too high a price for the comfort they feel.

The price I paid for walking in those fields was higher, and I never felt comfort or peace or oneness with nature. That is all a game. Do not believe everything my generation says. I knew only fear there, a sense of disquiet. Every coppice I passed seemed alive with mingling shadows. But it was not just shadows. It was presences. It was the knowledge that here, where green fields gave way to moor, I was more vulnerable than ever. Something was waiting for me, something I could neither name nor envision. But I knew, as I turned each corner of that road, that it was hiding, biding its time.

I reached the village of Kirkwhelpington early on the third day. "Barras Lodge, near Kirkwhelpington" was the address I still remembered my mother writing on the envelope when she asked my father's cousins for help. It was a small bleak hamlet on the edge of nowhere, with an ancient parish church, a school, and very little else. The world seemed to end here, in scrub and moor and forest.

I found a little public house where they sold me bread and cheese and small ale to wash it down. It was a rough place, with no more than a couple of unpolished tables and a few wooden stools. When I had finished, the publican's daughter came to clear my table. She was a girl not much above my own age, red-faced and well built, but not at all pretty.

"Can you tell me where to find Barras Hall?" I asked.

"Barras Hall? Whatever do you want to go there for?"

"My brother's there," I said. "I have to find him."

"What business has your brother with the likes of them?"

"You mean the Ayrtons?"

"Who else would I mean? They'll give him no work, if that's what he's looking for. Nobody goes to Barras Hall in search of work."

"Why's that?"

"They just don't."

"Nevertheless I believe he's there. Can you tell me how to find it?"

She hesitated, then nodded.

"Keep on the main road as you leave here, that's the Cambo Road. Stay on it through Cambo to Scots' Gap. There's a turning past there on your left, before you come to Hartburn. That'll take you up to Barras Hall. You can't miss it. There are walls all around and but the one way in."

I thanked her and left. Outside, there was a threat of snow in the air. On the grass verges, the morning's frost had not lifted. I passed dark woods in which the frosted branches of leafless trees stood out against the conifers like plumes of smoke. No one passed me on the road.

At Cambo, I asked the way again. My shoes were almost worn through by now, and I wondered how much longer I could walk in them. The road was badly surfaced, and I had started to limp by the time I got to Scots' Gap. Not far past, another road, little more than a lane, turned northward between tall, winter-struck hedges.

The wall started soon after that. It was high and thick, intended to keep people out. Grass grew right up against it and moss covered its top. Beyond it, a screen of trees prevented me from seeing any further. There was no sign of a house. On my left, tall crags cast sharp shadows against the flatness of the sky.

I must have walked two miles or more before I came to a break in that long line of stone. Tall posts flanked a high rusted gate. Behind them, I could make out a sort of lodge, its door boarded up, its windows broken.

I pushed open the gate and stepped inside.

CHAPTER 8

I AM WIDE AWAKE NOW, WIDE AWAKE BUT DREAMING OF MY past. A long path or drive lay in front of me, though from where I stood only a little portion of it was visible. On either side, dense evergreen shrubbery grew close to the edge, hemming in the path and blocking the view. The sky was obscured by tall, leafless trees that rose out of the bushes. They grew thicker and more tangled as they receded into the distance, until at last they became mere shadows through which I could see nothing.

It was as though, stepping through that gate, I had severed myself from all contact with the world outside, as though my universe had abruptly shrunk to the narrow dimensions of this solitary gravel path thick with weeds. I glanced behind me. The heavy gate had closed of its own accord, unheard by me, as though acting in harmony with the trees and shrubs, working in silence to enclose and contain whatever came within their reach. To enclose within, but also, I sensed, to shut out.

Strangely that thought comforted me, for was not the world from which I had come indeed something to be repelled? The walls and gate which had at first seemed so forbidding to me now took on a quite different aspect, as the outriders of a fortress within which—should all go well and against my expectations—I might at last find once more the security that my father's death had snatched away. Behind those high walls I could forget the shabbiness and poverty of that other existence. If only it could be so. I shut my eyes tight and offered up a prayer. If only it could be so.

The path was evidently seldom attended to. Moss and weeds choked it, and I began to fear that Barras Hall might, after all, be deserted or in a state of decay. Was this why there had been no reply to my mother's letter? The trees, a mixture of oaks, beeches, and sycamores, had been left to grow without proper care. I remembered the splendid old trees in our garden at home, and all the pruning and lopping Tom our gardener had said was essential to their health. Here, clumps of dull green moss and splotches of unsightly fungi clung dispiritedly to the trunks, pitting and ruining the bark. I noticed several that had died and one, struck by lightning, that leaned heavily on its nearest neighbor, weighing it down.

I must have walked for almost half an hour. The gravel gave way in places to patches of half-frozen mud, across which I made my way with difficulty.

Turning a sharp corner, I found myself suddenly in full view of the house. Beneath a shrunken sky, from which it could have been cut out and deposited on the ground, it stood facing me like a wall of gray stone. I felt my knees go weak as I looked at it, wondering why I had ever been so stupid as to come here, so naive as to imagine I might ever be received with cousinly pity or concern.

You have seen houses like it on your travels. The drivers with their National Trust cards and their flasks of milky coffee visit them on weekends, to walk, silent-footed, in a daze of admiration, about their stiff, furnished rooms. I have never shared their fascination, but I suppose they look within themselves for memories of a past they never knew.

I had arrived at the end of my road. I knew that if I were forced to turn back down that path and seek the open road again, I would have nowhere to go, that I would in all certainty die in a ditch somewhere.

The facade was a long granite slab with high windows set on the ground floor and smaller, squarer ones on the first. In its center stood a rectangular portico of thick, evenly spaced pillars, topped by a pediment. Other than that, the house was devoid of ornament. Not even the clumps of ivy that rambled in patches over the stone could offset the impression of severity conveyed by its every angle. This was not the severity to which I was accustomed, the grim utilitarianism of the workhouse or the factory, but something of quite a different order.

There was grandeur in it—for the house dwarfed everything around it—and a certain aloofness. Yet the severity of its lines suggested something else. Hauteur mixed with . . . what? Savagery? Not quite, something tamer than that, tamer and yet more ancient, if that were possible.

Hesitantly I climbed the steps to the door. I stood there for a long time, suspended between conflicting fears. Several times I reached out for the handle that pulled the bell, and each time I drew away again. All the time, light was draining from the afternoon sky. I could feel the imminence of night. The cold had grown even more bitter. It was that which hurried my hand to the bell at last. I pulled it hard, a single, determined tug, followed by a long, scarcely bearable silence.

And then, barely perceptible at first, I could hear footsteps coming nearer. The door opened soundlessly and I saw, framed in the doorway by shimmering candlelight, a tall woman dressed in black. Her waist was tightly clasped by a wide leather belt from which hung a huge ring filled with keys. In one hand she held a tall glass lamp in which a candle burned.

"Well, girl, what is it? What brings you here?"

Her voice was sharp and unwelcoming. I stammered my long-rehearsed reply.

"Please, m-ma'am. I . . . I've come to see Mr. and Miss Ayrton. I mean Sir Anthony and Miss Antonia."

I think she almost laughed. There must, after all, have been much in my appearance and the directness of my request that was droll, even absurd. But if she felt any humor in the situation, she suppressed it readily enough.

"Get on your way, you cheeky young baggage, before I tell Hutton to set the dogs on you."

"No, ma'am, please." Fear overcame my hesitancy. "I've walked a long way. From Newcastle. I must speak with them. They're my cousins. That is. . . ."

She had been about to shut the door in my face, but at the word "cousins" she froze.

"What? What did you say, child?"

"I meant . . . My father was their cousin. So I suppose I must be. . . ."

I think my accent had caught her ear. She looked me up and down.

"Father? You say your father? What is your name?"

"Charlotte, ma'am. Charlotte Metcalf."

For a moment something like real pity moved across her face. I could not understand the look she gave me. She frowned and pursed her lips.

"Wait here, girl. Don't move from that spot if you value your life."

She closed the door with a bang. I heard her footsteps move away across the black and white marble floor whose shining face I had seen through the shadows in the entrance hall behind her.

It was growing very cold. I was so tired, I wanted to lie down on the doorstep and go to sleep. Even inside the partial protection of the portico, the biting wind found its way to me. Behind the house, a dog barked loudly, and I wondered if the tall woman had gone to set the beasts on me as she had threatened. Shivering, I waited. I had nowhere else to go.

The door opened again. The woman in black was there again, her face still impassive, looking down at me as though I were a species of snail that had crept into her path.

"You are to come with me," she said. "Stay close behind me and keep your hands to your sides."

I took a deep breath and crossed the threshold. How simple that is to write: "I crossed the threshold." But there are certain steps that take us farther than we think, and once we have taken them we can never go back. That movement of two or three paces was one such. I have never gone back. I can never again be that child on the doorstep, that shivering, half-clad wretch with so little to hope for.

She closed the door behind me. I found myself standing in a high, shadow-filled hall lit by a huge candelabra in the center. Neither gas nor electric lighting had reached that far from town, even by that late date. Here they still used candles or oil.

All around the borders of the hall were pillars of dark pink marble atop which were set busts of Roman emperors in white stone. There was an enormous fireplace of white marble, unlit, and above it a great mirror in which tiny reflected candles sparkled. I had expected decay, and instead here was opulence such as I had never seen. Barras Hall may not have been the grandest of houses—it lacked the stateliness of nearby Wallington or Seaton Delaval—but coming as I did out of such an utter wasteland, everything in it filled me with awe.

The tall woman went ahead of me along a long unlit corridor, then along a side passage lit by a single oil lamp, at the end of which we came to a narrow flight of stairs.

"Watch your step here," she said. "The steps are worn, and you'll break your neck if you slip."

I followed her up gingerly. We entered a wide corridor into which the rays of the setting sun were falling through a line of sash windows. Everything had turned red, for the sun had crept out from beneath its covering of cloud. Between the windows, hanging from long cords, were large portraits done in oils, men and women dressed in the fashions of one hundred and more years ago. All along the corridor, small Chinese cabinets and gold-painted chairs captured the sunlight. I almost stumbled on the faded carpet, realizing with a shock that it was the first on which I had set foot in years, apart from the one in the Lincott's drawing room. The feeling of softness beneath my feet was almost sinful.

We came at last to a high, gilded door. The tall woman paused, holding her candle at chest height, then knocked. A weak voice answered, and she opened the door.

"You are to go in," she said. "Miss Antonia is waiting for you."

I felt so frightened. What had I come to do? To claim an inheritance to which I knew I had no right? To thrust myself on a relative who had already turned my family away empty-handed? The tall woman had made no reference to Arthur. He must not have made it here after all. I shivered as I stepped into the room.

I had expected . . . I do not know quite what. Something infinitely grand and imposing, a salon filled with gilded furniture and rich tapestries, a room in which soirées were held, glittering, full of glittering people. But this was only a small drawing room, lit by row upon row of candles, comfortably furnished in a thoroughly Victorian style. There were no mirrors: that struck me almost at once, so intense had been my expectation that the room would be filled with them. A log fire burned in the grate, a massive fire, whose heat reached into every corner of the little chamber.

On a low divan set against the wall facing the fireplace sat the most striking woman I had ever seen. I held my breath the moment I set eyes on her. She was slender and fair and very, very beautiful. I could not then guess her age very well, but I think now she must have been in her middle or late thirties. She was one of those women whose beauty is not mere prettiness, whose features have the strength to survive the disappearance of early youth. As her eyes fell on me I sensed at once a clutter of emotions: pleasure, curiosity, and, more deeply hidden, an inexplicable sadness.

She was dressed in a fine black gown of shot silk, the collar and sleeves edged with violet, as though she were in half mourning. The whole effect, whether intentional or not, was thoroughly Victorian, as though the woman in front of me still lived twenty or thirty years in the past.

I stood uneasily by the door, not knowing whether to curtsy, step forward, or retreat. She held me with those perfect, unblinking, all-seeing eyes, as though ingesting me by sight alone, in small, satisfactory bites.

"Come here, child."

The softness of her voice surprised and, curiously, comforted me. Its musicality swiftly undermined all my reservations. There was not the least harshness or rebuke in it. At once I felt less afraid than I had been.

"Don't be afraid. I want to look at you."

I stepped toward her tentatively, as though afraid my legs would snap and send me toppling on my face. I could not speak. All the time, I kept my eyes on the carpet.

"Let me see your face," she whispered when I was only a few feet away.

I looked up. Her soft blue eyes were regarding me with an expression of mingled curiosity and pity. I felt like crying out.

"You say you are my cousin Charlotte. Is that so?"

"I . . ." The words froze on my lips.

"Don't worry, child. There's nothing to be afraid of. I won't harm you. Even if there be no truth in your story, I should not send you away empty-handed. There is nothing to fear. Speak up."

"Yes, ma'am. That is, my father was your cousin."

"Your father? And what was his name?"

Her voice was so gentle, her manner so reassuring.

"His name was Douglas Metcalf. We lived in Kenton Lodge, in Gosforth. That is, until he died."

"I see. You mean Gosforth in Newcastle, of course."
I nodded.

"When and how did your father come to die?"

I told her the date and circumstances. Her eyes widened, as though she were hearing of his death for the first time.

"Child, how do you come to know this?"

"I've told you," I said. "He was my father."

"But . . ." She hesitated. "But how do you come to be dressed like this? In rags. Surely—"

"We wrote to you. That is, my mother did. She told you how we had lost our money."

Her mouth opened. She seemed alarmed, startled by my revelation.

"Wrote? Lost your money? When was this?" Her voice took on an urgency that had not been there before.

"Why, soon after Father died. You did not answer. No one answered. No one wanted to help us. We had to go into the workhouse." I found it impossible to keep the bitterness out of my voice. While this beautiful woman had been living here in style, my poor mother had been forced to take my brother and me to that terrible place.

"But, my sweet child . . ."

She stood suddenly, looking down at me.

"Tell me this isn't true," she said. "That you're making it up."

I shook my head.

"It's all true," I said. I lifted my bag. "I have photographs. Of my father and myself. Of my mother. You can see them if you like. There are letters. It's all true. Every word."

"And your mother and brother? Where are they?"

"My mother's dead. She died in the workhouse."

Her hand flew to her mouth. She sank slowly back onto the divan.

"Dear God," she whispered. "We received no letter. No letter, do you hear me?"

She looked at me in horror, in what I took for unfeigned horror.

"Oh, my sweet child. What have we done to you? What have we done?"

There were tears in her eyes. She reached out her hands, held her arms open. In so many years, no one had opened her arms to me like that. I felt a cry spring to my lips, a dreadful cry of misery and loneliness. And the next thing I knew, I had thrown myself on her and been taken into her embrace.

CHAPTER 9

I<small>T WAS LATER THAT NIGHT</small>. I <small>HAD BEEN HANDED ALMOST</small> ceremoniously to the tall woman—whose name, I learned, was Mrs. Johnson, and whose function was that of housekeeper—to be divested of my rags, bathed, powdered, perfumed, and dressed in proper clothes. These latter presented something of a problem, for no children or adolescents lived at Barras Hall, and it was hard to see how Mrs. Johnson could conjure up a wardrobe for me out of nothing. However, leaving me in the bath, she disappeared for about twenty minutes. When she returned, an entire outfit of clothes was cradled in her arms, all of my size. They were a little old-fashioned, dating from perhaps twenty or thirty years before, like the dress my cousin Antonia had been wearing, but very well preserved and of the highest quality.

Women wore so many items of clothing then, most of them underclothes. I started out with long woolen combinations, buttoned and frilled, and black woolen stockings; over these I slipped on a pair of cotton drawers, followed by a white petticoat bodice, exquisitely embroidered and fully equipped with its own array of buttons and frills; over that went a shorter, flannel petticoat and a flounced alpaca petticoat; and finally, a lovely blue silk dress, the most beautiful thing I had ever worn in my life.

Now, bathed and brushed, with my hair combed and teased into something resembling respectability, transformed, in short, from an urchin to a young lady, I was back once more in the little drawing room. This latter, I now realized, was an anteroom that communicated through a double door with a much larger room beyond. With me were my half-cousin, who had already insisted that I address her by the name Antonia, and her brother Anthony. Antonia and I were seated side by side and hand in hand on a little chaise longue while Anthony, a slim man in his early forties, stood by the mantelpiece, almost a parody of a Victorian gentleman. I thought him very handsome, but a little daunting.

I had been brought a light supper of lamb with peas and mashed potatoes, washed down with a little wine. There had been sweet pears for dessert. I was feeling satisfied and warm for the first time in years. I pressed Antonia's hand and struggled to concentrate on what my cousin Anthony was saying.

"You say your brother left Newcastle to come here?"

He spoke in a gentle voice, but so little accustomed was I to male company that I found myself scarcely able to answer his questions. I nodded.

"And how long ago was that?"

I shook my head.

"I don't know, sir. A few months ago, I think."

"You think?"

Antonia leaned forward.

"Anthony, you must not be so hard on her. Only think what she has been through. I am sure she is doing her best to remember things."

"Of course, my dear, of course." He turned his face to me and smiled. "My dear Charlotte, you must not call me sir. I am your cousin and, I trust, your friend. You may call me Cousin Anthony, if you wish."

I could say nothing. I was overwhelmed. In such a short space of time, to have ceased to be an outcast and to be—I held my breath very tightly whenever I thought of this—part of a family once again. My only anxiety at that moment was to know what had become of my brother Arthur.

"Thank you, sir. I mean, thank you, Cousin Anthony."

He smiled broadly.

"Now, let us get back to the subject of your young brother. Are you sure he knew the name of this house? Or that he knew our name, the name Ayrton?"

"I . . . I think so. When I mentioned the names to Annie, she seemed to recognize them."

"But Arthur is rather younger than yourself and may well have been confused. Northumberland is a big place, a young man could easily get lost."

I nodded. My own experience had taught me how easy it was to go astray in this bleak countryside.

"I will have to find him," I said. "He's my responsibility. I should never forgive myself if anything happened to him."

"Nor should we," said Antonia, pressing my hand. "But I hardly think it is such a good idea for you to go in search of him. You would not know where to begin. Would she, Anthony?"

He leaned back against the mantel.

"Not at all. It is a job for a professional. I shall have a detective brought up from London. A trained man, someone with the resources to execute a proper search. If he uses assistants, they will track young Arthur down in no time at all."

"But—" I began.

"Anthony is right, my dear," Antonia broke in. "You would accomplish nothing on your own. It is very nearly the middle of winter. Let Anthony take care of the matter. Arthur shall be found. You have our word."

I hesitated to say what was in my mind.

"Thank you," I said. "Thank you for saying you will find Arthur. And for all this." I indicated the clothes in which I had been newly dressed. "But I . . . What is to happen to me while Arthur is being looked for?"

Antonia looked at me in surprise.

"Happen? Why, my dear Charlotte, nothing is to happen. You are to stay here with us. Surely you cannot have thought otherwise. After all that has taken place. Anthony and I have already spoken about it. You are to live with us. Here at Barras Hall. I take it the house meets your requirements."

I opened my mouth wide. For though I had hoped and prayed for just such an outcome, I had every reason to distrust my fate. I must have looked very foolish, for Antonia laughed, then reached out and drew me into another embrace.

When I drew away at last, I saw Anthony still standing by the fireplace, watching us both with a curious expression in his eyes. Seeing me catch his gaze, he smiled.

"I am very moved," he whispered. "Yes, very moved. I wish Mother had lived to see this. Is that not so, Antonia?"

She parted from me, nodding gently. I remembered my own mother's visit to Morpeth, how she had been sent away in disgrace, but I said nothing. Would it have made any difference if I had?

"And now that that is settled," said Antonia, "we must get you to bed. You seem extremely tired."

Her brother tugged a bellpull next to the mantelpiece, and a few moments later Mrs. Johnson appeared, as though she had been waiting to be summoned.

"You shall have your own bedroom in due course," Antonia said. "But for the moment you may sleep in the west wing. There is a room there entirely suitable for a girl of your age. And such a pretty girl at that. Isn't she, Anthony? Isn't she pretty?"

"She is indeed, my dear. Very pretty indeed. I have no doubt she will grow to be a beauty like you."

"He is such a flatterer, Charlotte. You will find that out in time. Believe only half of what he tells you. But I know he is telling the truth when he remarks on your fine looks."

She paused.

"Johnson," she said, "Miss Charlotte is to remain with us. She is to be one of the family, for she is, indeed, our cousin. Is the pink bedroom ready yet?"

Johnson nodded. In my newfound security, I was less in awe of her and able to examine her more closely. She wore her hair tied back severely in a bun. I would have guessed her to be around fifty, but she had the appearance of someone who had always looked that age. There was an unchangeableness about her. It was almost as though she had always been there and always would be. Her lips were very thin, her cheeks drawn, her eyes sleepy, yet capable of coming instantly alert, like the eyes of a cat.

"Yes, my lady. I've given the room an airing, and the bed as well. They're still a little damp, but I've got a good fire going. I'm sure Miss Charlotte will be very comfortable."

I was a little puzzled that Mrs. Johnson should have undertaken all these tasks herself, but I soon enough learned that she and the man Hutton were almost the only servants in the house. Hutton carried out all the heavy and unpleasant tasks, but most of the housework was done by Johnson, aided by an older woman by the name of Hepple, who seemed to live in the depths of the house and to venture very seldom aboveground. At that time I put all this down to the remoteness of the place and the difficulty that must create for finding staff.

We said our good nights, arranging to meet again at breakfast, and Johnson led me out, her candle held aloft as before. Ahead of us stretched the corridor with windows, in darkness now save for small pools of candlelight at regular intervals. I shivered, finding the cold more bitter after the very considerable warmth of the drawing room.

"You need to wrap up warmly here of nights, miss," said Johnson. "I'll search out a wrap for you. You'll have it in the morning."

There was so much darkness, I could make little sense of where I was led, only that I passed through long, empty corridors, up and down little flights of stairs, past the doors of silent rooms. What light there was came from oil lamps or candles in brackets. I had been brought up in a world of gas and electric light, and though I had worked by candlelight often enough, it had never been in a place so vast or so full of lurking shadows.

But, though the shadows unsettled me a little at first, they did not awaken real fears, so full was I with the sheer happiness I felt boiling up inside me. I had never known such happiness, not even in my years at home with my mother and father. For then I had known nothing else, I had no standards of comparison, no grief or dismay to set against the cosseted life I led. Now the only thing that marred my joy was the knowledge that Arthur was not here to share it with me. But even that weight was much lifted from my shoulders. The thought that a team of trained men—from London, no less—might soon set about searching for Arthur relieved me of my anxiety more thoroughly than I had thought possible. I believed it only a matter of time, of very little time, before I should see him again. I vowed then that once we were reunited, nothing—not marriage, not a career, not children—should ever keep us apart again.

We arrived finally at a low door near the end of a corridor with a curious ceiling, a ceiling painted with angels, their wings just visible in the dim light. Mrs. Johnson opened the door and stood aside to let me pass.

"You'll sleep here tonight, miss. Until we can fix up another room."

I stepped inside. As I did so, for just a moment, I felt a shiver pass straight through me. I put it down to the temperature, yet it seemed strange, for I had stepped from a cold corridor into a room where a warm fire was burning brightly.

Thinking back, I find it hard to separate my first impressions of the room from those I finally took away with me. The walls were covered in a delicate paper depicting a trellis bearing climbing roses and peonies. The bed took my breath away. It was set high off the floor on fluted legs, and over it lay a cloth of rich brocade, embroidered in a Persian pattern. High above it a circular canopy was suspended from the ceiling, and from this two long curtains, tied back at their ends, hung near its head.

Someone had laid a nightgown on top of the bed and drawn the sheets back.

"I told Hepple to put a jar in. You can leave the fire to burn down: it'll help keep off the damp. Breakfast is at seven o'clock, but Miss Ayrton says you're to be allowed to sleep on if you wish. Just ring for me when you wake up. There's a bellpull beside the bed."

I thanked her and stood indecisively in the center of the room. As she reached the door I stepped forward tentatively.

"Mrs. Johnson . . ."

She turned. There was no emotion in her face.

"Yes, Miss Charlotte?"

"I . . . just wanted to thank you."

"You *have* just thanked me."

"No . . . I meant, for believing me. When I came to the door, you were going to turn me away. But you didn't. You went to my cousin Antonia and told her who I was. If it hadn't been for that—"

"I'm sure we're all very happy things have worked out for the best, miss. God looks after us. In His way."

When she was gone, I found a chair and drew it up to the fire. I sat for a long time, watching the flames flicker, watching sparks chase one another up the chimney. Outside, I could hear the wind passing through the tall trees. From time to time the window rattled. But I felt secure and at peace, for I knew no wind could reach me here. No wind, no cold, no hunger. I fell asleep in the chair, thinking I was back in my nursery at home.

CHAPTER 10

I WOKE THE FOLLOWING MORNING TO FIND ANTONIA BENDING over me.

"My dear Charlotte, I am so sorry. I hope I didn't wake you."

I rubbed my eyes and made to raise myself. I was still in the chair where I had fallen asleep.

"Here, let me help you. You must be a mass of aches after a night in that chair." She smiled. "I merely came to reassure myself that you were all right. It is very late, and I know you would not wish to miss so much of the day."

Blinking, I stared at her, then slowly around the room. Someone had pulled back the curtains. It seemed impossible that this could be true, that I had not been dreaming. At the thought of dreams, I recollected something that slipped as quickly away from me again. There had been something in my dreams, something important, something I wanted to remember, but could not.

"Johnson will be here shortly to help you change into fresh clothes. You must not be afraid of her. She has been with us so long, we are quite used to her, but I know she can appear quite alarming at times to those who do not know her."

She reached out a hand and straightened a lock of my hair, which had fallen over my face.

"When you are up and dressed, Charlotte, ask Johnson to show you the way to the morning room. Breakfast finished some time ago, but I'm sure we can find something for you. I'll see to it myself. I'll be waiting for you there."

"What time is it, please?"

"Why, after ten o'clock, my dear. I trust you will not prove to be a sleepyhead."

I shook my head.

"Well, we must find you a clock. This house is quite full of them, though I confess they do not all keep good time."

With that, she smiled once more and glided from the room. It was chilly without a fire, but I was well accustomed to rising before dawn in the cold. Johnson appeared soon after, carrying over her arm a selection of dresses, one of which she said I might choose to wear. I selected a bright yellow satin dress edged with silk.

"We'll have these taken in for you, miss, if you'll have the patience to wear just a couple of them while I see to the others. I'm sorry they're not more fashionable."

They could have been a hundred years and more out of date for all I cared. She helped me out of the blue dress, badly crumpled from my night in the chair, and helped me on with the yellow. When that was done, she sat me down at the dressing table and brushed my hair.

It was growing long again, and I could scarcely believe that the face I saw in the mirror was the same one that had stared back at me, hollow-cheeked, from the shining pots and pans of the Lincotts' kitchen not so many days before.

When I had finished dressing, I crossed to the window and, leaning across the seat set into its bay, looked out for the first time. There were no clouds. Bright sunshine fell on the winter grass and the naked branches of the trees, slanting sideways out of an open sky. A large, formal garden, poorly tended and blighted now by winter, stretched away toward a thick coppice of denuded trees. Around a central lawn stood statues of some sort, their outlines blurred and indistinguishable from where I stood. At the center of the lawn was an ornate fountain, and farther back I could make out what seemed to be the edge of a large maze.

"You'd better hurry along, miss. Miss Antonia will be waiting downstairs."

As we left the room I had my first glimpse of old Hepple. She came shuffling in, carrying a heavy bucket of coals and some kindling, dressed in a dirty apron, and wearing on her head a mobcap that had seen better days. I smiled at her, thinking sympathetically of my own condition in Mrs. Lincott's house, but she looked away and scurried off.

Antonia was waiting for me in the morning room, as promised. Now, looking back across the years, I can still see that room clearly, as it first impressed itself upon my gaze. A room of mirrors and artifice, I had almost said deceit. Paintings of fruit and flowers decorated the walls and ceilings. A large mirror at one end gave the impression of endless space. Gilded furniture shimmered in the sunlight. Antonia sat on a low divan, smoothing the folds of her wedding dress.

She had prepared a small spread of cold meat, eggs, honey, preserves, and freshly baked brioche, all laid out on a white damask cloth over a low table, on the most exquisite plates I had ever set eyes on. They were Sèvres porcelain, fragile and delicately patterned. Steam wafted from a hole in the lid of a silver *chocolatière.* When I had seated myself, she poured chocolate into my cup and offered it to me with a smile.

I felt all my former awkwardness, my diffidence and self-consciousness, rush over me again. As I took the saucer my hand shook, toppling the cup, sending a stream of hot brown liquid across the cloth. The cup struck the floor and smashed into a hundred fragments. For a second something like anger flashed through Antonia's eyes, then she was on her feet, mopping the table with a large napkin.

"Leave it, leave it," she murmured. "It doesn't matter, really it doesn't. It was only a cup."

I stood, looked round me, saw myself reflected in twenty mirrors, and burst into tears.

"I should . . . never . . . have come here," I blubbered. "It's only . . . taking advantage . . . of your kindness. All . . . I wanted . . . was a place . . . here. I can . . . work as a maid. Really . . . That's what I am. I've . . . no right . . . to be . . . in here with you."

Making soothing noises, Antonia dropped the napkin and took me in her arms and kissed me.

"What is all this nonsense about? You are my cousin, my long-lost cousin. Never let me hear you speak of such things again. You are not a servant, Charlotte, you are a young lady of breeding who has passed through a time of difficulty, that is all. Thankfully your difficulties are at an end. From now on you are to live here with Anthony and myself as one of our family. It is your destiny, Charlotte. Your destiny. You are to be the younger sister I never had.

"So let me hear no more talk of your unworthiness. Come, dry your tears and eat your breakfast, or it will soon be time for lunch. I'll set a fresh place for you."

Laughing lightly, she embraced me once more, then sat me at the other side of the table, moving my plate and bringing a cup from a little dresser. It was to become a ritual before long, our taking breakfast together in the morning room, just the two of us.

"I do not expect Anthony back until this evening," she said. "He has gone into Morpeth on business. Business which includes a visit to his solicitors. He intends to instruct them to hire men in London to carry out the search for your dear brother Arthur. They are to set about their task at once. No expense is to be spared. You must put all worries out of your mind now. He will be found. You may rest easy about that."

"I do believe so," I said, for, more than anything, it was what I wanted, needed, to believe. To have found all this—a house, kind relations, comfort—and to think of Arthur in a factory or down a pit somewhere, scraping a living with his bare hands, unsettled me terribly.

"Now, dear Charlotte, what are we to do today?"

"Do?" I swallowed a mouthful of scrambled egg. "Why, I should be perfectly happy to do nothing."

"Well, it is not good to be idle. I am sure your dear mother taught you that. I shall show you a little of the house, of course. You must get to know your way around. And it is not so labyrinthine as it seems. If it is not too cold outside, we shall go for a walk in the garden. Later there will be time to go further afield. There is only

Hutton to do the work, I fear, and the grounds are not as well kept as they were in my father's time, but you will no doubt find some small portions to please you. There is a maze, and a folly, and in the spring there are little wooded dells that fill up wonderfully with wild flowers. If that is to your taste."

"Oh, yes. I should love to see flowers. There were never any flowers . . . where I was."

A shadow passed over her face.

"You shall tell me your . . . adventures this afternoon. Unless, of course, it would pain you to speak of them."

I shook my head.

"If you have time to listen, Antonia. I mean for you to know all about me. Every little thing."

"I intend to know all there is to know. And, tell me, Charlotte—do you read well?"

"Read?"

"Do you ever read aloud?"

"I can, yes. I have not had much practice. But my father used to read to me, and Mother sometimes, so I know how it is done. If the book is not full of hard words, I should not find it too difficult, I'm sure."

"Excellent. Then you must read to me. It is often tedious here, Charlotte. We are so much in the countryside. And the countryside is frequently dull, especially in winter, when no one comes to visit. I have often longed for a companion, someone to share these long days with. We have a large library, shelves full of books, but I have little patience for reading alone. Would you mind that, Charlotte? Reading to me?"

"Oh, no, I should love it. I cannot think of anything I would rather do."

"Then it is settled. You shall read to me. We shall

begin today." She paused. "But we must not neglect your own interests, Charlotte. It would be extremely selfish of me to monopolize your time, much as I would love to do so."

"But it would not be selfish. I should so much like to spend my time with you, Antonia. I feel very happy in your company."

She smiled.

"And it makes me happy to hear it. You shall be happier still, I assure you. But you are still young, and I regret to say that you have lost a great deal of time during these past few years. We must consider your education."

"I had lessons in the workhouse. I can read and count well enough."

She tutted, shaking her head.

"Nonsense, child, that is not what I mean by education. You are not to be a clerk or a governess. I don't want you locked up all day in some dusty schoolroom. You have no need for arithmetic or geography, I assure you. But you are, I think, in need of some polish. It will not be long before you enter society. We must ensure that you are properly equipped for your station in life. A little French, some Italian, a proficiency at the piano, a knowledge of painting, fashion, haute cuisine. You will not mind that, will you?"

"Why, no. I . . . I think I should rather like it."

"Very well. The matter is settled. We are too isolated here to engage a governess. They will not come, they dislike what they call being 'buried in the countryside.'" She smiled winningly. "Well, perhaps they are right. We are a little dull here at times. So I shall have to take charge of your improvement myself. In return for the hours you will spend reading to me. Isn't that a fair bargain?"

Her smile was so engaging, her eyes captivated me. She stood.

"Now, Charlotte, I think it is time we got moving. Do you want to see inside first, or are you more in the mood for a walk outside?"

"Outside, I think. It is such a lovely morning. Not at all like yesterday. It is as though the whole world has changed."

"Indeed it is. It has changed for all of us, has it not?"

Antonia lent me a warm cape and a hand muff, and we set off together, leaving the house through a small door in the rear. It was sharply cold, but bright. A flight of steps took us down into the rear section of the garden, set with low hedges and flower beds, among which weather-beaten wooden benches were scattered.

Antonia took my hand in hers and drew me toward the path leading to the fountain.

"The fountain was built in 1760 by an Italian architect called Zefferino Puccianti. It doesn't look like much at the moment, but in the spring we'll get the water going again. Then it will look very grand."

"I think it's very grand already," I said.

"Wait until you get closer."

I thought how it had looked earlier, spied from my bedroom window. And I wondered if I could guess which was my window from here. Letting go of Antonia's hand, I turned and gazed up at the house, at the windows on the first floor of the west wing. There was a slight movement behind one window near the end. I could see a face. Someone was watching us.

"Antonia," I said, "isn't that Anthony up there?"

She let go of my hand and turned.

"What did you say?"

I pointed toward the window. The face had now disappeared.

"I thought I saw Anthony watching us."

"Anthony? But, gracious child, I already told you that he has gone to Morpeth. He is with his solicitor. It must have been Johnson that you saw. Why don't you wave?"

"There's no one there now."

"No. No, there isn't."

She turned and smiled at me.

"No one at all."

CHAPTER 11

WE DINED THAT NIGHT AT EIGHT. IT WAS A STRANGE EXPERI-ence for me. All the time my father was alive, I had never dined with him or my mother, for they, of course, ate in the dining room downstairs—often with guests—while Arthur and I took our meals with my governess in the nursery. And after that there had been small, simple meals with Arthur and Mother, or a spartan supper in a vast hall with two hundred other women, or scraps snatched from the servants' leftovers in the Lincotts' house. I scarcely knew what table manners were, what knife and fork I ought to use and in what order, how to converse between mouthfuls. In the workhouse I had learned to bolt my food or starve. The taste of wine was wholly new to me, and at first unpleasant.

Antonia and Anthony put up with all this with the best grace. I caught an occasional sideways glance between them, and a little frown on Antonia's face from time to time, but neither said anything. I watched Antonia when I could, as I had watched her all day long, trying to guess her age, for at fourteen it is far from easy to estimate the years of one's seniors. She seemed younger than I remembered my mother, more beautiful, though less soft. Her mouth had a slight hardness and the expression in her eyes was at times brittle. Yet when she smiled, she became quite radiant, quite irresistible.

When it was time for pudding, a long-forgotten luxury, Cousin Anthony leaned across the table with a look of great seriousness.

"Charlotte," he began, "you will be pleased to hear that I have instigated a search for your brother. My solicitors have engaged a London company called the Endicott Detection Bureau. They have offices in Charing Cross, and I am told they are the capital's most reliable investigators. Mr. Melrose, my solicitor, sent a telegram to Endicott himself today, in order to retain his services and give him basic particulars. I have his reply here."

He placed a little pair of half-moon spectacles on his nose, then took from his inside pocket a folded sheet of paper. When he had unfolded it, he held it at a little distance and cleared his throat.

"I shall insert the words omitted by Endicott for the purposes of economy. The telegram reads as follows: 'Stephen Melrose, Esq. Sir: I beg to acknowledge your communication dated this morning, respecting a request by Sir Anthony Ayrton for the assistance of this bureau in tracing the whereabouts of his cousin Arthur Metcalf. In view of the urgency of the situation and your client's generous offer to increase our normal fee, we should be most happy to undertake the task. I propose to arrive in Newcastle tomorrow in the company of two of my best men. Can you please arrange for someone to meet us at the station and for accommodations in a suitable hotel?

Will you also please ensure that we are supplied with a full description of the boy, with a photograph, if possible, and details of how he came to be missing? The services of a clerk with good local knowledge would prove invaluable. I am, sir, your faithful servant, Josiah Endicott.' "

Anthony returned the paper to his pocket, then looking across the table at me, asked, "How do you find the roly-poly, Charlotte? It is to your liking, I trust?"

"Oh, yes, very much."

"And the custard? It is not too thin, I hope?"

I shook my head violently.

"No, no, not at all. It is quite how I like it. Quite how I . . ."

I hesitated.

"Remember it?" asked Antonia.

I nodded. Was that why they had arranged for nursery food to be served at dinner, to awaken a memory in me?

"Mrs. Johnson made it specially. Do remember to thank her later."

"I shall. I shall indeed."

"Now, Charlotte," resumed Anthony, "you realize that I shall have to ask you for details of Arthur. To send to Mr. Endicott."

"Send to him?" I glanced up. "But surely he will come here?"

Anthony shook his head.

"Why, no. It is much too out of the way here. It would only cause an unnecessary delay."

"I see. But surely he will wish to speak to me. Perhaps I should go to Newcastle. I can tell him everything I remember. And I have some lovely photographs."

"That will not be necessary, Charlotte dear." Antonia smiled. "You are still fatigued by your journey here. A description will suffice."

"You and I shall sit down after dinner, Charlotte," Anthony continued, "and you shall tell me all there is to know about your brother. And I will put the photographs into Mr. Endicott's hands personally. You have my word. Now, you must have another helping of roly-poly. And I shall have another as well: it must be twenty years and more since I had any, and I do confess, it is still my favorite."

He cut another fat slice and slipped it onto my plate. Jam ran out onto the dish, staining it red. Then yellow custard was poured over it. I felt a little sick. My stomach, unused to such rich food, was turning ever so slightly.

"Mrs. Johnson will be sorely disappointed if you do not do justice to her cooking, Charlotte. She wants to see red roses in your cheeks again. As do we all."

I smiled and picked up my spoon. As I did so I shivered. The room had grown suddenly cold, as though a draft had rushed in from somewhere, but there was a Chinese screen between us and the door. The fire was still blazing as redly as ever. I saw a look pass between my cousins. They had noticed the sudden chill as well.

"I think you should close a window, Anthony. It has grown quite chilly in here."

Anthony gave her a strange look, then nodded and got to his feet. He went across the room and made as though pushing the sash more firmly shut. But when he returned to his seat, the temperature in the room was still low. The problem did not lie in a partly open window, I was sure of that. But why the pantomime?

Antonia smiled at me and reached for her wineglass. I noticed that her hand shook slightly. She lifted the glass and sipped a little wine. The room began to feel warm again, as quickly as it had grown cold. Antonia glanced at me.

"Charlotte has been reading to me, Anthony."

He raised one eyebrow.

"Really? How splendid. I hope she has been reading something improving. You are much in need of improvement, my dear."

"That is unkind of you. She has been reading from Charlotte Brontë. *Jane Eyre.* We have already made considerable progress. This afternoon we reached the part where Jane meets Mr. Lloyd, the apothecary."

"That is most excellent progress." He turned to me. "Do not let her tire you, Charlotte. My sister will listen to the telling of tales quite remorselessly, she will quite wear you into the ground. You must resist. You must tell her when you are tired, you must put the book down and say you will read no more."

"She has a delightful voice, Anthony, a most delightful voice. A little coarsened by her companionship of the past few years, but possessed of a most winning modulation. I already have great hopes of her. Which brings me to our good news. You will be pleased to learn that I have decided to act as Charlotte's governess."

He raised his eyebrows, looking at me.

"Indeed?" He paused. "That sounds eminently sensible."

"I intend to polish her, Anthony. To make her ready for the station in life to which her destiny calls her."

It was not the first time I had heard Antonia speak of my destiny, yet I still found it a curious turn of phrase for what was, after all, no more than the chance falling out of events.

"You really should not take so much trouble on my behalf," I protested.

"Let us be the judges of that, Charlotte," said Antonia. "What you call 'trouble' is both a duty and a pleasure. I rarely find the opportunity to combine them. Surely you will not begrudge me my chance."

Mrs. Johnson chose that moment to come in to take the plates away. I thanked her for the roly-poly.

"There's nothing to it, miss. Just a bit of suet and some jam. What would you like tomorrow night?"

"Whatever you think best."

"Oh, no, it's not for me to say. You must choose. Was there anything you dreamed of when you were in . . . before you came here?"

I looked at Antonia, then at Anthony. They both smiled encouragingly.

"Well," I said, "there was one thing Cook used to make me on Sundays. Bread-and-butter pudding."

"Capital," shouted Anthony, "capital. That was another of my favorites. Yes, Johnson, you must make some bread-and-butter pud."

"Very well, sir. Miss Charlotte. Bread-and-butter pudding it shall be."

We retired to the little drawing room, the antechamber in which we had been the night before. Mrs. Johnson brought coffee for Antonia and a cup of cocoa for me. Anthony poured himself a glass of brandy from a large decanter. Balancing it carefully on the broad arm of his chair, he again slipped on his spectacles. They gave him a schoolmasterly air, a little pedantic and fussy. Taking a small notebook from his pocket, he turned to me.

"Now, Charlotte, you must tell me all you know about your brother and his movements. Omit nothing that may be of the slightest assistance to the diligent Mr. Endicott."

I told him what I could, which was not, in reality, very much.

"No matter," he said, putting his pencil and notebook away. "He has no money, so he will not have traveled far. You will find that he has taken employment between Newcastle and here, with a farmer perhaps. Put your mind at ease, he will turn up."

Antonia glanced at the clock.

"It is almost ten o'clock, Charlotte. I'm afraid I have tired you today with our walks. Tomorrow shall be less strenuous, I promise. But now I think it is time for you to get some sleep. Do you think you know your way to your bedroom now?"

I nodded, but I had really hoped that someone might take me there. The thought of negotiating those long, dark passages alone was daunting.

"I'm sure you will not get lost. You're not a child, after all. Take that lamp in the corner, I believe it's full."

I picked up a tall oil lamp. Anthony kindly rose from his seat in order to light it for me. He kissed me on the forehead and bade me good night. Antonia also rose. She kissed me lightly on the lips.

"Good night, Charlotte. I know we shall be very happy here together. Anthony and I are so pleased that you have come."

It was a long way to my room. I wanted to walk quickly, but I feared getting lost and was obliged to pause every so often in order to ascertain my precise whereabouts. By night, the house was quite a different place than what I remembered from my tour that afternoon. What had appeared quite a simple route now showed itself a maze of interlacing corridors and tangled shadows. The sound of my dress rustling in the silence alarmed me. My own footsteps echoed on the stone and wooden floors over which I passed.

Seen by night, the west wing appeared desolate. I prayed that it would not be long before a room could be made ready for me in the main part of the house. Last night, I had been too tired and bewildered to give it much thought; but tonight, I found the idea of sleeping so far from the rest of the household disturbing.

I reached my room at last, and slipped inside. The warmth of the fire was welcome after the bitter cold of the passages. I undressed quickly and slipped in between the warm sheets, resting my feet on the stone bottle, yet another luxury I had almost forgotten. I blew out the oil lamp, but left a candle burning.

Lying there, I thought of Annie, still in the maid's room at the Lincotts'. She had no fire or hot-water jar, no silk dresses, no puddings topped with custard. I determined then and there that as soon as I was securely established here, I would ask Antonia to help do something for her. She had, after all, rescued me from the slavery of working for the Lincotts and had sent me on my way here with money she could ill afford to spare. I owed her everything. I fell asleep thinking happy thoughts of how we would meet again, become best friends, and spend the rest of our lives together.

CHAPTER 12

Days passed. The frost lifted for a time, then came down harder than ever. The grass was white most days, the sky clouded over and stayed cloudy. Every morning Antonia and I would walk in the gardens, wrapped up against the ever-deepening cold. We wore hooded capes and our hands were encased in thick muffs of expensive fur. Mrs. Johnson had worked hard to remake several of the dresses to fit me more comfortably, and I was able to change into a different one most days.

Sometimes I tried to imagine how we looked, Antonia and I, two women walking in long dresses through a frosted garden. There was something old-fashioned about the scene, as though time had stood still. I remembered the bustle of Newcastle: trams and motorcars on the roads, steamships on the river, trains hurrying in and out of Central Station. Where was all that now? It was as if it had never existed, as though there had never been anything but this quiet place among winter trees.

I could have believed that time itself had slipped under a coat of frost and become perfectly still.

In the afternoons and sometimes after dinner, I would read to Antonia for an hour or more at a time. She was an attentive and indefatigable listener. We finished *Jane Eyre* and moved on to *Pride and Prejudice*. She often corrected my reading of a word, my pronunciation or intonation, and frequently she was obliged to explain something for me, an allusion or historical reference. I thought her quite clever then, though on reflection I think hers was a superficial knowledge, having no other purpose but to impress. I do not mean she affected learning in order to seem superior, as many people do nowadays. She was wholly free of that sort of vice, believing as she did in an innate superiority of breeding that needed no outward show to bolster it. The display of knowledge was merely part of being an accomplished person, someone capable of joining in conversations at dinner without appearing wholly vacuous. There was nothing in her of the game-show contestant or the autodidact desperate for praise.

Her tutoring of me rested on the same assumptions. She was at first assiduous, embarking straight after breakfast on the first of the day's allotted tasks, dreamed up by her the night before. In the first few weeks, I learned some basic Italian and brushed up the little French I had learned years before and now almost wholly forgotten. From the library, Antonia brought massive volumes on the history of art, stuffed with sepia reproductions of works by the great masters, accompanied by dreary commentaries that she quickly discarded in favor of her own lighter remarks, remarks I now perceive to have been deeply misinformed.

We found an old harpsichord, rather out of tune,

under a dust sheet in a long-unused music room on the first floor. For half an hour each day she and I would sit facing this instrument while I, with clumsy fingers, attempted pieces by Bach and Mozart. Antonia herself played tolerably well, but without feeling. At intervals, she would instruct me in the names of exotic dishes, the vintages of wines, or the latest Parisian fashions, all without any apparent guiding principles.

For languages, music, deportment, and all the rest were, I soon discovered, a cause of infinite ennui to my cousin. Often in the middle of a session, or as I was finishing a sonata, she would drift into a little reverie, out of which I feared to rouse her; or talk about her childhood and early youth; or suggest that we take a walk about the grounds, hand in hand over frosted grass.

The one thing she did enjoy was horse riding, and she was determined to make a good horsewoman of me. She herself rode a sorrel gelding called Coriolanus, while I was presented with a two-year-old by the name of Petrarch. It cannot have been much fun for Antonia, for what she wanted was a riding companion with whom she could gallop for miles through the open fields, whereas I, wholly untrained, could barely keep a saddle. She persevered, however, and in a week or two I had at least learned how to sit up straight without tumbling to the ground.

There were, of course, frequent intervals in which I was free to explore the house and grounds alone. I never walked far, never out of sight of the hall.

A large stream ran through the estate for over a mile. Anthony explained that it was a tributary of the River Coquet and that its name was the Hartwell. The folly Antonia had told me about stood on a low hill overlooking the stream across a short grass sward. It was a small Greek temple, complete with Doric columns. A small door behind the portico formed the only entrance, but when I first went there, I found it locked. I thought briefly of asking Antonia for a key, but in the end thought better of it. The little temple repelled me somehow. There was a sinister feeling about it and the area for some distance around.

Returning from it the first time, I asked Antonia who had built it. She seemed almost reluctant to answer, then smiled her very best smile and sat me down beside her.

"It's almost as old as the house, my dear. One of our Ayrton ancestors had it built, a man called Sir James Ayrton. It was his father, William, who built Barras Hall. William was a Whig who stayed loyal to the Earl of Sunderland after his fall in 1710. It's a thing our family has always prided itself on—its loyalty, its consistency. William's faithfulness brought him a rich reward. Sunderland became first lord of the treasury eight years later, and he did not forget the Ayrtons. When the hall was completed, the earl himself gave Sir William many books out of his own collection, and in time a great library was created here."

"Is that the same library I like to read in?"

A wistful look crossed her face.

"No, my dear. I'm afraid it's no longer what it was. Our grandfather incurred debts—gambling debts, if you want to know the truth—and to pay them off he sold over half the volumes. Most of the really valuable books have gone."

"And what about the folly?"

"The folly? Oh, yes, of course. Well, James Ayrton, Sir William's son, built the west wing, where you sleep. He was widely traveled. I believe he got as far as India, and afterward he was the British ambassador in Constantinople for a time. Later I'll show you some of the treasures he brought back from his travels. He built the folly in 1740 as a place to hold parties. That was all the rage in his day."

"What does the inscription mean?"

"Inscription?"

"Over the doorway. 'They shall inherit it forever.'"

For a moment she seemed uneasy, as though the words had carried uncomfortable associations for her. Then she smiled and nodded.

"Oh, you mean our family motto. It's a verse from the book of Exodus: 'I will multiply your seed as the stars of heaven, and all this land that I have spoken of will I give unto your seed, and they shall inherit it forever.' Well, perhaps so, but the old folly has seen its best days, I'm afraid. We've not had much use for it since Sir James's time. It's cold and damp inside. Anthony talks of having it knocked down before it gets to be an eyesore. It's not in good repair. Hutton thinks it may be dangerous. I'd stay away from it if I were you."

There was a steeliness in her voice that startled me. As though she were afraid I might go to the folly, afraid I might see something she did not want me to see. She changed the subject then, and I said no more of it.

There was another part of the grounds Antonia wished me to avoid. Not far from the folly, a steep path wound its way down through thick undergrowth toward the river. Passing it once, I asked Antonia if it led anywhere interesting.

"Why, no . . ." She faltered. "There are . . . some very dull ruins. An old church used to stand there. But it was too far from the house for comfort, and my grandfather had it pulled down. You'll find nothing there now but a few old stones. But I would rather you stayed away from the place, Charlotte. The path is muddy and treacherous, even dangerous in parts, and you might very easily slip and break a leg, or worse. We might not find you for days."

I agreed, but mentally reserved the possibility of an exploratory visit in the spring or summer, when the mud would have dried up. The thought of old ruins, however sparse, thrilled me.

I spent more and more time in the library. Sir William Ayrton's original library had been shut up and the books removed to a gloomy chamber on the first floor, a place full of shadows, little visited, dusty, and ill lit. The books had been left to fall, as it were, into a dust-induced slumber, seldom disturbed, unread, unloved. I came to believe it was my mission to wake them up and bring some sort of light back into their existence. Whenever I got the chance, I would go to the library to browse or read until the cold forced me to leave again. Finally Antonia said she would ask Hepple to light a fire there for me in the afternoons. It became part of her educational project for me.

Yet her manner was changing almost imperceptibly. I would often find her preoccupied. Sometimes, in the middle of a passage, she would stand and tell me to stop reading. Very often, she would go to the window and stand staring out into the garden, almost as though expecting to see someone appear there and come toward her. Once, as I watched, I saw her start, but when I asked if she was all right, she assured me that she was perfectly well. And yet, when she turned, I saw that her face had gone quite pale and that she was trembling.

At certain times this nervousness became more

marked. On two further occasions it grew cold during dinner, as it had done soon after my arrival. Each time Antonia turned noticeably pale and looked at her brother anxiously. From the corridor leading to my room a small branch passage broke off. At its end, only yards from the main corridor, a short flight of stairs led up to a low wooden door, drab and untended in appearance, as though the room to which it belonged had been long neglected. During our first tour of the house, Antonia had told me that the door was kept locked, that the room was used for storage and never entered. Yet I could not repress a faint shudder every time I passed the opening that led to it, for it seemed darker than the rest of the house, and very sad, as though it had once been the scene of an unhappy or terrible event. I observed that whenever she passed that way, Antonia very deliberately kept her gaze fixed in front of her, quickening her pace a little, and biting her lip.

I saw little of Anthony. He was often away during the day, but it was never made entirely clear to me what business took him from Barras Hall. We dined together most evenings, and every night I would ask what progress had been made in the search for my brother. Generally Anthony would reply that there was no fresh news; but from time to time he would pull from his pocket a letter from Endicott, detailing the progress of the investigation. So far they had traced Arthur to two lodging houses in the west of Newcastle, then to a jobbing carpenter's shop in Fleece Court and a farm on the outskirts of the city, at Kenton. There was a possibility that he had been seen a little farther north than that, at Ponteland, through which I had myself passed on my way to Barras Hall. It seemed that he was on his way here, and I began to think he would arrive at the front door in person, as

I myself had done, long before Endicott and his men could track him down.

And then, quite unexpectedly, there came a report that he was back in Newcastle, for he had been seen there in a city-center shop one week earlier.

"He must have taken fright at the cold weather," said Anthony. "And he would be right. This is no time of year for a boy like him to be trudging through the countryside. He has made the right decision to get back to the town."

"But when will I see him? You said it would not be long."

He reached across the table and took my hand.

"My dear, I fear we may have to wait for spring before he risks the road again. But don't fret. He won't slip through the net we've woven for him. Endicott has posted a fine reward in every public house and lodging this side of Newcastle. He has men scouring the city every day. Arthur won't get far. You'll be together again in time for Christmas. I promise you."

That night I went to bed quite distressed, for in spite of Anthony's reassurances, my former fears for Arthur's safety had surfaced again. In the workhouse, I had heard people speak repeatedly about how hard winter was for the poor. Everyone had known friends and relatives who had died from cold or hunger when the temperature dropped too far or there was snow on the ground. Could Arthur, alone and without resources, survive to the spring? If he was now in the city, would Endicott be able to find him in time?

CHAPTER 13

THE DAYS DRIFTED. WINTER GREW MORE SEVERE, THERE WAS snow at the end of November, deep enough to keep us confined to the house for almost a week. I resigned myself to the likelihood that Arthur would remain undiscovered for another few weeks at least and gave up hoping to be reunited with him by Christmas.

"Did you love your brother very much?" Antonia asked me one morning.

"Yes, of course."

"There is no 'of course' in it," she replied. "Take Anthony and myself. We are very loving, but we were not always so. When we were children, we positively hated one another. Or so it seemed at the time."

"It cannot have been true. You are very happy together. Like a husband and wife."

She raised her eyes from the tapestry she had been working on.

"You think so, do you?"

I nodded.

"Were your parents like that? Very loving toward one another, I mean?"

"Yes. Oh, very much indeed."

"Then you were very lucky. It is not always so."

I already had a good idea that such was the case, from conversations overheard in the workhouse. But I had rather thought the lack of love those women spoke of owed a great deal to poverty. The middle and upper classes, I still fondly imagined, were free of the terrible vices and unbearable pressures that split working-class families apart.

"When I grow up," I said, "I think I would like not to marry, but to live in a house like this with Arthur."

Antonia snapped off the thread she had been working with and tossed her needle into the basket.

"I am delighted to hear it," she said. "Now, if you will excuse me . . ."

She stood and left the room, leaving me puzzled by the abruptness of her departure. I remained in the morning room to finish off a small piece of embroidery I had begun two weeks earlier. When it was done, I saw that more than an hour had passed. I wanted to show Antonia my completed work and therefore set off in search of her.

I could find her nowhere on the ground floor. The house was quite silent: Anthony had gone out to visit a farm on the estate, Mrs. Johnson and Hepple were preparing lunch in the kitchen. Upstairs, I headed directly for Antonia's bedroom, a large, mirrored chamber set almost in the center of the building, with a superb view over the garden.

As I worked on the embroidery, which involved some complicated pieces of raised needle weaving and cloud-filling stitches, Antonia had regularly complimented me. I was proud of the finished article, still tightly fastened in its tambour, and now wanted to surprise her with it, for she had expected me to take another day at least over its completion.

She had left the door of the room open. Rather than call out and draw attention to my presence, I approached the door quietly, meaning to surprise her. But as I reached the opening I caught sight of her in one of the large mirrors that hung on the wall facing me. Her back was turned, and at first I could only see her partially. There was, however, something about her manner that cautioned me to be careful and, above all, not let myself be seen.

She had changed her clothes, and now, as she turned slightly, I could see that she was no longer wearing the dress she had been wearing when she left the morning room, but a wedding gown. It had once been a lovely thing of lace and satin and embroidered panels, white and delicate and soft, but was now rather faded and even tattered in places, as though it had been torn and clumsily repaired. As I watched I saw that Antonia was admiring herself in another mirror on the opposite side of the room, turning, bending, straightening, for all the world like a young bride on the morning of her wedding.

And then, abruptly, her hands flew to her face. As though stricken, she stood thus for a few moments before sinking onto the bed behind her, sobbing like a child. Embarrassed now and frightened, I turned and sneaked away along the corridor and down the stairs.

All during lunch, Antonia seemed very strained, and if I looked closely, I could see the redness in her eyes. She admired my embroidery without real enthusiasm and ate distractedly. Returning to the subject of the morning, she inquired more closely about Arthur: what he had been like, what things he took pleasure in, what he found distasteful, what he most liked to eat, and so on—no end of trivialities, to which I offered the best answers I could.

The afternoon I spent alone in the library at Antonia's suggestion, reading a novel called *Ardath* by Marie Corelli. She was at the height of her fame in those days, though I fancy even you, Doctor, have never heard of her. And very lucky you are, too, for she was a dreadful prig and a worse writer, and she deserved none of the success that public opinion of the time heaped upon her.

Anthony spent almost the whole of dinner regaling us both with stories of the tenant farmers and the extra work they had to put in when it snowed. One man had already lost three sheep in snowdrifts. Another farm was wholly out of reach, even on horseback. Antonia listened politely while her brother spoke, but I saw that she was still out of sorts, pale, and thinking of other matters, matters whose nature I could only vaguely guess.

I reached my bedroom a little early to find Johnson turning down the sheets. She seemed a bit startled by my sudden arrival. I asked her if she thought Antonia was ill, for she did not seem to be herself.

"She's not ill, miss, no. It's just that sometimes . . ."

"Sometimes what?"

"Nothing, miss. When you're older, you'll understand better. You have to be kind to Miss Antonia. She hasn't had an easy life. In spite of appearances."

She turned to go, then, pausing, looked back at me.

"Be sure to keep your door locked tonight, miss. Once I've gone."

"Locked? Whatever for?"

She looked steadily at me.

"This is an old house, miss. The doors are old. Sometimes a wind blows on the moors. The corridor can be drafty, and these doors don't hold as fast as they used to. Best to keep it locked. I have a key. I can let myself in when I bring your hot water in the morning."

I must have fallen into a deep sleep. I had sat up reading and must have dozed off in my chair. When I woke, I felt stiff and awkward. The fire had died down almost to nothing. My candle was still alight, but it had burned down low. Something must have wakened me. As I sat there the first thing I heard was the wind. And then, above it, another sound. The sound of footsteps coming along the passage outside my room.

I sat stock-still, straining my ears. The footsteps continued. They reached my door and stopped. With a shock, I realized that I had forgotten to lock the door as Mrs. Johnson had instructed. The key was in the lock. My heart beating, I rose and tiptoed across the room, fearful that at any moment someone would open the door. My finger reached the key and turned it softly. I fancied I could hear breathing, but could not be sure it was not my own.

And then I heard the footsteps again, moving away this time. When they had quite faded away, I could hear nothing but the wind in the branches.

CHAPTER 14

ANTONIA SEEMED IN BETTER SPIRITS THE NEXT MORNING, AS though recovered from her preoccupations of the day before. When I came down for breakfast, she greeted me warmly.

"I'm sorry I was such poor company yesterday," she said. "I had a sick headache. They afflict me from time to time."

I sympathized with her and asked if she had slept well.

"I did. And you?"

"Did you . . . pass my room in the night?" I asked.

"Pass your room? Why, whatever for?"

"I . . . thought I heard footsteps at my door."

A slight frown ran over her face, then she smiled reassuringly.

"You must have dreamed it, my dear. Everything here is still strange to you, you are not yet familiar with the sights and sounds of the house. But I assure you no one would go down there to disturb you."

"Yes," I said, "it must have been a dream."

But the memory was too clear. Was it possible that things could happen here without my cousin's knowledge?

It was sunny for a change, and after breakfast we went out for our first walk in over a week. The gardens were still deep in snow, but Hutton had cleared some of the paths sufficiently for us to take our "constitutional" without having to trudge through drifts.

Ever since my arrival at Barras Hall, something had been niggling at the back of my mind, and that morning I realized for the first time just what it was.

"Antonia," I said, "can you tell me why it is there are no birds in the garden?"

"No birds?"

"Not here, not in the woods, not anywhere on the estate so far as I can tell."

"But, my dear, they've all gone south for the winter—surely you know that. It's called migration."

"Of course, I was taught about it at school. But our teacher said that a few birds stay on, even in winter. Robins and suchlike. But I can't see any of them."

Antonia glanced at me uneasily and smiled. It was a forced smile, one she kept in reserve for situations like this. I had begun to find my cousin a little false.

"Well, my dear, they must be there if you say they should be. But I am sure they keep to their nests in weather such as this. They'll venture out in due course. You'll see."

I nodded, unconvinced, but in no position to argue. I was a city girl, I had no understanding of the ways of the countryside. Perhaps Antonia was right, perhaps even the robins kept to their homes in colder weather.

But surely there had been no birds even before that, before the snow fell or the ice froze on the ponds. I could not wholly dispel a growing fear that there was something unnatural about Barras Hall and its grounds.

That night I locked my door as soon as I got to my room. I sat up reading again, but this time I did not fall asleep, and I heard no footsteps in the passage. Eventually I went to bed as usual and fell asleep almost at once.

It must have been very late when I woke. My candle had burned out, and it was pitch-dark. For a moment I thought there must be footsteps again, but though I strained, I could hear nothing. And then, just for a moment, there was something. Like a child's laugh, cut short.

I sat up. It was very cold, and I was frightened.

"Is someone there?" I whispered. But there was only silence. Fearfully I reached out for the box of matches I had left on my bedside table. I struck one, holding it up as it flared into flame. The room was empty. The match burned down and went out.

The next moment I heard something else. I could not tell at first what it was. A scratching sound. Very faint. I listened intently, trying to determine from what direction it might be coming. It must be a mouse, I thought with relief. And that other noise must have been it squeaking. I was not afraid of mice, I had seen plenty in the Lincotts' scullery after dark.

The scratching continued. After a few minutes I had to admit that it was no mouse. It was too regular, too deliberate for that. And I now knew from which direction it was coming. From the window. I remembered the dream I had had, the dream in which I had seen Arthur at a window, first outside, then within, scratching on the pane. I had thought that just a dream. But now I was wide-awake, listening to the same sound. For the first time, I do not know why, the thought passed through my mind that Arthur might be dead. It was such a silly, disturbing notion, I dismissed it instantly.

The scratching still continued. I could not bear to lie there any longer, just listening to it. I struck another match and got out of bed. Using a third match, I lit the oil lamp. Its more powerful flame cheered me instantly. I hesitated only a moment before crossing to the curtains and pulling them aside.

As I did so the scratching stopped. I saw myself reflected in the windowpanes, a ghostlike figure in a white nightgown that trailed around my feet, a light held aloft in one hand. Putting the lamp on my dressing table, I returned to the window and pressed my face to the glass.

There was a little moonlight. I could see the garden below, stark and still, frost thinly laid across its surface, trees in the distance, visible only as shadow. I caught sight of something moving, very slowly and deliberately, across the grass, a little in front of the fountain. My breath clouded the glass, and I rubbed it. I looked out again, at the spot where I had seen the movement. All was stillness. There was nothing there.

CHAPTER 15

I SAID NOTHING AT BREAKFAST OF WHAT I HAD HEARD AND seen. For, indeed, by the time morning came I could no longer be sure I had actually seen or heard something. The shadow on the lawn might have been anything—a fox or a squirrel: the countryside was full of things about which I knew next to nothing.

The cold weather had returned, and with it fine rain and a threat of storms. We stayed indoors, Anthony in his study, Antonia and I in the drawing room, where we painted insipid watercolors of wildflowers copied from books. Rain shone on the windows, the fire crackled and blazed, a tall clock ticked on the mantelpiece and another by the door, the world around me seemed at peace at last, and I put all disquieting thoughts out of my head. If only Arthur were here, my happiness would be complete, I thought.

About three o'clock a sharp wind began to rise. The flames in the fireplace were blown hither and thither, soot fell down the chimney and spilled out onto the hearth, the windows began to bang annoyingly. Antonia looked up from her painting.

"Charlotte, dear, would you be so good as to fasten the window more tightly? It's making such a racket. And why not draw the curtains while you're at it?"

I had been sitting on a low divan near the window. Putting down my board and brush, I crossed to it and fumbled with the catch, which either Johnson or Hepple had left unfastened. As I did so I glanced out into the darkening garden.

There may have been a movement, I am not sure, but something drew my attention to a point near the far end of the lawn, just where the garden ended and the screen of trees began. It was at first impossible to distinguish with any clarity, but moments later I saw someone step away from the trees and onto the lawn. It was a woman or girl, wearing a full-length gray dress, with long fair hair that fell below her shoulders. She was coming toward us quite quickly, not running, but moving rapidly somehow. As she drew closer I saw that she was quite young, about my own age or a little older.

I turned my head to Antonia.

"Who is the young lady in the garden?"

Antonia's paintbrush seemed to freeze in mid-stroke.

"I don't understand," she said. "What young lady?"

"Why, come and see. She's coming this way."

If ever in my life I have seen someone turn pale, it was then. Antonia stood and joined me at the window, somewhat reluctantly, I thought. When I looked down again, there was no one there. Just wind and the last of the thin rain.

"Where?" Antonia demanded. She had grabbed my wrist hard and her voice was strangely hoarse.

"Why, there." I pointed toward the spot where I had last seen the figure in the gray dress. "Well, I can't think where she can have gone."

"What . . . did she look like? What was she wearing?"

I described her as best I could, and as I did so Antonia drew away from the window.

"Draw the curtains, child, quickly."

"Why, what is it, Antonia? You're shivering. Whatever's wrong?"

She was in the middle of the room now, clearly struggling to retain possession of herself.

"Wrong?" She smiled horridly. "Nothing's wrong. Why should you think that? I just felt a chill, that's all. Hurry and close those curtains, there's a draft in here."

I did as she asked, then returned to my seat on the divan.

"Do you know who she was?" I asked.

"Who?"

"Why, the girl in the garden, of course."

Affecting disinterest, she picked up her brush and started painting with short, nervous strokes.

"It must have been Rington's girl, from the Low Farm. He sometimes sends her over with accounts for Anthony. She'll have to hurry if she wants to get home before dark."

But she had been coming this way, not away from the house but toward it. And quickly, as though running. But she had not been running. I said nothing more. But of one thing I was certain. Whatever I had seen on the lawn the night before, it had not been the girl from Low Farm.

* * *

That night at dinner, as though prompted by his sister—as I suspect he had been—Anthony spoke of the visitor he had received that afternoon.

"Young Clara. She's almost a woman now. It won't be long before Rington marries her off to one of the local lads."

He turned and smiled at me.

"Have you ever been to a wedding, Charlotte?"

I said I had not.

"Then we must see that Clara's is a proper occasion. We'll have the whole countryside in and give the young couple a feast. There hasn't been a wedding on the estate for as long as I can remember. Has there, Antonia?"

Antonia shook her head but said nothing. I sensed the tension in her posture and silence, and remembered stumbling upon her the day before, in a wedding gown, in tears.

Later, when I got to my room, Mrs. Johnson was tending to the fire, which had been blown about by the storm. I watched her brush soot from the hearth and poke the remaining logs back into flame. A smell of resin wafted through the room.

"What sort of girl is Clara?" I asked.

She straightened, looking at me with a puzzled expression.

"Clara? Who exactly do you mean, miss?"

"Why, Clara Rington. The girl from Low Farm."

Her face lightened.

"That Clara? Well, I see very little of her. A dull enough girl she is, and fat like her mother. Lazy, too, by all accounts."

This did not sound much like the slim creature in a gray dress I had seen on the lawn.

"I've heard her hair is very fine," I said.

"Her hair?"

"She has lovely long fair hair, doesn't she?"

Mrs. Johnson shook her head.

"Why, bless me, no. She's as dark as the devil himself, is Clara Rington. Whatever do you want to know all this about her for, anyway?"

"Oh, nothing. I just thought I saw her today when she visited the house."

"Visited . . . ?" She looked at me strangely. "Why, no, you must be mistaken, miss. There've been no visitors today. And, as I say, Clara Rington is dark, not fair."

"Then who was it I saw this afternoon, walking across the garden?"

Her face did not turn pale as Antonia's had, but nonetheless I saw her expression change and a sort of hoodedness fall over her eyes. I described the girl I had seen in as much detail as I could muster.

"You must have been mistaken, miss," was all she said when I had finished. "There was no one here like that today. The rain plays tricks. The light, late in the afternoon."

"But I saw her clearly. I . . ."

She shook her head decisively.

"No, miss. There was no one in the garden today."

"But I tell you, I saw someone. She—"

"Please, miss. It's better you don't say any more. The mind can play all sorts of tricks. When my boy—"

She pulled herself up suddenly, as though she had said something out of place, and started abruptly for the door.

"You were going to say something about your son,

Mrs. Johnson. I didn't know you had children. Does he live nearby?"

She seemed about to twist away from me, but I would not let her go.

"Yes," she said flatly, "I had a son. A boy about your age, miss, a lovely boy with a voice like an angel. He used to sing in the choir at Kirkwhelpington. He . . . he died. My husband left us soon after that, there've been no others."

Her voice had clouded over, and I felt embarrassed to have opened an old wound so clumsily.

"I'm sorry, I—"

"It's all right, miss. It was a long time ago. I'm over it now. Well over it."

"What were you about to say about him?"

She hesitated.

"Only . . . Only that after he passed on, I sometimes thought I saw him. In the house here, out in the grounds, places I'd seen him when he was alive. But it was fancy, miss, that's all. Fancy and grief. They make a bad pair. It passed in time. But I know the mind does queer things. Like what you fancied you seen today."

I said nothing in reply. She gazed at me hard for a moment, as though torn, as though there were more she could say, but dared not. At last she seemed to think better of it.

"Remember to keep your door locked as I told you, miss. The storm is set for worsening tonight. Keep it locked and you'll not be wakened."

When she had gone, I sat for a long time by the fire, listening to the sound of my clock ticking, to the ashes falling into the grate. Outside, the wind was still rising. I could hear it blowing in gusts across the tops of the trees, hurling itself against the high roof of the house.

My window rattled constantly, and from time to time the thin curtain would move in a little trembling dance. Cold drafts crept into the room, toying with the flame of my lamp, making me shiver.

I went to bed soon after midnight and fell asleep, worn out by thinking about the girl I had seen in the garden and about whom everyone was lying to me. Sometime in the middle of the night I was startled into wakefulness by a loud noise. I sat up in bed, listening carefully. The wind was howling fearfully by now, cracking and bumping around the house like a questing beast. The noise came again, a banging sound from outside. I lit my candle and clambered out of bed. It was bitterly cold. The fire had long since died to ashes. Still half-asleep, I threw on my shawl and stumbled to the window. When I drew the curtain, I found I could see out quite clearly, for the wind had blown the clouds away.

There were stables at the end of the east wing, and I saw now that one of the wooden doors had come unhooked and was banging against the wall. Even as I watched I saw someone appear from the house and make his way across the courtyard to the stables. It was Hutton, carrying a storm lantern. He made the door fast and returned to the house. All became still again, except for the wind, which, as if frustrated by this interference in its work, seemed to be blowing harder than ever.

I thought I would never manage to get back to sleep, what with the terrible noise and the drafts blowing through every crack in my window frame. As I prepared to draw back the curtain, however, I noticed that the window had inside shutters. They would certainly help deaden the noise and keep the drafts out.

At first I thought they must be stuck fast. Certainly they had not been opened in a very long time. But I exerted all my strength and managed to get one wing open. Inside, it was full of dust and cobwebs. The hinges were jammed with rust, but I pushed and pulled until they gave and the shutter moved into place.

I had expected the second wing to give me the same trouble, but to my surprise it came open with very little effort, as though it had been regularly used not so very long ago. I pushed it shut and turned away.

At that moment I felt something very like a draft pass through the room. It reminded me of the cold I had experienced on those three occasions in the dining room. No sooner had it vanished than I became aware that I could hear something. I felt my flesh crawl, thinking the sound came from within the room. But, as I listened, I realized that I was mistaken, that it came in fact from the corridor. And that it was the sound of someone sobbing bitterly.

I stood in perfect silence, straining to hear. The howling of the wind was muted now by the shutters. I had not been mistaken. Someone was weeping, very softly, in another room. I lit the oil lamp on my dressing table. Taking a deep breath, I lifted it and stepped to the door. Taking care to make as little noise as possible, I turned the key and opened the door a fraction. The passage outside was pitch-dark and cold, very cold, colder even than my room. I listened attentively, trying to ascertain from which direction the sound was coming. It seemed to issue from my left, where the locked room was situated. The sobbing was pitiful now, rising and falling without pause, as though someone's heart was broken.

The more I listened, the more certain I became that it was a young woman or a girl of about my own age. I felt an awful sense of dread creep into me. My legs were like lead, I could hardly move from where I stood, and yet

I knew I had to go farther. I could not return to my room and leave unanswered the question drumming through my mind.

Slowly, like someone moving in a dream, I walked to the opening where the short passage branched off. It stretched ahead of me, flickering with shadows stirred by the light. At its end the stairs led to the door. It was just as I remembered it, but for one thing: it was half-open.

The weeping continued, every sob chilling me to the bone. In the shadows, the door seemed to beckon to me. I wanted to run, to pick up the hem of my nightdress, turn tail and flee back along the corridor, hurry to my room and slip inside and turn the key and take refuge in my bed. But I knew I could not. Not now.

I must have stood there shaking for a very long time, I could not say how long. Everywhere shadows bobbed up and down, for the lamp was trembling in my hand. That such a simple thing as a girl weeping should have filled me with such fear may appear ridiculous to you. But you were not there, you did not have to see the darkness behind the door, you did not have to listen to the endlessness of that voice.

It took me a long time to cross the short distance separating me from the stairs. My heart pounded painfully as I climbed up. At the top I leaned forward.

"Who's there?" I called. "What's wrong?"

At that instant the crying stopped. It did not falter or fade away, it just halted. Nowadays we would say "as though someone had turned a switch." And at that very moment I heard a voice behind me.

"Charlotte. What are you doing out here? What can you be thinking of?"

I turned, my heart beating loud enough to fill all that

sudden silence. Antonia was standing behind me, a candle in her hand. She was dressed in a long white nightgown, and her loose hair hung down over her shoulders like a veil.

"Do you know what time it is?" she demanded.

"I . . . I . . ." I faltered. "I heard something."

"Heard? What did you hear?"

"Why, didn't you notice it? You must have. She was weeping so loudly. It went on for such a long time. And she must be in there now. I have to find her, I have to go to her."

"Weeping? Someone in there? What sort of nonsense is this? The only sound I have heard is the wind. The wind singing outside. You have mistaken the wind for something else."

Nimbly she slipped past me and closed the door. There was a key in the lock. She turned it and took it from the door, clutching it tightly in her hand.

"Come away from here at once," she commanded. "You will catch your death of cold."

"But . . . ," I tried again.

She looked very coldly into my eyes.

"There was nothing there," she said. "A door blown open by the wind, and the storm howling outside. Do not deceive yourself any further, Charlotte. Go back to bed."

There was nothing more I could do. I walked quickly back to my room and slipped inside. As I turned to lock the door I felt something brush my cheek. It was . . . as though someone had touched me softly with their hand. The touch was followed by a rustling sound, very gentle, like a woman's dress. And then the sound of my clock ticking. And the wind outside, crying across the night.

CHAPTER 16

I DID NOT SLEEP AGAIN THAT NIGHT. DEAR GOD, I CAN STILL remember how I sat in that semidarkened room, listening to the cries of the wind, imagining at every moment a movement beginning among the shadows or a whisper forming at my ear. I opened the shutters once more, fearing that if I left them as they were, it would never grow light in that room again.

A little before dawn the wind died down, and I heard the crying again, softer now, or weaker, and more pitiful than I remembered. It stopped when the first light struggled into my room. I may have slept a little after that, but I truly do not recall.

Not long after that, I dressed in order to make myself a little warmer. As the daylight strengthened I began to feel less apprehensive. It is curious how our desire for normality can override even the most powerful impressions of the strange or the terrible. At moments I almost started to believe that Antonia had been telling the truth, that I had indeed heard nothing but the wind. And that I had seen nothing in the garden the day before, only rain falling and the light of the sun in its descent. I determined to ask Antonia outright about the incident.

It was a little before eight, when I normally went down to breakfast, that I heard someone moving in the corridor. As a rule, neither Hepple nor Mrs. Johnson came that way so early. I recalled Antonia's haste to close and lock the door of the room above the stairs, and I now wondered whether the footsteps I had just heard might not be connected with it in some way.

Hastily gathering my long skirts above my ankle to stop them brushing against the floor, I sneaked out of my room and turned toward the stairs. Someone had lit a light farther down. At the corner, where the short passage branched off, I flattened myself against the wall. Now, quite distinctly, I could hear noises coming from the end of the passage. Footsteps and an occasional bump. There was someone there after all.

Gingerly I edged my head partly around the corner. A single light burned at the foot of the stairs. The door was ajar, and through the narrow gap I could make out a soft glow as of daylight. I was working up enough courage to go forward when the door opened. A moment later Mrs. Johnson appeared in the entrance. She seemed tired and gray, and her movements were sluggish, in marked contrast to her accustomed nimbleness. From where I stood, I could only see that she was carrying an earthenware bowl filled with strips of white cloth. The cloths appeared to be wet and stained with patches of red. As I watched she turned and closed the door behind her, locking it with a key on the large ring I knew she always carried with her.

I had seen enough. Running on tiptoe, I got back to

my room before she had time to reach the main corridor. Her footsteps sounded briefly in the passage, then gently faded into silence.

Ten minutes later I appeared in the breakfast room. Antonia was waiting for me as usual. She explained that Anthony had had to go out early to inspect the estate for damage in the wake of the storm. I thought she seemed more subdued than usual. There were rings under her eyes. It was that look I had seen on those earlier occasions when it had grown cold in the dining room.

She poured chocolate for me, hot and thick, filling the thin white cup of Sèvres porcelain that had been set aside as mine. When it was full, she set down the *chocolatlère* and smiled. I sensed that to do so cost her an effort.

"I hope you got back to sleep without trouble, my dear. After being so rudely wakened by the wind."

I shook my head.

"I couldn't sleep," I said. "That sound . . . I couldn't get that sound out of my head."

"What sound was that?"

"The sound I told you about. As though someone was crying. As though her heart was fit to break."

Antonia frowned.

"I told you, Charlotte, there was no one crying. Just the wind making a nuisance of itself, as it is inclined to do in these parts. Put it out of your head."

"But I *did* hear it! Not the wind, that can't have been it. I heard the noise again later, long after the wind had stopped. . . ."

She looked at me strangely. I find it hard to describe that look properly. A mixture of fear and pity and . . . loathing. Yes, I think all three emotions were present. And yet, throwing my mind back across the years, I think her feelings were directed less at me than at herself. For Antonia loathed herself above all others. And her very life was measured and controlled by fear.

She put down the cup of chocolate she was drinking, settling it in its fragile saucer with the greatest deliberation.

"Just what is it, Charlotte, that you are accusing us of? That we are harboring someone in that room? Keeping her there against her will, perhaps? Or a madwoman, maybe, like Mrs. Rochester in *Jane Eyre?* Is that what you think?"

"I . . . I truly do not know what to think, Antonia. If you say there is no one else in the house, I am sure I must believe you. I cannot do otherwise, after all your kindnesses to me. But I do know what I heard."

"If you insist, Charlotte. I cannot very well deny that you must have heard something, for you are not to be persuaded otherwise. But you must think what you are saying, child. If what you heard was neither the sound of the wind nor the voice of a living person, then you leave yourself with only one other possibility, do you not?"

She looked at me intently, as though challenging me to say what she knew I was thinking. But to speak it, to give it reality in speech, that was something quite beyond my powers.

"I think . . ." I started to say, then looked away, bending my head.

"You think the house is haunted, don't you, Charlotte? That the sounds you heard—or think you heard—last night were made by a ghost. That possibly the figure you think you saw in the garden yesterday was a phantom. That is what you think, is it not?"

I looked up with a sort of defiance. She had said the words I could not bring myself to utter. Her face was set and pale, but her eyes challenged me to contradict her. Helplessly I nodded. There was a long silence. I could hear the clock ticking behind me.

"Well," Antonia said at last, "that is not so very hard to understand. This is a large house, a house full of shadows. Everywhere there are boards that creak, and chimneys that whistle, and cracks that magnify the slightest gust of wind. I have lived here all my life, I have learned to understand the house's moods and manners. You are fresh to it, and it is easy for me to forget that."

She lifted her cup and took a sip.

"Very well, my dear. It seems that I shall have to set your mind at rest. After breakfast, we shall go to your mysterious room and see for ourselves. I assure you, we shall find no languishing prisoner. And no waiting ghost."

She smiled as though we had found a joke to share. But I could still sense an underlying uneasiness. She was like someone whistling in the dark. The rest of breakfast passed in an uncomfortable silence. I was aware for the first time that I had begun to fear my cousin, though I could not as yet say exactly why. I did not mention that I had seen Mrs. Johnson coming from the locked room, nor did I voice my suspicion that what I had seen on the cloths she carried had been blood.

When we had finished, Antonia stood.

"Well, Charlotte, are you still game for a visit to your haunted room?"

I nodded reluctantly. I was sure that whatever had been in there was now gone. For I was by no means convinced that the sounds I had heard had indeed been of supernatural origin. What if they had really been holding someone? And what if that someone had now been done away with and their room cleared of all traces of their presence?

There was a stillness about the house that I had not perceived before. It was as though my own senses were being sharpened or growing attuned to an atmosphere of menace that had at first been concealed from me. We went quickly upstairs, Antonia always a few paces ahead. When we reached the passage, it was dark. Mrs. Johnson had extinguished the light. It felt very cold.

Antonia relit the lamp. Around her neck she wore a gold chain at the end of which were several keys. One of these fit the door. She opened it and pushed it slowly open. My heart was beating fast, yet I knew I would see nothing.

A cold winter light falling through high windows revealed an empty room. It was bleak and unfurnished, and its walls had been painted a dull white. The floorboards were bare and unpolished. The only thing that relieved the bareness was a fireplace in the wall opposite. It did not seem to have been lit in a very long time. A cage of iron bars covered the windows from top to bottom.

I cannot describe exactly what it was I felt as I followed Antonia over the threshold. Despair does not describe it, or anguish. It was more like a wave of loneliness, of abandonment. Very like what I had felt the day my father died, and the days that followed it. Or that dreadful moment when my mother and I set foot inside the workhouse. Above all, it was like the day Mrs. Moss came to tell me that my mother, too, was dead. It was as though the room itself acted as an amplifying chamber for those worst feelings of my childhood.

"You see," said Antonia, turning to me. "It is as I

said. There is nothing here. What you heard was nothing but the wind."

"You told me this was a storeroom," I said. "You said it was locked and only used for storing things nobody wanted."

For a second Antonia was thrown. She must have forgotten her earlier explanation. But she recovered almost instantly.

"You're perfectly correct. But since your arrival, I've decided to make a few changes. You need a better room in which to paint. This room receives excellent light, even in the winter. Mrs. Johnson has been clearing everything out of it. I think she finished cleaning it this morning. It will soon be ready for your first lesson, as soon as I can get the paint and other things from town. I had been hoping to save it as a surprise, but you've rather forced me to spoil it. Never mind. I'm sure you're going to be very happy here."

Suddenly she stopped speaking. The next moment I felt it, too, the abrupt drop in temperature. I saw the sudden fear in her eyes.

"Come, Charlotte. We've spent long enough in here already. There are things to be done."

So saying, she grabbed my arm and pulled me through the door. She had scarcely locked it before she set off, hurrying ahead of me back to the main house. I followed, distracted and unsettled. But of all the impressions that that empty room left on me, the greatest was that of overwhelming loneliness.

CHAPTER 17

I COULD NOT CONCENTRATE FOR THE REST OF THAT MORNING. Nor, I noticed, could Antonia. She knew, I think, that I did not believe her, that I still harbored nagging suspicions about what was going on at Barras Hall. A change had come over our relationship, a cloud that would not easily be blown away.

At lunch, Anthony told us of the damage the storm had caused in the woods. Trees had been blown down, a stream had been blocked by subsidence, some of the outbuildings had suffered the loss of slates or bricks. I paid little attention to this recital, for half the places he mentioned were unknown to me. But one remark did attract my notice briefly.

"We shall have to have someone in to look at the folly," he said. "There's been damage to the roof. A branch fell on it and took some of the stone cladding away. I'm afraid it will cost a lot to put right."

"Shouldn't we just have it pulled down, Anthony? It's

in a bad enough state as it is." Antonia's face was flushed. She had taken wine with her meal, something I had only observed her do at dinner.

Anthony looked at her more sharply than seemed warranted by the question.

"I think not, Antonia. On the contrary, this may be the right moment to have it put in good repair. We'll see what Kettlewell says."

"You know he won't work there, Anthony. Nor his men."

Anthony shot a quick glance at me, then back at his sister.

"They will if I pay them enough. They're common laborers, Antonia, they'll swallow anything for cash. If need be, I'll bring men in from Newcastle." He paused. "I'll go straight into Morpeth after lunch. Don't expect me back until dinner. But don't wait for me if I'm late: I can always eat alone."

When he had gone, Antonia turned to me. The wine had made her more relaxed. She smiled, a ghost of the winning smile she had summoned up so easily before.

"I know you are tired, Charlotte, after your wakeful night. So I propose we cancel all our lessons for the rest of today. I have been thinking. You are often alone here. I know how dull that must be for a girl your age. You are unaccustomed to our country stillnesses. Clearly it unsettles you. Now, I really cannot have my dear cousin unsettled. You must have a companion."

I looked at her uncomprehendingly.

"Don't look so startled, my dear. I have thought of the very thing. We'll put on our wraps and bonnets and take a turn through the grounds. I'd like to see for myself a little of this famous damage Anthony has been telling us about."

Mrs. Johnson brought our things and we set off. It was bitterly cold. The wind had torn yesterday's clouds clean out of the sky, and the rain had cleared most of the snow away, but Antonia said she thought there might be more snow in the air. We headed past the stables to an area I had never visited. This was Hutton's domain, a place of potting sheds, vegetable gardens, and kennels. I could hear the dogs barking long before we arrived.

Hutton appeared as though from nowhere, doffing his cap as he watched us approach. I had kept myself well out of his way until now, fearing his surly manner and unkempt appearance.

"Miss Antonia, Miss Charlotte. What can I do for you?"

He never smiled, did Hutton. I guessed him to be in his late fifties or thereabouts, a beetle-browed, stony-faced, ill-proportioned man of few words. He had, I fancied, a temper. And for all that he acted subserviently toward Anthony or his sister, I had detected a freeness in his manner that suggested ill-suppressed insolence. Hutton was not downtrodden. It was almost as though he held some power over my cousins, or as if all three shared some secret.

"Hutton, your bitch Sarah gave birth to pups last year, did she not?"

"Hmm, that she did."

"What's become of them?"

"Drowned, ma'am."

"What, all of them?"

He shook his head slowly.

"No, not all. I kept two. Was you wanting one, miss?"

"Not for myself. I thought Miss Charlotte might like one for company."

"They're not lapdogs, miss. I keep them for working dogs. They're hardly suitable for a young lady."

"What breed? I think Anthony said they were lurchers."

"No, ma'am. Springer spaniels. Nothing fancy about them, mind you. Not much pedigree to speak of."

Antonia turned to me, smiling.

"You won't mind if they don't have pedigree, will you, Charlotte?"

"I . . . No, of . . . of course not," I stammered. I had never had a dog, never owned a pet of any description. All my fears seemed to have been eclipsed by this sudden, delicious surprise. As Antonia had intended they should be.

"Let's see them, Hutton. We don't want to keep Miss Charlotte waiting."

He led the way to a low shed near a rubbish heap filled with shards of garden crockery. As we approached, high-pitched barking broke out from inside the shed. Hutton opened a narrow door, stopped, and went inside. Moments later he came out holding two spaniel pups, one under each arm. They were both well grown.

"This is the bitch," he said, indicating the animal wriggling under his left arm. "And this here's the dog."

"Well, Charlotte, it looks as though you have a choice."

But my mind was already made up. The male had a black flash on his forehead, and appealing eyes that were already fixed on me. I reached out to take him.

"May I?"

Hutton said nothing. He let me take the dog, as though it had been no more than a sack of potatoes. He was unshaved, and, close up, I could tell he was unwashed.

The pup squirmed for a moment, then reached up to my face with his wet nose and began to nuzzle me. I laughed out loud, pulling my face away. His warm fur smelled dark and exciting.

"How old is he?" I asked.

"A year," muttered Hutton. "More or less."

"What will you call him?" asked Antonia.

"Perhaps he already has a name."

Hutton shook his head.

"No need for a name. Not as yet. Call him what you want."

"Then I shall call him Jasper."

Antonia looked at me in surprise.

"Jasper? Wherever did you get such a name?"

"My friend Alice had a cat called Jasper."

"It's an excellent name. I'll get Hepple to fix up a corner for him in the house. He can sleep in the kitchen. But you'll have to get him house-trained."

"He's trained already, Miss Antonia. I'd rather not have to clean the shed out after him."

"Well done, Hutton. And thank you." She turned to me. "Say thank you, Charlotte."

I thanked Hutton. He disappeared into the little hut with the other dog, then reemerged holding a length of rope attached to a shorter piece.

"You can use this till you get a collar and lead for him," he said. "He's used to it."

He slipped the collar around Jasper's neck with a movement that I found surprisingly deft.

"He was never intended for a pet," he said. "But he'll do well enough if you look after him and don't pamper him. When he's a bit older, bring him to me for training."

He paused and straightened.

"Now, if you don't mind, Miss Antonia, I've got work to do. This storm has made a fine mess of things."

He stomped off, leaving us with Jasper.

"Well," said Antonia, "what will you do with your new friend? Shall we take him back to the house?"

I shook my head.

"If you don't mind, Antonia, I'd like to take him for a walk."

She looked at me doubtfully for a moment, then nodded.

"Why, of course, he'll be in need of exercise after being kept cooped up in that old shed. I won't come with you. There are some matters I have to attend to back at the house."

She kissed me on both cheeks and left. I noticed that someone was watching her from an upstairs window as she made her way back.

Jasper knew at once what was up. After running circles around me, he suddenly tried to break away, pulling on his makeshift lead. I made a loop in it and slipped it around my wrist. He was not strong, but I was unaccustomed to animals and found him hard to control at first. We walked through the gardens at a snail's pace: everywhere we found new scents and new sights for Jasper to investigate.

In time, I learned to pull on the lead to get him moving, and before an hour had passed we had become firm friends. Antonia's choice of distraction for me had been inspired. Jasper could be engrossed in anything: a root, a leaf, an old bird's nest lying on the ground. The smallest object could become his world for minutes at a time. In the woods, he was almost uncontrollable. There were animal smells, the spoor of rabbits and squirrels, the trails of badgers. In his enthusiasm, I forgot to be preoccupied with my own fears.

The afternoon sun grew hot enough to lift a mist from the damp ground. I paid little attention to this at first, for the mist was nothing more than a fine, hazy film between the leaves. But as time went by it grew more dense in places. We had strayed close to the river, and here larger patches of thick mist had accumulated on the banks and somewhat farther back. I had little fear of losing my way, though I was concerned not to wander too far from the path, however attractive some parts of the undergrowth might be to Jasper.

Then, without warning, after a particularly involved chase around the backs of some rhododendron bushes, I realized that I was indeed lost. I was not unduly worried, for I knew that as long as I found a path and stayed on it, I would eventually find my way to a part I knew. Antonia had taught me that during our first walks through the grounds. Jasper was tiring by now, and our progress was made much easier.

My confidence began to ebb when, after some twenty minutes, I found myself still in unfamiliar territory. It was growing chilly and damp, and I could sense that the sun was sinking low. I felt the first prickings of fear then, realizing that if I did not find my way to a familiar path soon, I might very well be stranded by sunset in the middle of the woods. For some reason, it now mattered greatly to me that there were no birds anywhere. Why did they stay away? Was it merely a freak of nature, or something more sinister? Uncomfortable fears began to crowd in on me. Somehow they communicated themselves to Jasper, for he grew quite subdued. I pressed on, desperately seeking some sign that I was within striking distance of the house.

My relief was enormous when, turning a corner, I caught sight of the folly, its outline much obscured by a tangle of winter foliage and folding mist. For all that I disliked the place, I knew that it would lead me to safety, and I hurried to get nearer, in search of a vantage point from which I could discern my way.

I must have been within about thirty yards of the temple when I first became aware that Jasper was dragging on his lead. The little dog was pulling back, as though reluctant to follow me. Somewhat accustomed to his ways by now, I merely pulled harder on my end, getting him some way farther toward the folly. We were almost clear of the woods now, just a short expanse of grass and low undergrowth separating us from the ruin, when Jasper's reluctance grew more frantic. He began to whimper, then simply refused to go an inch farther. When I turned to look at him, I felt my heart turn cold, for his eyes were distended with fear, his ears lay flat against his head, and every hair on his body was standing on end.

"What is it, Jasper? What is it? What do you see?"

He just moaned, the most pitiful moans imaginable, and continued to pull hard against the rope. I was certain he could see or hear something. My every impulse was to turn tail and run with Jasper until we were out of sight of the folly. But this urge was tempered by the fear I had that if I did so, I might become irreparably lost.

Jasper was lying flat now, whimpering and burying his snout between his front paws. And then, suddenly, he started to snarl and tried to back away. A moment later he fell utterly silent. And in the silence I heard something. I could barely make it out at first, so soft it was, but as I listened I began to realize that it was the low sound of voices singing. Soft voices. Children's voices. And the singing, faint as it was, was coming unmistakably from inside the folly.

CHAPTER 18

THEY DID NOT SING FOR VERY LONG. A FEW MOMENTS, HALF A minute at the most, then silence, a silence that completely filled the woods. The singing reawakened in me the emotions of the morning, those feelings of desolation and abandonment that had assailed me in the empty room. I hunkered down alongside Jasper, stroking him, whispering words of encouragement while all the time I kept my eyes fixed on the folly, on the shifting outline of its ivy-covered walls. Only the mist moved. I wanted to leave, to run breathless from that terrible spot, but something held me transfixed.

Suddenly I heard the sound of a door opening then slamming shut. It was followed by the unmistakable rattle of a key turning in a heavy lock. A moment later I saw a figure leaving the folly. It was my cousin Antonia.

She stood on the steps for a moment, then turned her head as someone else appeared behind her. I caught my breath. It was Anthony. He came up to her, kissed her softly on the neck, then on the mouth. Not softly, not at all softly, but with a violence and—I understand it now—a passion that left me stunned. I had never seen a man and woman embrace like that, I was bewildered by the eagerness with which they kissed, bewildered and, in a way I could not understand, a party to it all. I could feel their need for one another even at that distance, even in my ignorance of what it really meant. They kissed for a long time, then parted slowly and at last walked away, hand in hand, until they were swallowed up by the mist.

I remained crouching there, my hand on Jasper's neck, confused, tearful, as frightened by my cousins' behavior as by the singing that had preceded it. There were no more sounds anywhere, but all around me the shadows were growing, and I knew it was time to leave. It was not hard for me to find my own way back, now that I had my bearings. Jasper became his old self again the moment we got a little distance from the folly, though he was too tired to run around much. It was nearly dark when we got back to the house. Mrs. Johnson had prepared a basket and food bowl for Jasper in the scullery. He was unsure of them at first, but within minutes had eaten and then rolled himself into a ball and fallen fast asleep. I envied him the ease with which he could throw off his fears.

"Miss Antonia wants to see you upstairs, miss." Mrs. Johnson looked at me strangely, as though trying to guess what I was thinking. Had she caught sight of me spying on her that morning?

"I'll go up shortly."

"She's been expecting you back for tea this long time, miss."

That was hardly the truth, and I guessed Mrs. Johnson knew it. I nodded and left, after saying good-bye to Jasper.

Antonia was in the drawing room with the tea things spread out in front of her.

"The tea's stone cold, Charlotte. Where on earth have you been?"

"We got lost in the woods," I said. "It's misty outside. Jasper went all over the place and I had to follow him."

She glanced at me sharply.

"You'll have to train him better than that. I'll get a proper lead sent up from Morpeth. Now you must be hungry. I'll have Mrs. Johnson bring some fresh water."

"That's all right, Antonia. I'm a little tired after my walk. If you don't mind, I'd like to go to my room to rest."

"Very well. But remember that dinner will be at the usual time. It's just the two of us this evening."

A fire was burning in my room, as it always was at this time of day. I sat in my usual chair, staring at the flames. Nothing could conceal from me that my cousins shared a dark secret, but its nature and extent I could not begin to guess.

I felt a draft at my side. The curtains had not been drawn, but it was dark outside now, so I decided to close them. As I pulled the left-hand curtain across, I noticed something on the floor, just at the foot of the window, almost out of sight. Picking it up, I saw that it was a small book bound in red leather and covered in dust. In a flash, I realized that it must have fallen from the narrow space inside the shutters when I opened them the night before. I finished drawing the curtain, then went back to my chair with the book.

With my handkerchief, I wiped most of the dust away. There was no title on the cover or spine. When I opened the little volume, I saw why: it was only a note-book, though rather an expensive one. Most of its pages were covered in a fine, elegant hand. Flicking through them, my eye fell on one line:

I lock my door at night now, but the footsteps never cease, and I still hear whispers where there should be no whispers.

With a shaking hand, I closed the book. It was as though the writer had been here with me on that night when I had listened to footsteps outside my own door, this very door. For no explicable reason, I got up and turned the key in the lock, as I was growing accustomed to doing much later, when I retired to sleep. I had realized what it was I held in my hand: a journal. A journal, if I guessed right, that had been kept by someone who had lived in this very room.

For a long time I just sat there, unable to move, scarcely able to think. The journal frightened me. For some reason, it had linked itself in my mind with the weeping I had heard in the night. If someone else had slept here and written down their recollections, perhaps I would find that they, too, had heard the sobbing. If so, I would know that it had not been a figment of my imagination.

At last I plucked up enough courage to begin reading.

I have moved to the west wing at last. Mother says I am quite grown up now, and must have a room of my own. It is such a pretty room, with the loveliest blue paper all covered in roses. I can see most of the garden from my window. It is a little bleak just now, with winter setting in, but in the summer I shall have such a gorgeous view. I'll ask Hutton to plant some rosebushes just outside, where I will be able to see them first thing every morning.

I was in such a tizzy yesterday, getting everything ready for the big move. It was so exciting, thinking of being in a proper grown-up room instead of that old nursery. I got to hate the nursery so much. The best thing about this room is that I have a wardrobe of my own to keep my dresses in. We went to Morpeth last week to have a fitting at Madame Doubtfire's. She's the funniest old thing: she wears a red wig and the most awful rouge on her cheeks. Mother thinks her rather common, but she is the best dressmaker for miles and miles, so everybody puts up with her. I am so looking forward to my treasures. They'll be ready before Christmas, or so she says.

I've decided to keep a proper diary. From now on I intend to have a thoroughly interesting life. It can be so dull here. There are scarcely any visitors. And I do miss Signorina Rocca, even if she was a hard old stick at times. Mother gives me my lessons herself now, but her mind isn't on it half the time. She says I'm to have a new governess after Christmas, but it won't be easy getting anybody decent to come and live out here. I wish we were nearer Morpeth. It's so cut off here in the country.

November 4, 1892. I must make sure I put the date on these entries. The diary was a present from Uncle Anthony, who says I should use it to organize my thoughts.

I stopped reading, arrested by the reference to someone called Anthony. I assumed this must be my cousin. No one had ever mentioned a niece to me. In fact, I realized that apart from their mother and my father, both of whom were now dead, not a word had been said to me about the rest of Anthony and Antonia's family. Nor, for that matter, of the breach that had come between them and my father. The diary entry was almost exactly ten years old. I calculated that if its writer had then been around my age, she must be in her midtwenties by now. I read on.

Entry followed entry, one for almost every day to the end of November. My predecessor's life seemed very like the one I lived: art and music lessons with her mother, walks in the garden or the woods, whole afternoons reading in the library. She had a pony called Oliver, however, and whenever the weather permitted, she would take him for long rides, often venturing onto the moors, although her mother had strictly forbidden this. Sometimes she had visits from cousins who lived in Elsdon, but it seems they were rather younger than she was and not ideal company. She seemed content enough with the way things were, but at times a terrible sadness would reveal itself. One passage dated late November particularly struck me.

How I wish I had a friend here, someone I could share my thoughts with. Mother is no good, all she wants to do is bury herself in this place and write letters to friends who never come. She says I am to be "brought out" when I am eighteen. But that is three years away, or will be on my birthday next month. In the meantime, what am I to do? Everyone here is so much older than I, and in any case, the servants are no use. I need someone my own age. There are so many things I can never talk about.

Sometimes I read a sad story and end up in floods of tears. Mother would not understand, and Anthony would only laugh. Or I come back from a ride on Oliver, and I've seen something new that I want to tell them about, but they all act bored because they've seen it before and it isn't new or exciting to them. And I'm frightened that when it's time for me to go to balls and such things, I'll be so old and wizened inside that even if I met the most handsome man in the world, I wouldn't know if I was in love or if he loved me back. I'd give anything to leave Barras Hall right now, tomorrow, as soon as there's a chance. But I know there won't be a chance and that I'll just have to stay here forever. Nobody will want to marry me, just like Mother.

It felt cold. I went back to the window, thinking there was still a draft, but the sash was tightly closed and the curtains drawn fast. Back at the fire, I could still feel it, cool against my throat. I shivered and continued reading.

20 November. We went into Morpeth today for the fitting of the first dresses by Madame Doubtfire. Mother and I, that is. For some reason, Madame D. refuses to come to the hall. Mother says she had a little set-to with Grandmama, when she lived here. It's a pity, because the journey was terribly muddy and slow, and once we almost went off the road. Hutton drives the horses too hard. I've spoken to him about it, but he pays no attention. He won't whip them in my presence, though, he knows better than that. He drowned three kittens last week. I only found out yesterday, much too late to do anything about it. I can't bear the thought of the poor little things in a sack tossed into that cold water. How can people be so cruel? Mother says it's just the way of the country folk, but I don't think that's any excuse.

After the fitting, Mother went again to Mrs. Manners in Copper Chase, leaving me at the Queen's Head with Hutton, which I hated. Mother says it relieves her mind to see that woman, but I wish she did not go. They say she holds séances to bring back the dead. Mother calls her a medium, and says she gives her messages from the departed. I don't like the idea at all. It makes me shudder to think of such things, though Mother says it is harmless and can only do good as consolation for the bereaved.

The dresses are lovely. My favorite is a long gray dress with black beading, all in pure silk. It has a beautiful lavender panel set into the front. Madame Doubtfire says the materials were sent specially from Paris.

I halted in confusion. A gray dress with a lavender panel and black beading! Surely that was the very dress I had been wearing two days ago, one of the collection I had been given on my arrival at the hall. Of course: the writer of the diary would have grown out of them and left them behind when she was finally "brought out." No doubt she had married soon after that and gone away to live with her husband, leaving all her childhood possessions behind. I so hoped so; I hoped she had escaped from the dullness of her life on the moors.

*Madame Doubtfire is such a funny little woman.
She reminds me of that character in Dickens, Uriah
Heep. Always running about after her clients, "her
ladies," as she calls them, simpering and dropping
little curtsies at the slightest opportunity. "Is that
to your satisfaction, Miss Caroline?" Or "Such a
slim figure, Miss Caroline. You will be such a
beauty at your first ball."*

    *Mind you, I get the feeling she's afraid of
Mother. It's funny that, thinking of people being
afraid of her. I'm often sorry for her, and I know
there is some sort of embarrassment because I
don't have a father; but I've never thought of her as
frightening. Grandmama is frightening, but she no
longer lives with us, thank God. Not since Grandfather died. But old Doubtfire really scoots around
Mother as though she were about to eat her up.
"I'm sorry, Miss Antonia," or "Whatever can I have
been thinking of, Miss Antonia?"*

I almost let the book fall from my hands. "Miss
Antonia"? Did that mean . . . ? Surely it could not mean
that Antonia had a daughter. She was not married. I had
seen her wear a wedding dress, but she . . . A very
different sort of chill stabbed at my heart. Antonia had
a daughter ten years older than I, a daughter of whom
she never spoke. I knew enough to understand a little of
what this meant. Caroline had been illegitimate.

    I glanced up in alarm, thinking I had heard some-
thing, a cough or snarl in the room behind me. There was
nothing there. The curtain seemed to move. I decided not
to go to the window: if there was a draft, Mrs. Johnson
would see to it. I would tell her at dinner. I started
reading again.

22 November. Nothing in my diary yesterday. It was rather a peculiar day. Mother was tired after her drive to Morpeth the day before. Anthony said he had to do some work on the estate. He wants to bring friends here to shoot next season. I don't even ask him about it. Why can't they leave the poor birds alone? The weather had picked up a bit. I took Oliver for a long canter out on Todcrag Moss. On our way back, I passed by the old folly. It always gives me the creeps, but it is the shortest way through the woods from the Harwood side, and Oliver was tired. I was walking him, stretching my legs a bit, and we were going rather slowly.

What happened next was rather queer, but I know I didn't imagine it. Just as I passed near the folly Oliver reared up and broke away. He seemed terrified of something, behavior I've never seen in him before. He's usually such a placid old thing. He knocked me to the ground and ran off in the direction of the hall, keeping to the path, thank God. I was quite winded at first. By the time I got to my feet, he was out of sight. I prayed he wouldn't go far.

I couldn't guess what had spooked him. There hadn't been a sound, and I had not noticed anything running across his path. Well, I thought, it must have been a squirrel. Horses will do that sometimes, though it's odd. But then I did hear something. The woods were very quiet, and I couldn't have been mistaken. I heard . . . Well, I'm not quite certain, but it sounded like somebody singing. Several people, actually, as though a little band of children were near me. I thought for a moment that it must be some village children, practicing their Christmas carols perhaps. But that was silly, they never come near here, they pretend there's a "curse" on the hall.

Actually I thought the sound came from inside the folly. It went on for half a minute or so, then stopped. It stopped dead, just like that, and it was quiet again. I've never liked the folly much, and never been inside, but I went up to the door and tried it. It was locked as usual, so nobody can have sneaked in. I couldn't stand round listening, not while Oliver was straying, so I set off after him. He wasn't far away after all. I caught him munching some grass just off the path. He seemed right as rain, but I scolded him for giving me such a fright. Mind you, I wonder if he hadn't heard those voices before I did. They were a little spooky, and it could have frightened him.

Dear God, I felt as cold as ice. I had no need of drafts to chill me. She had heard them, too. Ten years ago. They had frightened her horse as they had frightened my dog. She had heard them in the same place and for the same length of time. It was no coincidence.

At that moment the weeping started again.

CHAPTER 19

"PLEASE," I WHISPERED, "PLEASE STOP CRYING. PLEASE, I can't bear it."

To my astonishment, the crying did stop, as though I had been heard. But in the very instant that it did so, I knew something else was wrong. Even now, I cannot think of the sensation I experienced without feeling acutely nervous. I was certain, mortally certain, that someone was standing behind me, someone who did not wish me well. They were watching me with a look of intense malice, unwavering and unblinking. I felt the skin crawl on the back of my neck. That is the sort of thing you read in books, it has become utterly hackneyed, even risible; but if you have ever felt it, ever really felt it under circumstances like those, you will know how incredibly horrible it is.

I can't say how long I sat there, feeling that terrible staring presence behind me, frozen to the spot. It cannot have been more than a minute, two at the outside, for I am certain I could not have borne it longer than that. But it felt like an age, with every second stretched out unnaturally. I remember gripping the arms of my chair and forcing myself, against every instinct, to turn and confront whoever or whatever was watching me.

And I did turn. I turned, expecting some tremendous horror, and saw nothing. There was absolutely nothing there.

"Oh, God," I remember praying, "please, please help me. I don't understand what's happening here, but I need Your help."

The silence that followed left me feeling more uncomfortable than I had before. My gentle God was elsewhere evidently, tending other sheep. Deep inside, I think I understood that He would not accept my invitation to step into the nightmare I could feel closing around me. But I have never forgiven Him for abandoning me so thoughtlessly in my hour of need.

I was still sitting there when I heard footsteps, then a knock on the door.

"It's time for dinner, miss. Miss Antonia says you're to get a move on."

Johnson's voice brought such a sense of normality with it that for a moment I forgot her involvement with the events in the locked room. I hurried to my feet and unlocked the door. She was standing in the dark corridor holding a single candle. My fear must still have been visible, for the moment she caught sight of me, a look of concern crossed her features.

"Are you all right, miss? Nothing's happened, has it?"

I shook my head hastily. I could not trust her and feared to take her into my confidence.

"No," I lied, "nothing at all. I'm perfectly all right. Just a little tired. I've been asleep in my chair."

She continued to scrutinize my face, but said nothing further.

"Wait there," I said. "I'll get the lamp."

I closed the door. Crossing to the dressing table, I stopped to take Caroline's diary from the chair. I thought it best that no one learn of my discovery. Hurriedly I slid it to the back of one of the dressing-table drawers and shut it.

Mrs. Johnson was still waiting for me.

"Why was your door locked so early, miss?" she asked pointedly. "It's more a bedtime matter, surely."

"I felt tired after my walk, and I was afraid of it being open if I should fall asleep."

She paused and turned to me.

"You must try not to worry, miss. If you hear things. Or . . . see things."

"Hear things? What do you mean, Johnson?"

"I think you already know very well, miss."

She seemed very nervous, again on the verge of saying more than she ought.

"Please, miss, go on doing as I told you and keep your door firmly locked."

"Whatever good will that do? It won't stop me hearing things, will it?"

"No matter, miss, just you do it. And take this. Take it and wear it."

She slipped from around her neck a small silver cross on a fine chain. I was unused to such things, and greatly surprised that Mrs. Johnson wore one, for it was something I associated with Catholics. She sensed my hesitation, but reached out and looped the chain over my neck.

"Tuck it into your dress, miss—where it's out of sight, but where you'll know it's there. In case of need."

"What sort of need?"

But she only looked at me sharply and continued walking.

Antonia was waiting impatiently at the table.

"Charlotte, I expected you down fifteen minutes ago. That's twice today you've kept me waiting."

"I'm sorry, Antonia. I fell asleep at the fire. It was such a long walk today. I promise it won't happen again."

She looked scarcely mollified, but, rising, ushered me to my seat. Moments later Mrs. Johnson appeared with our soup on a tray, and dinner began.

The atmosphere was strained. All through the meal, I felt a terrible urge to ask about Caroline, Antonia's daughter.

"What did you do before I came?" I asked. "Whenever Anthony went away."

"I dined alone," she said.

"But surely there can't always have been two of you?"

"Ever since my dear mother left, yes. She hated living in such a big house after my father died. That's why she bought her villa in Morpeth."

"Who lives there now?" I asked, wondering if the house might not have come into Caroline's possession.

"It's empty for the moment. We'll look for tenants in the summer. No one takes on property at this time of year."

"Don't you have any other relations who might take it over?"

She looked at me very attentively. Could she have sensed that I knew or guessed something? Possibly.

"No," she said emphatically. "There's no one now,

apart from yourself. And your brother Arthur, of course." She hesitated. "I did not want to tell you this, Charlotte; at least not yet. But Anthony and I have considered . . ." She looked intently at me. "Well, my dear, we have considered whether it might not be possible for us to adopt you. And Arthur later on, naturally, once he has been found. Do you understand what I am saying? We mean to have you legally adopted by ourselves."

I stared openmouthed at her. I could not think what to say.

"There's no need to say anything now, my dear. It will take you time to get used to it. But I hope you will be pleased. You will no longer be an orphan. And it would mean so much to us. Neither of us having children of our own, of course."

It was as though she had guessed exactly what had been going through my mind and was now supplying a direct denial of Caroline's existence. I decided I must be more direct.

"But . . ." I began hesitantly, conscious of a need for extreme caution. "If you . . ."

"Yes?"

"What if you were to marry? Surely you are not yet too old to have a child of your own."

Something between a smile and a sneer crossed her face.

"You are mistaken, child. It is entirely out of the question, I assure you. Even if I were to marry, I am too old to give birth. But marriage is impossible in any case." She paused. "Well, I suppose you are old enough to know something of my past. I was . . ." She hesitated again. "I was once engaged to be married. I will not trouble you with the details. He was a wealthy man, an important man, that is all I will say. The wedding plans were made, the date had been set, the banns called, the church reserved, the invitations sent. And then Simon . . ." A look of pain settled in her eyes. "And then, without warning, and with only weeks to go, my fiancé broke his pledge. He wrote to me saying he could not go through with the marriage after all. A week later he left for the colonies."

Her voice on the verge of breaking, she fell silent. I sat staring at her, frightened to speak, yet desperate to know the answers to so many questions.

"How . . . long ago was that?" I asked.

She looked up. There was a haunted expression in her eyes.

"How long? Twenty years ago," she whispered. "A very long time. I was seventeen years old."

Seventeen. Only two years older than I would be in a few weeks' time.

Anthony arrived soon after that and began his meal while we finished ours. He seemed tired and preoccupied, and Antonia and I soon went to the drawing room, leaving him to finish eating alone.

"You are very close to Anthony," I said.

"Yes, of course. Only a few years separate us. We have shared our lives."

I hesitated, then plunged in again.

"I am surprised that he has never married. He is as handsome as you are beautiful."

She seemed flattered by my words.

"Thank you for that compliment, my dear. Yes, you are right, Anthony is a good-looking man. More than one young lady has been left crying on her pillow for his sake. But while Mother lived here he considered it his duty to look after her. And then . . . And then he stayed single to look after me. He has made a very great sacrifice. But I try to be a comfort to him."

"Why," I said, "it is almost as though you two were married."

She looked at me rather coldly.

"Yes," she said, "it seems quite like that, does it not?"

Anthony came in then.

"Isn't it time you were in bed?" he asked, rather brusquely.

It was still a little early, but I nodded. I wished them both good night and went off to my room. Caroline's diary was still in the drawer where I had placed it. I settled down before the fire and began to read where I had left off.

CHAPTER **20**

23 November. Last night I heard something at my window. As though someone was scratching on the panes. But when I looked, there was no one there. I asked Mother this morning if she had ever heard of ghosts at Barras Hall, but she said I was being silly and told me to say my prayers with a better will.

24 November. Scratching again. It woke me twice. I said nothing to Mother.

27 November. There was singing last night. I tried to make out the words, but they were indistinct. It is not a Christmas carol. I'm frightened now, but I daren't say anything to Mother or Uncle Anthony.

28 November. Voices in my room. I can't make out what they say. Terrible fear all night, and more scratching.

29 November. I lock my door at night now, but the footsteps never cease, and I still hear whispers where there should be no whispers. Dear God, make it stop. I think I may be going mad.

3 December. They have started in the daytime now. I am frightened to be alone, and spend every moment I can with Mother. The old man was on the stairs again yesterday.

Mother says there are to be special celebrations for my birthday. I am trying to concentrate on that, to take my mind off other things. It's only two weeks, but the eighteenth seems as though it will never come.

The eighteenth. I looked at the page in disbelief. That was the date of my own birthday. And it was less than a week away. Suddenly I remembered how Antonia had talked so often about my destiny. Did it have something to do with her daughter? She had dressed me in her clothes, and I guessed that many of the other things I had been given had once belonged to her. Tonight she had talked of adopting me. She would have two daughters, both born on the same date. She and Anthony would take the place of my parents, and I would take the place of Caroline. . . . With mounting horror, I began to understand. I remembered Antonia and her brother coming out of the folly together, the kiss he had given her, their walking away together hand in hand. Had Anthony been Caroline's father? God knows, I understood little enough of such things. But the possibility was undeniable.

So, too, was another possibility that now forced its way into my consciousness: that Caroline might no longer be alive. That she had died and that . . . I could not bear to follow the train of thought to which this led me. Hastily I returned to the diary.

5 December. The old man again. He was in my room last night. I could not see him, but I know he was there, watching me. When I see him on the stairs, there is such a look of hatred in his eyes. I'm more frightened of him than of anyone. He means me harm, I know he does, and I don't know how to stop him.

There are children in the house. I heard some of them laughing on the back stairs yesterday. I take the back stairs now when I can, to avoid the old man. I think they are the same ones I heard singing in the folly, and again in the garden. What can they want?

10 December. There was something on the lawn last night. I watched it for a long time, creeping across as slowly as a tortoise. It was too far away to make out the shape properly, but it seems to be black and about four feet long. It has arms and legs, though I am not sure how many. I think it may be there every night, only I cannot see it when it is too dark.

11 December. It was there last night again. Moving toward the house. I think it was closer than on the night before. It may not take it much longer to reach the hall. God will not answer my prayers.

I have asked Mother to invite the Reverend Watkins, but she says he will not come here. It has something to do with an old quarrel. I have decided to ride down to the village tomorrow with Oliver. I need to talk to someone.

He was in the old place today. Darker and more solid every time he appears. No matter where I go, he manages to find me.

12 December. I saw the minister today. He is a young man and has only been two years in the parish. I asked him, and he says he knows nothing about a quarrel. He sat and listened while I told him all I have seen and heard. At first I think he believed me touched, but after a little while he fell very silent. He asked me many questions, and at the end spoke with me most earnestly. He says my life may be in danger if I stay at the hall. When I asked him why, he merely said that he had heard things about the house, things some of his oldest parishioners had told him. I pressed him for details, but he claimed that was all he knew, that the house has a bad name in the district. He knows more than that, I'm sure of it. At least he has promised to visit.

Mother asked where I had been. I said, to the blacksmith's to have one of Oliver's shoes reset. She looked as though she did not believe it, but she said nothing. She and Uncle Anthony are together much recently.

Noises tonight. No night without them now. The thing in the garden is almost at the wall. There is something in the corridor while I sleep. I hear it rustling. Is it enough to lock my door?

13 December. Reverend Watkins came today, but Mother sent him away as though he had been the devil himself, and not a man of God. She guessed that I had been to see him. In the end, I told her

everything. She looked at me as though she thought I was mad, as I had feared she would.

At dinner, Uncle Anthony told me I was to say no more about what he called my "delusions." Otherwise they might have to have me locked up. On my way to bed I noticed—oh, please help me, somebody—that a new lock had been put on the door of the little chamber at the top of the stairs near my bedroom. I saw Johnson there earlier today. If I can, I shall escape tomorrow. Reverend Watkins will help me.

Nothing in the garden. I think it is here now. Inside the house. It will be a long night. I saw him in the passage outside my room this evening.

That was the last entry. The rest of the pages were blank. I sat shivering, as though I had turned to ice. More than anything, I wanted to believe that Caroline had escaped as planned. And yet the book I held in my hands was surely the best evidence against that. For surely she would not have left it behind, however carefully hidden. Unless . . .

The only hope I saw was that an opportunity for flight had suggested itself unexpectedly and that there had been no time to worry about such trivial things as her diary or her dresses. I wondered if she had taken Oliver, if that was how she had managed to get away.

And yet, however much I wanted to believe in Caroline's escape, in my heart I knew it was unlikely. She had written her diary that night and placed it behind the shutter as usual, for me to find all those years later. The next day something had happened, and she had never returned to her room. I thought of that other room, the one with bars on the windows, and Antonia's threat to have her daughter locked up. Was it her weeping that I had heard?

A terrible thought struck me. What if they had kept her locked up until now, a lonely prisoner in that awful room, with Johnson as her jailer? That would explain so many things. Perhaps she had indeed been mad, perhaps she had imagined all those things she said she had seen or heard. And perhaps—I shuddered at the thought—she was allowed out of her cell at night, to take a little exercise while Antonia slept. Those footsteps I had heard outside my door, might they not have been hers? That would explain Mrs. Johnson's insistence that I lock my door. She might be given to violence. That could explain the blood I had seen on those white cloths. And was it possible that the figure I had seen in the garden two days before, the young girl in a gray dress, had been none other than Caroline, allowed out by mistake?

This explanation, disturbing as it was, nevertheless gave me a little comfort. I deliberately put out of my thoughts my own memories of voices singing at the folly or a dark shape creeping slowly across the lawn.

In order to reassure myself further, I determined that I should approach the Reverend Watkins myself. Mrs. Johnson would surely know if he was still vicar of Kirkwhelpington. Or, if he had since been moved, as was probable, the new vicar would be certain to know an address to which I could direct a letter containing my inquiries.

And yet, if my mind were to be set to rest on Caroline's account, I had to acknowledge that further information could leave me a prey to darker thoughts. What if she had indeed escaped? What if the minister had smuggled her away from here and was now willing to tell me that she was alive and well in another part of the country, married possibly, as I had first imagined her? In that case, if Caroline was not mad, had never been locked up in that room, whom had I heard weeping? Whom had I seen in the garden? And what was it that Caroline had seen and heard in Barras Hall all those years ago?

Mental excitement kept me awake longer than usual, but in the end, exhausted by my thoughts and the day's exertions, I undressed and slipped into bed. Sleep came quickly.

It was very dark when I woke. I did not emerge from sleep slowly, as I usually did, but quite abruptly, with almost no transition. One moment I was sleeping, the next I was lying fully conscious in that darkened room. It is important that you understand this, Doctor, that I was not asleep. What happened next was not a dream.

I knew with absolute certainty, just as I had known earlier, that someone else was in the room with me. There was no sound, not even the sound of breathing, but I knew I was not alone. I lay there for a very long time while the most terrible thoughts passed through my head. At last I could stand it no longer. Whatever might come of it, I determined to have a light with which to confront my visitor.

A candle and a box of matches always lay by the bed, on a little low table on my right-hand side. Gingerly I stretched out for them. Fumbling in the darkness, my hand touched something soft and unfamiliar. My heart almost stopped beating as I moved my hand again, sick at the touch. And as I did so I realized what lay beneath my fingers. Human hair, long and thick, on a level with the edge of the bed.

I screamed loudly and tore my hand away, rolling frantically to the other side of the bed, scrambling out of my sheets and blankets, and finally tumbling to the floor. My mind was not working at all, I was in a blind, animal panic, utterly terrified by that single, repulsive touch. I lay in the darkness like someone stunned, unable to think or act.

On the other side of the bed there now began a singularly unpleasant rustling sound. Even now, all these years later, I can still hear it if I am ever foolish enough to let my mind go blank. It is impossible to describe it adequately. Dry, insectlike, powdery, as though something long dead were alive and moving. It seemed to be creeping closer. As it did so I slid fearfully back across the floor until my back struck something hard and angular.

I realized that it must be a leg of my dressing table. And in the next instant I remembered that the oil lamp was still on it. I was confronted by an intolerable choice: I could sit there in the darkness, listening to the sound slowly approaching me, or I could light the lamp and see it face-to-face. Either prospect filled me with horror.

Yet to remain in the dark, waiting for it to reach me, was more than I could bear. I scrambled to my feet and found the matches in their usual place by the lamp. It was a matter of moments to scratch a flame into life. With a trembling hand, I raised the glass and put the flame to the wick.

Steeling myself, I turned. The still-flickering flame cast an uneven light across the room. Shadows bounced against the walls and then grew still. There was nothing. The rustling noise had stopped, and the room was empty.

Then, suddenly, I caught sight of something out of

the corner of my eye. As I turned my head I saw her: a young woman in a gray dress, watching me intently. The next second, a shadow covered her. When I looked again, there was no one there.

CHAPTER 21

JASPER WAS WAITING FOR ME THE NEXT MORNING IN THE kitchen, full of energy, eager for a walk. I went out with him after breakfast. Anything to be away from the house. Antonia seemed distracted and had no time for lessons. I was rather relieved, for I found it hard to be with her, knowing all I did. At lunch, Anthony told me there was news of Arthur and that they still hoped to find him in time for Christmas. For the first time I suspected that he might not be telling me the whole truth.

The events of the previous night remained imprinted on my thoughts all day, the way a nightmare lingers, only much more real and solid. I became steadily more preoccupied with the question of what had happened to Caroline, and wondered if a similar fate awaited me. But what exactly *had* been her fate?

After lunch, while feeding Jasper in the kitchen, I asked Mrs. Johnson what she knew of the vicar.

"The vicar, miss? Whatever will you be wanting him for?"

I lied as well as I could.

"I want to ask him if he will let my mother be buried in the churchyard at Kirkwhelpington. I hate to think of her in that place where they put her. They bury them in quicklime in the yard."

She looked at me quizzically.

"I'm sure the vicar would have no say in that. You'd have to approach the proper authorities."

"Nevertheless he'd know if it was possible."

"Haven't you mentioned this to Sir Anthony? He has lawyers and such who can make inquiries."

"I'd rather not trouble him. Perhaps the vicar won't have her. She wasn't from his parish."

Mrs. Johnson paused. I suspected that she wanted to keep the vicar and me apart.

"Well, miss, if you've a fancy to move her, you could always have her buried here. At the house."

"At the house? I don't understand."

"There used to be a chapel at Barras Hall, years and years ago. In Sir Anthony's great-grandfather's day, I think it was. There's still a little graveyard left, near where the chapel stood. All the family tombs are there. Surely you've passed it."

I shook my head.

"No. Where is it?"

"Not far from the folly, miss. You turn off the path after it goes over the bridge, then a little down again. All the Ayrtons are buried there for ever so far back. I'm sure Sir Anthony would have no objections to letting your dear mother be put there with the rest of them. It would be more fitting."

"I'll ask. Thank you, Johnson." But I had already guessed that the place she meant was the site of the ruins, about which I had been warned by Antonia, though she had not said a word then about the presence of family tombs.

Jasper had finished eating. I said I would take him into the garden for a few minutes. As I was about to go I turned back to Mrs. Johnson.

"Does he ever come here?"

"Who, miss?"

"The vicar. Surely he must visit Barras Hall sometimes. It's the biggest house in the neighborhood."

She shook her head slowly.

"Well, miss, your cousins are not churchgoing people. Their mother, the late Lady Ayrton, had a . . . disagreement with the vicar in her day. You'll not see them down there or him up here."

"That's a pity," I said. "My parents used to take me to church every Sunday. I liked some of the hymns they sang. What's the vicar's name? If I'm ever in the village, I should quite like to call on him."

"He's a man called Collins. I've seen him once or twice when I've had business in the village. A runty little man with spectacles. Not much of a man, and not much of a vicar, I'll be bound. I'd not waste your time on him."

"Has he been here long?"

"Goodness, so many questions. I've got work to do, miss, or perhaps you hadn't noticed. No, Collins is a new man. Only been here a couple of years. There was Watkins before him, but he left. Went to a big parish in Yorkshire, I believe. Or maybe Lancashire. One of those parts."

She stopped.

"What am I doing prattling on to you like this? Get on with you. And take that dog out of here: he's been in my hair all morning. He should be in a proper kennel outside."

That afternoon I wrote a long letter to the Reverend Watkins, addressing it "care of Rev. Collins, the Vicarage, Kirkwhelpington," and enclosing a covering note in which I implored the new vicar to send it straight on to his predecessor. The postman was due the following morning—he paid us two visits a week—and I had resolved to lie in wait for him after he called, in order to put my missive directly into his hands. I had some stamps in my drawer, left over from several given me by Antonia a couple of weeks previously, for letters I had written to Annie and to a couple of other friends I thought were still in the workhouse.

I slipped the sealed letter into the pocket of the dress I was to wear to dinner that evening, for I feared that were Mrs. Johnson to find it, her suspicions would be aroused. Rather than remain in my room as it grew dark, I decided I would take my bath a little earlier than usual.

The only proper bathroom in the house was an old one situated above the kitchens. It was walled with dark wooden paneling, and in its center stood a huge Victorian tub into which one had to lower oneself with the aid of brass handles. I rather hated it, for it was cold and dark, unlike the rather pretty bathroom my mother had created at home, in which I had spent many happy hours soaking in hot water and playing with little wooden boats my father had made for me.

In the bathroom, I found that Hepple had already heated the stove, from which the water was heated. The room was not warm, but enough of the chill had been taken off the air to make it bearable. As had become my custom, I filled the tub with as much hot water as possible before starting to undress, for the steam helped warm the air further. I did not really mind the discomfort, for the privacy and leisure of bathing here were considerable luxuries to me after the communal bathing rooms of the workhouse. After all, I was still very young, and acutely embarrassed by the changes that had been taking place in my body over the past year or more.

I undressed now, not fully at ease even on my own, and climbed carefully into the huge bath. Far above me, the light of my lamp glimmered on the glass skylight. Once, I had seen the moon hanging above me while I bathed, but tonight there was nothing there but darkness. The bathroom was full of echoes. Each time I splashed, lifting a leg or an arm to rub myself with the enormous sponge Antonia had given me, the sound of the water would be amplified. I tried to keep as still as possible, for there was something I disliked about those sounds.

I had almost finished when, for no perceptible reason, I began to feel terribly afraid. Holding my breath, I lay perfectly still. Not a ripple disturbed the water. There was no sound. I think I expected to hear that abominable rustling again, but there was nothing. Then I looked up, at the door.

The upper half of the door consisted of a pane of frosted glass surrounded by smaller, colored panes, some with stars inset. Against the center pane, blurred by the rough texture of the glass, lay a shadow. Someone was standing outside.

"Who's there?" I called out. "Is that you, Antonia?"

The shadow moved, but there was no answer.

"Mrs. Johnson? Are you there?"

Still no answer. A horrible suspicion came to me.

"Caroline? Is that you?"

Silence. And then the sound of the doorknob rattling, turning and rattling. I lay frozen by fear. The rattling continued for about twenty seconds, then stopped abruptly. The shadow hovered in front of the door for a few moments more, then turned and moved away.

I remember sitting in the bath, unable to move a muscle, while the water grew cold. All the time a sentence from Caroline's diary kept going through my head: *He was in my room last night. I could not see him, but I know he was there, watching me.*

I was brought back to my senses by a knock on the door and Mrs. Johnson's voice.

"Are you all right, Miss Charlotte? You've been in there nearly two hours now. It'll soon be time for dinner."

"I . . . I'm all right, Johnson. I must have dozed off. Don't worry, I'm coming now."

I hurriedly stepped out of the now freezing water and began to towel some warmth back into myself. My clothes were waiting for me over a low stool. When I had dressed, I turned to straighten my hair in the large mirror that hung near the door.

Though it was no longer steamed up, I could still make out on its surface the traces of letters, as though someone had been writing on it. I could remember doing so myself when younger. Holding the lamp at different angles, I succeeded in reading the words traced on the glass: CHARLOTTE, YOU MUST LEAVE THIS HOUSE AT ONCE. At the end there was a final word, almost impossible to decipher.

It was only when I stood back that I realized what it was. A signature:

CAROLINE.

CHAPTER 22

I SPENT THAT EVENING SHIVERING IN MY ROOM, MISSING DIN-
ner on the pretext that I had a headache. Antonia visited
me and helped me get into bed. I am sure she noticed the
cross around my neck, though she did not remark on it.
Once she was gone, I got up again, for I could not bear
to lie there like that, as though waiting for another visi-
tation to begin.

The message on the bathroom mirror had frightened me. The warning it conveyed fit only too closely my
own apprehensions, and I was now all the more determined to get my letter to the Reverend Watkins.

The crying began again after midnight and did not
cease till a little before dawn. I snatched some sleep,
starting awake every so often to see my lamp burning as
I had left it. Each time I would look nervously around at
the shadows with the most fearful expectation. I could
hear the crying, but could not summon up the courage to
venture out of my room. Nor would I have known what to
do if I had.

I was up and dressed earlier than usual, and went down well before breakfast, telling Mrs. Johnson that I wanted to take Jasper for an early walk. My aim was to catch the postman at the main gate, where he left letters and packages for the hall in a large metal box from which Hutton would fetch them later on.

He was on time. A little man in a peaked cap riding a bright red bicycle, one of the first in the district. He deposited a handful of letters and a parcel in the box and turned to go. I stepped out from behind the tree in whose shadow Jasper and I had been watching. Jasper growled threateningly while keeping himself well behind my skirts. Seeing me, the postman went pale and all but turned tail.

"Wait!" I shouted. "I have a letter for you to take."

He hesitated, then came up, wheeling his cycle beside him.

"Where's it for?" he asked.

"The vicar at Kirkwhelpington. Will you be sure to give it to him? It's important."

He looked at it, then at me, and finally slipped it into his bag.

"Aye, all right. I'll see he has it this afternoon."

"Thank you. It's most important. You will be sure to put it into his hand, won't you?"

"If he's home. Will he know who's written it?"

"My name's inside." I paused. "Tell me," I said, "when you first caught sight of me, I gave you a bit of a start, didn't I?"

"I wasn't expecting no one to be here."

"Is that all?"

He looked at me suspiciously, then turned his bicycle around.

"If that's everything, miss, I'd best be on my way."

"Did you think I was someone else?"

He cast an uneasy parting glance at me, then leaped on his cycle and pedaled furiously away. I watched him go, knowing that my life might depend on the letter he carried.

I got back to the hall well in time for breakfast, saying nothing of where my walk with Jasper had taken me. Antonia seemed tired and on edge that morning, but she insisted on our spending time together. A fire was lit in the library, and we stayed there until lunchtime, reading, neither of us with much concentration. Several times in the course of the morning, I caught her observing me closely. If I got up to fetch a book from one of the shelves, her eyes would follow me there and back again. If I rose to lay fresh logs on the fire, she would watch my every move. I sensed not concern for my well-being, but anxiety lest my actions escape scrutiny. Was I behaving strangely? I wondered. Did I betray my uneasiness in my posture, or nervousness in the way I moved? Did she guess what was going through my head, and was she now seeking for clues as to my possible intentions?

After lunch, she had me read to her again, and I had no choice but to acquiesce. I wanted to go outside again, for I had formulated a little plan that required the exploration of a spot deep within the grounds. After more than an hour of *Pride and Prejudice,* there was a lull. Antonia had already taken a pack of cards from a drawer in the sideboard—she was teaching me to play bezique (which she played by the Portland rules) and écarté—when I decided to face the issue.

"Please, Antonia, I must take Jasper for his walk. If you don't mind, that is. It will be dark soon, and he hasn't been out all day. Perhaps we can play later, after dinner."

She hesitated, as though reluctant that I should escape from her supervision. For a moment I thought she was about to offer to accompany me, but in the end she merely shrugged.

"In that case, I shall make do with a few games of Miss Milligan. Perhaps I can get it to come out this time. See you get back before dark. I shall expect you for tea at the usual time."

I thanked her and hurried from the room before she changed her mind. Jasper was waiting impatiently in the kitchen. I slipped on my cape and gloves, and we set out at once.

Despite its proximity to the folly, which I now feared more than ever, I had determined to visit the family graveyard Mrs. Johnson had spoken about. Jasper was in fine spirits, bounding and leaping ahead of me, sniffing quarry in every bush or heap of fallen leaves. The day was dull, with dark clouds and a threat of rain. As always, I scanned the sky for a sight of birds, but as always there were none. I had a good idea now why they stayed away from Barras Hall and its grounds.

Giving the folly as wide a berth as possible, I found the path Mrs. Johnson had spoken of, its entrance partly hidden behind a curtain of holly bushes. Fearing he might take fright again, I secured Jasper by his makeshift lead and kept a close eye on his behavior. As we pushed our way along the path, blocked at frequent intervals by low-hanging branches and patches of straying undergrowth, he grew a little subdued, keeping very close to me and almost tangling himself at times in the hem of my skirts.

It was dark here, much darker than in any other part of the grounds I had visited until now, partly because it was so low-lying, and partly because the vegetation had been allowed to grow wild, as though the path was little used. At one point I began to think I must have come the wrong way after all. Then I caught sight of a rusted iron fence running alongside the path among a riot of brambles and nettles. The ground at this point had once been paved, but the stones had long ago been displaced by weeds and wild grasses.

At the bottom, I came to a low stone wall in which an iron gate was set between thick stone pillars. On top of each pillar, almost swallowed up by the ivy that had entwined itself about everything, stood some stone figures. I could not at first distinguish what they were, but after careful scrutiny I made out the forms of two small men, hooded like monks and leaning on twisted staffs. Their features had been eroded by the passage of time and disfigured by a mottled patina of yellow lichen. Something about them made me uneasy, and I noticed that Jasper had stuck his tail between his legs and was hanging back.

I pushed the gate open with difficulty. There was no lock, but it was rusted and stuck fast at the bottom. I could only force an opening about a foot or a foot and a half wide, barely enough for me to squeeze through in my heavy clothes. Jasper hurried in after me, still huddling close to my side.

All about me the ground was choked with weeds and grass tussocks broken by clumps of reeds. Here, the path was even more overgrown than previously, winding along almost invisibly through a dense thicket of trees. Passing through these, I came into an open area beyond which I could make out the distinct outlines of broken walls. Between me and the ruins lay a scattered array of graves and tombs, all in a state of obvious abandonment. Several of the tombs were monumental, each one marked off from the surrounding area by a high iron fence. At ground level, several of the gravestones leaned sideways at alarming angles, and quite a few lay flat, almost buried beneath a carpet of grass and weeds.

Jasper whimpered, pressing his narrow body as close to mine as he was able. Ignoring him, I picked my way slowly along the path, past fallen urns and moss-covered angels with broken wings. It seemed even darker here than on the path outside, as though this deserted burial ground had little to do with daylight. It was the most desolate and mournful place I had ever set foot in. Phrases from the Bible flickered in and out of my consciousness, words of solace, offering resurrection and eternal life. I remembered the preacher intoning them at my father's funeral. Here they seemed nothing but empty platitudes.

But I had gone there to search for something, and I was determined to stay until I had discovered it or decided it was not there after all. My skirt and petticoats hampered my progress among the graves. Nevertheless I persevered at the cost of several rips to my dress, clearing away strands of ivy and brambles from one tombstone after the other. The earliest of the graves I uncovered dated back to the beginning of the eighteenth century.

This was a sadly dilapidated monument bearing the names of Sir William and Lady Beatrice Ayrton, the dates of whose deaths were 1723 and 1725. Near it were three smaller tombs, each belonging to a daughter of William and Beatrice's. I looked for Sir James Ayrton's resting place, but could not find it anywhere near those of his immediate relations.

The dead were for the most part members of the Ayrton family, though from time to time other names could be deciphered, in the majority of cases relatives by marriage. Toward the edge of the graveyard I found several constructions of more recent date: the tomb of Sir Percy and Lady Violet Ayrton, whom I took to be Anthony and Antonia's grandparents, and that of Miles and Edwina, their parents.

It was not far from there that I found what I had come for: Caroline's grave, a modest mound with a tombstone that already showed signs of wear. The date of her death was that of her fifteenth birthday, the eighteenth of December, 1892. Seeing it written so coldly in stone like that, the date we both shared, a shudder passed through me.

I had seen enough. Murmuring to Jasper, I turned to go. As I did so I caught sight of a largish tomb, set somewhat off from the others and until then concealed from view by a screen of tall juniper bushes. Though I had done what I had set out to do, I nonetheless felt myself drawn to this monument, with its classical outline and air of isolation. Why had it been built away from the others, for all that it was clearly the tomb of an important member of the family? It had started to grow dark. In my preoccupation with the search for Caroline's grave, I had let the time slip away thoughtlessly. Now the sun had sunk close to the horizon, and the sky was rapidly losing its brightness. If I did not leave soon, I would be caught in this dreadful place without light. It did not bear thinking about. And yet I could not leave without first examining this final tomb.

Hurrying, I fought my way through to it, my feet and clothes snared every few paces by thick tendrils of bramble. Even before I reached its walls, I had a good idea whose tomb it was. Its superficial resemblance to the folly was clue enough. And there, above a low, rusted door, I read the name, carved in square Roman letters into the stone: SIR JAMES STANDISH AYRTON, 1691–1779. Beneath this inscription was carved the Ayrton coat of arms, a tower flanked by two lilies, as on many of the other graves. But in this case, the shield was set in what is known as an achievement, topped by a helm and crest, backed by a mantling, and supported on either side. But where the supporters might conventionally have been lions or birds, here they consisted of two men in long, hooded tunics, the hoods concealing their faces, bent over and leaning on staffs. I was at once reminded of the figures I had seen atop the pillars guarding the entrance.

Just beyond James's tomb, as though radiating out from it, lay a row of low grass mounds without mark or favor, all heavily overgrown and in cases almost indistinguishable from their surroundings. I worked my way around to the side of the tomb, intending to cross that way toward the mounds, for I could see the traces of a path leading in their direction, and I was anxious to take a closer look.

As I came level with the center of the monument beside me, I noticed with a shudder that part of the wall had broken away, leaving a wide, gaping aperture that must have opened directly into the heart of the tomb itself. Suddenly I saw Jasper stiffen with fear. A low growl issued from his throat. Watching him, I felt myself grow cold. For I could feel it, too, that dark, revolting sensation of another presence which I had experienced twice in my room and once outside the bathroom.

I pulled Jasper to me, very close. His eyes were wide open, he was trembling, his gaze was fixed on the ragged opening in the side of the tomb. The next moment I felt as though a shadow had passed over me. I looked up.

He was standing barely ten feet away, in front of me. An old, old man, very bent, his weight thrown onto a tall staff topped with a knob of silver. He wore eighteenth-century clothes, entirely black, pumps and stockings and a short coat, the expensive garb of a gentleman. His head was bald, save for some wispy strands of white hair, and the skin was stretched tight across the face and skull as though about to tear away from the bone beneath.

I had begun to creep backward. My hand reached for the wall of the tomb for support when suddenly I felt something light brush my skirt. I thought it was a twig or branch and ignored it. I felt it again, more insistent this time. And then it touched my ankle. It was cold and dry, and it was wrapping itself about my leg.

I screamed and pulled away. Simultaneously Jasper howled and made a lunge in the direction of the hole. The grip on my ankle was momentarily relaxed. I pulled away hard and stumbled back until I was well clear of the tomb. Jasper growled once, then dashed after me.

CHAPTER 23

I RAN THROUGH THE GRAVEYARD, STUMBLING AMONG THE thickening shadows, unaware what direction I was headed in, sure my mind was going. Instinct rather than sense must have led me to the gate. As I came level with it I heard a voice call my name. Terrified, I ran even faster, Jasper always at my heels. As I rounded a bend in the tangled path, I made out a figure in front of me, blocking my way. I cried out in terror, then heard my name repeated and, looking, saw it was Mrs. Johnson. She was beckoning to me urgently, and shouting.

I stumbled toward her, Jasper running behind me, through clumps of stinging nettles. Every step cost me a tremendous effort, as though I were fighting, not only with the snares that caught at my legs, but with a much greater force that was pulling me back all the time. It was like trying to run through mud. All the while, Mrs. Johnson stood calling my name and urging me to hurry, but she seemed reluctant to approach any nearer to the graveyard.

Finally I reached her, sobbing and panting with the effort I had made.

"Come away from here, Miss Charlotte. Whatever were you thinking of to come down here on your own? If I'd thought you'd be so foolish, I'd never have mentioned this place to you. Let me take you back to the hall before you catch a fever."

As we walked back I caught hold of her arm.

"Who was he, Mrs. Johnson? That old man."

She looked at me sternly, but I could see that my words had frightened her.

"What man?"

I described the old man I had seen at James Ayrton's tomb. Mrs. Johnson only shook her head.

"No, miss, you must have been mistaken. There was no one there. No one at all."

I could get nothing more out of her. She fussed and worried over me, maintaining that the old graveyard was a place full of miasmatic vapors, its very air injurious to the health. My dress was in a dreadful mess, its hem covered with mud and torn in innumerable places.

"It's ruined, miss, it will hardly take patching. You'll have to change into another. A good thing Miss Antonia has ordered fresh for you."

Hot water was brought to my room and a fire lit. With my feet in a mustard bath and a towel around my hair, I was turned into a proper invalid. Mrs. Johnson prepared a bowl of hot mutton broth and insisted I drink it all. She instructed me on what to say to my cousin.

"Whatever you do, miss, don't let on to Miss Antonia that you've been down to the graveyard. She wouldn't like to know that, it would only upset her. She has a mortal fear of that place. Say you strayed after your dog down by the river and came back here in a mess. And not a word about my going after you."

"How did you know I was there?"

"Never mind. I found you. And a good thing, too."

A little later Antonia visited me, full of suppressed anger that was tempered only by concern lest I had injured myself. It seemed to be important to her that I should be kept in perfect health, for it was a topic to which she returned again and again. And yet I could not convince myself now that her inquiries had their origin in any genuine concern for my well-being. Discussing my state of health served some ulterior purpose, I thought, though I could not begin to guess what that might be.

That night there was no weeping. I could not go to bed, for my thoughts were filled with horrors, and I could not shake off the image of the old man staring at me out of that bloodless, skull-like face. That it had been James Ayrton I did not for one moment doubt. But what he wanted from me I could not surmise. Nor did I like to think too hard about what had touched me at the tomb. Was it the same abomination that crept, in the stillness of the night, across the lawn to the house?

Long after midnight, I thought I heard a door close somewhere. There was a sound of light footsteps on the flags outside. I went to the window and peered out. Illuminated by the lamp she carried, Antonia was walking across the garden, dressed in her wedding gown.

In a curious sense, fear had made me bolder. I was determined to get to the bottom of things. I was still dressed, and now, almost without thinking, I threw on my shawl and hurried out, carrying only a candle. By now I knew a shortcut to the back of the house down some little-used stairs that led to a small door originally built for the servants. I left the candle just inside to light my way on my return. Once in the garden, I got my bearings quickly. A good-sized moon had risen, and I found no difficulty in following the path I had seen Antonia take.

She had gone on down through the woods, along a little track that led, I knew, to the folly. I dared not hurry for fear of making too much noise, but I thought that if I stuck to the path, I was bound to stumble on her. And by now I was convinced that the folly itself was her destination.

In fact, I was mistaken. Between a clump of trees some five hundred yards before the building, I caught a glimmer of light. Approaching it, I saw Antonia in a small clearing, quite visible on account of the whiteness of her dress. I crept around the side of the clearing until I came to a tall holly bush, and from this vantage point I began to watch her.

She was kneeling on the ground, her head bent, weeping softly. Just in front of her lay a moss-covered mound that seemed unpleasantly similar in size and shape to the unmarked graves I had seen near James Ayrton's tomb that afternoon. I knew it could not be her daughter Caroline's grave, for I had seen that, clearly marked, in the little churchyard. But as I watched her a suspicion lodged itself in my mind, a suspicion that by degrees grew to near certainty. She had brought a bunch of winter flowers with her and was arranging them at the head of the grave, and I thought I heard her murmur more than once the name Simon: her fiancé's name, which she had let slip inadvertently. He had not gone abroad after all, but had died and been buried here in a secret grave at Barras Hall. Died or . . . I dared not formulate the thought that now entered my head.

She remained by the grave, intermittently weeping and conversing in whispers with her dead lover—if that was, indeed, who lay buried there. At last, with a great sigh that might have torn my heart had it not been for my own fears, she raised herself from the ground and set off back to the house. I waited until I was sure she was indoors, then retraced my steps through the moonlight. I did not cross the lawn, but skirted the garden with my heart in my mouth.

CHAPTER 24

I KEPT TO MY BED THE FOLLOWING MORNING, SAYING I HAD A cold. Antonia visited me after lunch. She was wearing outdoor clothes and showed no signs of the intense emotion she had suffered the night before.

"You don't seem too bad," she said. "You'll be down to dinner, I hope. Anthony and I are off to Morpeth this afternoon. I mean to get some things in for your birthday. It will be a small affair with just a few friends, but I mean it to be a happy day for you."

Shortly afterward, I saw Hutton getting the carriage horse from the stable. Slipping from my room, I made my way to the front of the house, where I could look out on the main driveway. A few minutes later Hutton appeared, leading the horse, which had been harnessed to a victoria. Anthony and Antonia emerged from the front door and seated themselves in the carriage. I watched them drive quickly away and disappear around a bend in the drive.

I was almost alone. Hepple spent most of her time between lunch and supper cleaning and scrubbing in the scullery. Mrs. Johnson, I knew, often took the chance most days of having a little sleep once the lunch things had been cleared away. Today was unlikely to be an exception. I waited in the corridor near her room until I heard her come upstairs and go inside. For the next few hours I would have the run of the house.

My object was to carry out a thorough search of Anthony's study, for I suspected that there must be papers that would answer some of the questions now perplexing me. Provided he and Antonia did not return unexpectedly, I was confident of getting away with my snooping unobserved. My only misgiving lay in the fact that the study windows overlooked not the front but the rear of the house. I had some time, but it would not be wise to linger.

The study door was unlocked. I closed it behind me and stepped briskly across to the window. With the curtains drawn back halfway, I had enough light to carry out my search. The walls were lined with tall mahogany bookcases filled with leather-bound volumes, the majority of which appeared, on first inspection, to be legal works. A deep armchair had been drawn close to the fireplace, and beside it was a low table on which various newspapers and popular magazines lay scattered.

My interest was immediately drawn, however, by a large *secrétaire* against the wall opposite the fireplace. The lid had been closed, and when I tried to pull it open, it turned out to be locked. I had expected as much and had come prepared. My workhouse education stood me in good stead for once. One of my friends there, a girl called Mary Pearce, had shown me how to pick a lock—something she had learned from her father. More than once we had gone together on expeditions to the kitchens late at night, gaining entry through a locked door and then picking the lock on one of the pantries. We never took enough to draw attention to our pilfering, but the extra rations had helped us both through some very hard times. Now I meant to put my skills to more serious use.

The lock on the desk was not particularly difficult. I used a bent hairpin as a skeleton key, and it took me only five or six attempts to get the lid open. Inside, I found a jumble of papers and a row of small drawers and pigeonholes. Systematically I began to go through these, taking the papers out and reading through them in strict order so I could replace them afterward without betraying that they had been disturbed.

One drawer contained nothing but bills. My cousin, it appeared, did business quite widely, for there were invoices here for goods from as far away as London and Brighton. They were mostly for small amounts, representing accounts for household items or equipment used on the estate. A few were for much larger sums, for coal or raw materials or transportation, relating, it seemed, to business transactions carried out at a number of localities and suggesting a range of commercial activities the nature of which I could only guess at.

In the pigeonholes I found yet more bills, various items of stationery, and assorted handbills advertising a wide variety of goods and services, many of them dating back twenty years or more. A second drawer held receipts. In a third I found bundles of letters, arranged more or less in alphabetical order.

I knew there would not possibly be time for me to read through these in full, but I went through them one at a time, taking mental note of the names of Anthony's correspondents and where they lived. Most of them were business letters, the contents of which appeared technical. There was a little pile of letters sent by their mother, from her house in Morpeth, and a bundle addressed to their father.

At the very bottom, quite apart from all of these, I found a single letter, still in its envelope, addressed to both Anthony and Antonia. Something about the writing seemed familiar. I opened it. It was about a page in length, written in a careful hand on fine paper with an embossed letterhead. The address was that of my old home in Gosforth. The signature at the bottom was my mother's. This was the letter she had written to my cousins after my father's death. The letter which Antonia had denied ever receiving, whose loss she had regretted with tears in her eyes. Of which Anthony had said it was a tragedy that it had not reached them, for if it had, our lives might have been different.

My hand shook as I replaced my mother's letter and closed the drawer. I wanted to shout and scream and call them liars to their faces. I wanted to go into a corner by myself and weep over their betrayal. But I did neither. I just continued searching, knowing that somewhere in here I would find more answers.

There were more letters in the next drawer. Among them was a bundle in identical blue envelopes, all unopened, with their stamps unfranked. I did not have to open them to guess their identity: these were the letters I had written to Annie and my other friends. At first I could not understand Anthony's motive in withholding them like this. How could it possibly benefit him not to post them? It was unlikely that they would suddenly receive a flood of unwelcome visitors as a result. And then, with a stab of fear, I thought I understood after all:

if no one had heard from me, no one would know I was at Barras Hall. I might as well be dead, for all anyone outside knew.

In the same drawer I came across a letter in a cheap envelope, bearing a Chester-le-Street postmark, and dated about three weeks earlier. It had been addressed to me: *Miss Charlotte, at the house of Mr. and Mrs. Ayrton, Esq., near by Kirkwhelpington, Northumberland.* I opened it and drew out a sheet of rough writing paper on both sides of which Annie had written, describing events at the Lincotts' following my disappearance, and telling me that a new girl had been found a day or two later. She looked forward to receiving news of me. And she hoped I had found Arthur and great happiness. Even this simple letter from an old friend had been kept out of my hands.

Alongside it I discovered Endicott's letters to Anthony, the ones he had read to me at the dinner table when recounting their mutual efforts to track down my brother. As I glanced through them I felt a little comforted by their reassurances and by the optimism they expressed that Arthur might soon be found. Perhaps, I thought, they might still find him in time for my birthday. What a present that would be!

Thinking to the future and the possibility that I might yet have to leave Barras Hall, I took a couple of the letters. I had no clear plan, but I rather thought they would serve as a sort of introduction for me to Endicott himself. The first one bore his London address, the later one just the heading "Newcastle" alongside the date.

I glanced at the clock on the mantelpiece. It was still only about half past two: there would be enough light to read by for a little while yet, and I was sure I would be done before a lamp grew necessary. I continued searching through the desk, knowing I might not find another opportunity like this.

A large drawer on the bottom contained a small chest of polished wood chased with brass. It was a moment's work to pick the lock. Inside were bundles of legal papers tied together with pink ribbon. I undid them carefully and read through them, finding nothing I could make much sense of until I came to a thick roll of what appeared to be shares in various companies. They meant very little to me, of course, for I had no proper conception of what stocks and shares involved. But the names of several of the companies did mean something.

Here were large quantities of holdings in the United Alkali Company, the firm which had forced all its Tyneside rivals, my father's company included, to close. Next to these were papers showing that Anthony had held stock in Tennant's, Allhuser's, and in large quantities, Newcastle Alkali and Chemical, my father's firm. There were also documents showing stock holdings in the Tyne Electrical Company, my father's short-lived attempt to rescue his fortunes.

After my father's death, my mother had spoken a great deal about stocks and shares, but everything she said had gone over my head. Even now I could extract no meaning from any of the papers in my cousin's desk. But it seemed a great coincidence that they should be here at all. And I wondered how it was that Anthony, if he had been so closely connected at one time to my father's business enterprises, should have expressed his ignorance of his bankruptcy and death.

Before I left the study, I made two other discoveries that, after their fashion, set all the others at nothing. These, if you like, were my only accidental discoveries, though even now I rather like to think my hand was guided. As I was closing the lid of the desk I noticed that beneath it, the Ayrton arms had been carved, the shield held, as on James Ayrton's tomb, by the figures of two hooded men. In my curiosity, I touched the figures, first one, then the other. As I did so I noticed that they seemed not to be quite firm. Returning my hands to them together, I pulled on them as though testing their solidity, and as I did so I observed a small panel open in the bottom of the desk.

I reached inside and drew out a folder bound with ribbon. The light was fading now, and I knew I should be gone, but the very secrecy with which it was invested made the folder irresistibly interesting to me. I carried it to the low table on which Anthony had strewn his newspapers and untied the ribbon.

Inside were dozens of newspaper cuttings, many of them yellow with age. Someone had written on them the name of the paper and the date of the issue from which they had been extracted. They came mainly from journals of local origin: the *Berwick Journal and North Northumbrian News,* the *Alnwick and County Gazette,* the *Hexham Courant,* the *Tyne Mercury,* and others. As I read them it was as though the frost now gathering on the grass and stones outside had entered me instead. It was then, I think, that a true consciousness of my situation was wakened in me and I became aware of the horror of my position.

One after another, the pieces in my hand—short, and expressed in the stilted language of the provincial journalist of the last century—chronicled a series of unconnected yet almost identical events. The disappearance over a period of ninety or more years of children and adolescents from farms or villages in a wide radius around Barras Hall. These were for the most part poor children, and little was reported beyond the fact that they had gone missing and that the proper authorities had been involved. From time to time there would be speculation as to their whereabouts. And in a number of cases, children from wealthier families would disappear, leading to more exhaustive and prolonged inquiries.

But—unless the cuttings assembled in that file were unusually selective—it seemed that in no instance was the errant child ever brought home or a body discovered. It was as though they had all disappeared into thin air.

Reaching inside the opening a second time, I drew out a small notebook, very old, bound in stiff leather that had rotted in places. Inside, I found scribbled notes in an old-fashioned hand. The name on the flyleaf was James Ayrton.

At that moment there was a sound of wheels on gravel. I rammed the cuttings back into the file and the file into its hiding place, sliding the panel back firmly. The little journal I slipped into my dress. By the time my cousins entered, I was well on my way back to my room. It was rapidly growing dark outside. But the true darkness was within me now.

CHAPTER 25

I SAT ALONE IN MY ROOM WATCHING SNOW FALL FROM A BLACK sky. I was crippled with thoughts. Antonia did not come to visit me. The snow went on falling; it would be heavy by nightfall. I picked up James Ayrton's journal and began to read.

> *12 January 1779. To the Temple last night. Read the Arbatel and the Lemegeton, but nothing came. Heard Something while in the Ascendant, but Voices only, and no Showing. There must be a fault, whether in the Recitation or the Performance I do not know. Will reread Trithemius; perhaps he has the answer.*

> *20 January. Two nights now and nothing has come. Pomponazzi counsels Patience, yet mine is sorely tried. All last night calling on Zabaath and Bahonym, but no Answer. Resolved to try again tonight, three times.*

15 February. This morning received the Book of Ebn Wahshiya from Amsterdam. It is full of Signs and must be digested thoroughly before using. Danger in confusing the Signs. Voices last night. They are becoming clearer. I have spoken twice with the Blind Man.

17 February. Wore the black Veil last night for the first time. It enhanced the Ritual as Trithemius said it would. I saw Shapes where there had been none previously. I must persevere and keep my courage.

20 February. There were feet outside my door again last night. I sense I am coming close. Think myself near to mastering the Signs of Belbeis and Cophtrim. Another week, then I shall make my attempt. Spent the morning reading in the Red Dragon *and the* Grimorium Verum. *Tomorrow seven times.*

28 February. Used the Signs last night for the first time. The Voices quite distinct. Saw Something, but not clear. I trust nothing was confused. Agrippa says there is great danger in it.

5 March. In the Temple all night. Redrew the Circle and used the Signs of King Berhemius. It appeared twice and spoke to me. I made it return the second time with much effort. Must read what Trithemius says about the Ascendant and Descendant.

6 March. Summoned It twice again last night. Would go back only unwillingly and with much coercion. It comes closer each time. I would perform in darkness, were it not that I need the light to read by, to avoid errors. It says It crouches by the door now.

8 March. Saw its Face last night. I must have mixed the Signs. It says It will not go back. I must spend today in the library to find an answer.

9 March. Saw something on the lawn. Very close. I can find nothing in either Pico or Paolini. If I cannot send It back . . . Dear God, if I cannot send It back!

Dinner that night was a torment. Several times, Antonia remarked on how preoccupied I was, how pale I looked.

"You are not feeling better, are you, my dear?"

I shook my head and continued to play with my food. She leaned across and whispered to me, "Perhaps it is your time of the month. You do know to what I am referring?"

I flushed and nodded quickly.

"Yes," I said, "that's what it is."

She did not look wholly convinced, but nonetheless smiled sympathetically. I was lying, of course: my periods had started not long before I left the workhouse, but during my months at the Lincotts' they had ceased again. I, in my innocence, thought they had ended for good, though I knew they were meant to continue much longer—until I got married and had children, as I then believed.

I excused myself from staying down for coffee after dinner, on the pretext that my headache had returned. Antonia kissed me good night and whispered that I should see her about my "problem" in the morning when she and I would be free to talk openly.

Sometime before, I had established that if one were to take a roundabout route from the drawing room, it was possible to reach the dining room from a different direction and to enter it by another door, one which—so Antonia had told me—had been used in the past for dinner parties but which now remained locked, ever since my cousins had started "keeping themselves to themselves."

I knew I would be taking a considerable risk, but I had resolved to make my way to the other side of the drawing room door in the hope of overhearing whatever conversation passed between Anthony and Antonia. I now desperately needed to know what they said to one another in my absence: whether they talked about me, whether Caroline's name was ever mentioned.

To my relief, the main dining room door was still unlocked, as it had been the day Antonia showed me through it. I opened it very slowly, terrified that the least creak of a hinge might alert my cousins. The room was in pitch darkness, but a faint crack of light showed on the far side, through the door to the drawing room. I left my lamp outside in the corridor, lest its light give me away.

All through that night's meal, I had observed the layout of the room closely in preparation for my work of espionage. I knew that if I kept to the north wall, there would be no obstacles between me and the door for which I was headed. Keeping my back against the wall, I shuffled closer. A murmur of low voices came through the door. I reached it in less than a minute and stood still, calming my breathing and the banging of my heart.

Pressing my ear against the keyhole, I found I could make out virtually everything that was said. My cousins were talking calmly about the work that had to be done to repair the damage caused by the storm. This went on for some five or ten minutes. Then there was a pause while Antonia poured fresh coffee. I heard a rustling of paper and realized that Anthony had opened a newspaper. Once a week he had several sent up from Morpeth, in order, so he said, to keep abreast of both local and national news. My heart sank, for it was possible he would continue to read now in silence and that, in another few minutes, Antonia would bid him good night and head for bed.

A few more minutes passed. The only sounds were the occasional clinking of a cup on a saucer or the crackling of Anthony's paper. Then I heard Antonia's voice, startlingly loud in the silence.

"Anthony, please put that paper down. We have to talk."

There was some loud rustling.

"Talk? What about?"

"You know as well as I do. Charlotte is growing suspicious."

"She saw Johnson coming out of the room, that's all."

"She heard the crying, Anthony. I've already told you that."

There was a sound of throat clearing.

"Yes, you have. But what of it? You reassured her. She thinks it was the wind."

"I doubt it very much, Anthony. Didn't you see her tonight?"

"You said yourself it's her time of the month."

"Possibly. But she was acting strangely earlier today as well. I think she has already started seeing them."

"Already?"

"Yes, I think so. A few of them at least. I fear she may have seen Caroline. She wears a crucifix around her neck. God knows where she got it from."

"Does she know Caroline is dead?"

There was another hesitation. I listened with my heart in my mouth, for now Caroline's existence and her death had been confirmed to me in almost the same instant. Would one of them let slip what had happened to her?

"Anthony, I think you should look at this. Johnson found it in Charlotte's room this morning."

"What is it?"

"Look for yourself."

A longer pause, then Anthony's voice, strained.

"A diary? Charlotte's?"

"No, you idiot. It belonged to Caroline."

"Good God. Where . . . ?"

"I don't know. It must have been hidden in the room. Charlotte obviously found it and will by now have read it."

"Does it . . . ?"

"It says enough. The child is clever. She will put the pieces together."

"Not all of them, surely?"

"No, Anthony, but enough to make her realize she may be in danger. She's been asking questions. Johnson says she was asking yesterday about the vicar."

"The vicar? What on earth for?"

"She said she wanted to have her mother's remains exhumed and moved to Kirkwhelpington. But I don't believe that for a moment. The . . . Caroline's diary mentions Watkins a couple of times."

"Does it? What's it say?"

"Here, let me see."

A longish pause and, just audible, the sound of pages being turned.

"Here we are: 'He says my life may be in danger if I stay at the hall.' And she mentions that time he tried to get in here and I had to send him packing."

"Nevertheless what did Watkins really know? A few tales the old villagers told him."

"That isn't the point. He believed Caroline. You can't have forgotten the fuss he made after her death. All that poking about."

"He found out nothing."

"He found out enough, Anthony. All he lacked was evidence that would stand up in a court of law. I think Charlotte may try to get in touch with him. He could cause trouble. Remember that he's not a parish priest any longer. I've heard he has the bishop's ear; and the bishop's a meddler."

"Durham's a long way from here. And there's nothing even he can do if we go through with the adoption."

"Anthony, I really believe you should think twice about that. It will only draw attention to her presence here. Once it's all over with, we don't want any legalities hanging over our heads. It was bad enough with Caroline."

"Nevertheless it would serve a purpose. I don't mean just the advantage of having Charlotte as our child in law. It would materially increase the meaning of the act if she were ours."

"Like Caroline?"

"Yes, in a sense."

"Nevertheless it's best we keep her presence here a secret. That way there will be no questions afterward."

"Perhaps you're right. Perhaps we can have her

adopted privately, dispense with the legalities. Melrose will know the best way to proceed."

There was a long silence, then Antonia's voice changed subtly in tone.

"I see them every day now, Anthony. You go riding, you visit Morpeth. Today is the first time I have been away from this place in over a month. Do you have any comprehension what it is like for me while you're away? They're growing hungry, Anthony."

"They promised to stay quiet. . . ."

"They stay quiet for a while, then they grow hungry. He above all. I don't think I can stand it much longer. It gets worse every time."

"We have no choice. If we don't give them what they want . . ."

"We could leave."

"And how far do you think we would get? Do you think distance means anything to them?"

"He was there this morning, Anthony. He has put on the veil."

"I know. I saw him, too."

"Sleep with me tonight. Please. I don't want to be alone if he comes."

"Very well." A pause. "How long is it now to the child's birthday?"

"Three days."

"Can you bear it for that long?"

"Not if it gets too strong."

"What about Johnson?"

"She's showing signs of weakness. I don't trust her, Anthony. We may have to . . . control her."

"Can't we just let her go?"

"You know we can't. She knows too much. And she can't hold that blessed tongue of hers."

"Do you think she'll try to interfere?"

"Possibly. She was upset by what happened to Caroline. And she still thinks of revenge for her son. You'll have to make the consequences of interference very clear to her."

"And the girl? What about her?"

"Yes. She will certainly have to be controlled. If she continues to be frightened."

"You say she has already heard Caroline? Perhaps even seen her. Well, it will not be long before the others show themselves. We shall have to ensure that all the preparations have been made for her birthday. If anything should go wrong at this stage . . ."

"I'm frightened, Anthony. I don't know if I can go through with it again."

"You have to. We both have to. It's the only way we can get any peace."

"Peace? We can never have real peace here. They'll be quiet for a while, and then the hunger will start again."

"Let's go to bed, Antonia. There's no use talking about this anymore. There's nothing we can do. I'll keep a closer eye on the girl, I promise."

"Will it ever end, my love?"

"Not in our lifetimes, no."

"And after that?"

There was a long pause.

"Perhaps not even then."

"I saw it last night, Anthony. In the garden. It's very close."

"Antonia . . ."

"It's getting closer all the time now. Caroline saw it. She wrote about it in her diary."

"Did she . . . Did she know what it was?"

"No. No, how could she?"

"What about Charlotte? Her window looks out in that direction."

"I don't know. She's read the diary. She may be curious."

"She would soon lose her curiosity if she saw it close at hand."

"Yes. Oh, God, let's speak no more of it, Anthony. Take me to bed."

The far door opened and closed. I was left in darkness and in silence. One thought repeated itself over and over in my mind: I had to leave Barras Hall that night. Otherwise I might never leave it at all.

CHAPTER 26

BY NOW I HAD LEARNED ENOUGH TO MAKE ME DREAD THE thought of even one more night under that roof. That my cousins meant me harm I no longer doubted. The problem was how to effect my escape. We were a good distance from any other habitation, and I knew I would not get very far on foot. There were no bicycles at Barras Hall, and even if there had been, I could not have ridden one. My only hope was to saddle Petrarch and make my way to Morpeth clinging to his reins.

Once there, it was my intention to seek out Anthony's solicitor, Mr. Melrose, and ask him to direct me to Endicott. This latter gentleman would, I had no doubt, be willing—in exchange for an adequate fee—to help reunite me with Arthur and see that we were both returned to a place of safety in Newcastle. If my suspicions were right, neither Anthony nor Antonia would dare follow us very far for fear of drawing attention to themselves.

I knew, of course, that Melrose would be puzzled by my appearance in his office. But he could not communicate with my cousins by telephone, and I was sure he would prove sympathetic to the urgency of my need to find Arthur. After all, I wanted nothing more than to see and speak with Endicott, and I was sure the lawyer would not begrudge me his address. Once I was on my way, he could tell Anthony what he pleased: I would be out of his clutches and, I prayed, reunited with my brother.

My two chief difficulties were how to find my way to Morpeth (for I had no firsthand knowledge of the district) and how to come by enough money to live on and to pay Endicott's fee. The first of these I had taken care of as well as I was able by tearing a map of the locality from a book in the library. It showed Barras Hall and the chief roads that led from it to the town.

The question of money was more difficult, chiefly because I felt an instinctive repugnance to the thought of stealing, which was the only means by which I might lay my hands on any. In the end, having revolved the dilemma in my mind for an hour or more, I decided to take with me several items of jewelry that had been loaned to me by Antonia. I would sell or pawn them once I got to Morpeth. Thinking of my cousins' treatment of my mother when she had approached them in desperation, I felt little compunction at this betrayal of trust.

It was, I thought, best to delay my departure until as near dawn as possible. Otherwise I might become hopelessly lost in the woods and waste precious time going in circles about the very place I wanted to escape from, or worse, I might end up riding in the opposite direction and end up miles from where I wanted to be.

Those hours of waiting proved a very great strain on

my resources, for I feared to sleep, partly because I might not wake until it was too late to make my getaway, and in part because I was terrified of letting go, terrified of waking in the middle of the night to find that I was no longer alone.

I left about an hour before first light. I had briefly considered leaving through the window, but the drop from the wall was sheer at that point, and since I have no head for heights, I was afraid to attempt the climb in my bulky outdoor clothes, even with the help of knotted sheets. In order to leave the house, I had to find my way downstairs in the dark, with only a candle for company. Against my wishes, I was forced to leave Jasper behind, for fear that his barking might draw someone's attention.

That was the hardest enterprise of my life until then, for I had every expectation of coming face-to-face with the man in black, the man I believed to be James Ayrton. And if not him, one of "the others" my cousins had mentioned. I started at the slightest sound or the smallest quivering of a shadow.

Petrarch was startled to see me at his stable so early, but a little fussing calmed him. I was still a novice at the art of harnessing and saddling, and in near darkness I got tangled up more than once in a web of straps and buckles. It must have taken half an hour to get the girth fastened tightly enough. The snaffle and reins proved easier, and by the time the sky was beginning to lighten, I was on my way down the main drive.

It was bitterly cold. I had scarcely joined the road when light flakes of snow began to fall, and I grew worried at the prospect of getting caught up in a blizzard. Judging by the map, I had to keep on that road for about three miles, then join another heading east through

Hartburn, Throphill, and Mitford. It was a journey of some eleven or twelve miles, but the numerous turns and windings of the road increased that figure to something closer to fourteen. Petrarch was fresh and evidently thrilled to be out on the road, in spite of the cold. As I grew in confidence I was able to give him his head a little and move at a respectable trot. At least the cold meant that the surface of the road was firm. A twisted fetlock would have spelled disaster.

Once on the main road, I allowed myself to doze a little, leaning my head against Petrarch's neck. The snow grew heavier. I began to think that it might work in my favor if it allowed me to reach Morpeth in safety and then came down even more heavily, cutting off Barras Hall and the possibility of pursuit. Perhaps someone was looking after me after all.

In spite of the weather, I rode with a lightening heart. Just to be away from Barras Hall was compensation enough for any hardships that might lie ahead. The open countryside seemed a perfect paradise. What had I to complain about? Not long ago I had been on these roads dressed in rags, penniless, and with nowhere to go. Now I wore fine clothes and rode a pony. I was already dreaming of the future: I would find Arthur and earn enough money to train as a teacher. I even began to think of marriage, when the right man came along.

I got some bread and milk at a farmhouse just past Throphill, paying with an extra pair of finely embroidered gloves I had slipped into my pocket. The farmer's wife would never wear them, but she knew they would fetch far more than the price of my simple breakfast at the next market. She asked where I had come from and I answered that I had ridden from Wallington Hall, a large house belonging to the Trevelyan family, a few miles south of my cousins' estate. To have told her the truth might well have been to forfeit her sympathy.

"Why ever are you out so early, miss? And in such bad weather?"

"I have urgent business in Morpeth," I said.

She looked suspiciously at me. Young women of good family did not go riding alone through the countryside in those days.

"More likely a man, I'll be bound," she remarked.

I blushed and said nothing to disabuse her of her illusion. She gave me a broad smile and turned back to her chores. I thought I might as well profit by her seeming complicity in what she no doubt took for an elopement.

"Please, don't tell anyone I've passed this way," I said.

She glanced at me with a look that suggested she knew all about these things and nodded.

"Your secret's safe with me." And to show herself in earnest, she made a point of returning my gloves. "You'll perhaps be in need of these," she said. "They're worth a sight more than a slice of bread and a mouthful of milk."

I arrived in Morpeth shortly after one o'clock. The snow had eased off slightly, but the sky showed signs of more to come. An old man on Dogger Bank gave me directions into the town center. I rode in along Newgate Street, past the old workhouse on the right. Though I had never seen the Morpeth Union before, I knew it for what it was. They were all alike, those places, built to a common plan, for a common purpose. I rode past with my head averted, knowing that if the worst happened, I would be taken there, and from there returned at the first opportunity to Chester-le-Street.

A boy gave me directions to the Queen's Head in

Bridge Street, where they fed and groomed Petrarch while I warmed myself by the fire. I was starving, but without ready cash dared not order anything to eat. The staff gave me plenty of curious looks, but I just smiled back at them and tried to look as natural as possible. As much as anything, I think my old-fashioned clothes must have raised a few eyebrows. But expensive garments, however out of fashion, create a very different impression than rags. As a pauper, I would have been sent packing. As a rich eccentric, I was as welcome as anyone.

I said I had business with Mr. Melrose, and this seemed to reassure them. Deflecting their inquiries as to my identity and where I had come from, I asked for directions to his office. A large, kind-faced woman, who seemed to be the manageress, told me exactly how to get there. As I turned to go she called after me.

"Will you be staying this evening, miss? It's likely to be a foul night once it gets dark."

"Yes," I said. "I'd like a room for the night, if you have one." Melrose would be sure to direct me to someone who would advance me some cash. And in the exhilaration of being so far from that dreadful place, I felt myself filled with a confidence I had never suspected I possessed.

"I'm sure we can manage that. Shall we expect you back for tea?"

"I'm sure you can," I said.

The offices of Melrose and Parker were situated in Newgate Street, in a low Georgian building. Their outward appearance was one of genteel prosperity: a highly polished brass knocker on a highly polished door, neatly glazed windows a little smudged with snow, a lamp glowing brightly behind the transom window on which their name was painted in fresh gold letters. Had it not been for my newfound confidence and the knowledge that I was dressed for my part, I should have slunk away from that shiny, intimidating doorway. The poor thing I had been only weeks before would have received a harsh welcome.

Coming here meant taking a risk, of course. But I counted on being away first thing in the morning, even that evening, if there was a coach to Newcastle. I calculated, too, on my ability to win Mr. Melrose's sympathies with my story. Anthony might be his client, but I reasoned that my fears of ill treatment might weigh more heavily with a man of the law, if only because he might see more clearly than most the possible consequences if I were to speak out in the wrong quarters.

I banged heavily on the knocker. Moments later the door was opened by a young boy in modest livery.

"I wish to see Mr. Melrose," I said.

"He's out."

"I've come a very long way."

"Doesn't make no difference. He's out."

"Well, when will he be back? Surely he can't have gone far on a day like this?"

The boy appeared to consider this.

"He might be an hour or more," he said.

"That's all right," I answered. "I can wait."

"Well, you can't wait here. I've got strict orders."

At that moment someone appeared behind the little doorman. This was a young man of about thirty, dressed in what we would have called in those days a gentleman's attire.

"What is it, Fenwick?"

"A woman, sir."

"I can see that."

The man pushed Fenwick out of the way and took his place in the doorway.

"Can I be of any assistance, miss?"

I repeated that I had come to see Mr. Melrose.

"Yes, of course. But I'm sorry, he has gone to visit a client and may not be back until very late. In fact, it is highly probable that he will not return this afternoon. The client is a recent widow, and I fear her affairs are somewhat complicated."

My face fell. To have come so far . . . .

"May I be of any help? I am Mr. Melrose's partner. John Parker."

I hesitated only momentarily, then nodded.

"Yes," I said. "Yes, I'm sure you can. I'm sure either of you would do."

"Well, I happen to be free. You must be freezing. Come in."

He ushered me inside, waving the boy out of the way, and led me into a room just off the hall. A fire was burning brightly in the hearth. He took me across to it, helped me off with my cape, and brought a chair across. Once I was settled, he offered me tea. The boy was called and sent off to make some. I felt very relaxed. This was all going to be much easier than I had feared.

"Now," he said, seating himself in a chair next to me, "tell me what I can do for you."

"I . . . hardly know where to begin."

"Well, what is your name? Perhaps we can start there."

"Of course. I'm sorry, I'm being very rude. It's just that . . . My name is Charlotte Metcalf. My father was Douglas Metcalf. He owned an alkali works near Newcastle. Perhaps you've heard of him."

"Metcalf? I . . . yes, I do believe I know who you

mean." He hesitated. "But isn't . . . ? Isn't your father dead?"

I nodded.

"But you will have heard of me, surely."

"Heard of you? No, I don't think I have."

"I'm a cousin of the Ayrtons. At Barras Hall. I believe they are clients of yours."

A look of total astonishment came into Parker's face.

"The Ayrtons? Why, I had no idea. . . . Of course, they are really Mr. Melrose's clients, although I have often dealt with Sir Anthony's more routine affairs. I'm the junior partner, you see. There are only two of us. But you do surprise me, Miss Metcalf. I had not the slightest idea that the Ayrtons had living relatives. I'm sure it will come as a great surprise to Mr. Melrose as well."

He paused.

"But you must forgive me. I am supposed to be listening to your explanation of what has brought you here."

Haltingly I told him as much as I could. My father's death, the workhouse, my mother's passing, my separation from Arthur, my visit to my cousins and their reception of me. About conditions after that, I thought it best to keep my own counsel for the present.

"I confess," he said when I had come to an end, "that you leave me a trifle confused. You say you have been living with your cousins and that they have shown themselves solicitous of your welfare. And yet you come here alone, on a bitterly cold day, in order to see Mr. Melrose. Surely your cousins could deal with any legal matters on your behalf. You are not telling me that you have ridden here without their knowledge, are you?"

"Sir, I do have reasons for wishing to absent myself

from Barras Hall. Let us say there has been a disagreement between my cousins and myself and leave it at that. It is not a matter I wish to enter into."

I fancied I caught a glimmer of understanding in his eye. He could not, of course, have understood the substance of what I was hinting at, but I think he did grasp from my appearance and tone of voice a little of its spirit.

"In that case, what brings you here?"

I explained about Arthur.

"I need to find Endicott as soon as possible," I said. "I don't want my brother taken to Barras Hall when they find him. I want him to be brought to me, I want him to live with me. I know Mr. Melrose engaged Endicott, and all I need to know is where I may find him now."

Parker looked at me strangely, as though I had said something out of place.

"Miss Metcalf," he said, "will you excuse me for a moment. I must make some inquiries. That is to say . . . I won't be a moment."

He was, in fact, several moments. Twenty minutes or more must have passed before he returned. I sat, sipping my sweet tea and listening to the sound of the clock on the mantelpiece ticking softly. It almost sent me to sleep.

Parker came back into the room and closed the door softly behind him. As he resumed his seat I noticed that he seemed worried about something.

"Miss Metcalf, forgive me for asking, but would you please explain to me again the circumstances under which your cousin came to engage the services of this Mr. Endicott?"

I repeated what Anthony had told me that second night over the dinner table.

"And you are sure you have got the name right?"

I nodded.

"I saw it several times," I said, "on the letters my cousin showed me."

"Miss Metcalf, I have to say that I think you must be mistaken. I have just checked Mr. Melrose's files and several directories. There is no record of his having engaged anyone called Endicott for the job you speak of. Nor has he ever mentioned it to me. Nor"—he paused— "nor is there any listing of a firm of that name in London or anywhere else."

"But that can't be," I protested. "Anthony said they were the biggest bureau in London. They must be in the directory."

He shook his head.

"I'm afraid not. I really have looked carefully. I'm sorry."

I reached inside my bag and drew out the small bundle of letters I had taken from Anthony's desk.

"But look at these," I said. "These are letters from Endicott himself. You can see for yourself."

He took them from me and glanced through them. I noticed him frown. He looked up at me, then started to read the letters more slowly. When he had finished, he laid them down on the arm of his chair and looked at me again.

"My dear Miss Metcalf, I have to say that these letters trouble me greatly."

"Why? What's wrong with them?"

I saw him hesitate, as though debating with himself whether to tell me or not.

"Well? What can possibly be wrong with them? Mr. Endicott wrote them himself."

Slowly he shook his head.

"I regret to say, Miss Metcalf, that you have been

the victim of a cruel deception. These letters are not in the handwriting of anyone called Endicott."

"But . . . ? How can you say that if you tell me you do not know anyone by the name of Endicott?"

"Because . . ." He paused thoughtfully. "Because they are all in the handwriting of your cousin Antonia Ayrton. Of that there cannot be the slightest doubt."

CHAPTER 27

A LONG TIME PASSED. I REMEMBER VERY LITTLE OF WHAT WAS said. I think I cried a lot, for the revelation of how I had been duped took away any hope I might still have had that Arthur was alive. My brother was dead, and I began to harbor the most incredible fear that my cousins had killed him. I told Parker of the newspaper cuttings I had found in Anthony's study. I told him about Caroline's diary. And I gave him James Ayrton's journal, which he placed in his desk, promising to read it later.

"How long ago do you say she died?"

"Exactly ten years ago. On the eighteenth of this month. It was her birthday. And mine, too."

"Ten years. That's well before my time. But I can check the facts."

"Then you believe me?"

"Believe you? I don't know what I should believe."

"I heard her."

"Heard her?"

"More than once. Crying at night. There's a room they usually keep closed up. The windows are barred. I think they kept her locked in there."

"I see."

I so much wanted this man to believe me. It was not just that he was so sympathetic. I felt that I could trust him. And how much I needed someone to trust.

"Can you help me?" I asked. "If they've killed Arthur, they must be stopped."

"We must have more evidence than this."

"Can you find it?"

He hesitated.

"I don't know. But I'll see what I can do."

At that moment the door opened and a second man entered the room. He was dressed in outdoor clothes and was shaking snow from a top hat. His face was round and florid, much reddened by the wind. I guessed him to be around sixty.

"John? What is going on? Tom tells me you've got a visitor."

Parker introduced us. The newcomer, as I had guessed, was his partner, Stephen Melrose. He looked a little oddly at me when Parker mentioned my name.

"Metcalf? Charlotte Metcalf? Not the Ayrton girl by any chance?"

I nodded.

"How very curious. Your cousin mentioned you once or twice. Yes, I see, there is a likeness. Rather a pretty thing, aren't you? But he omitted to mention that."

He shuffled off his scarf and heavy overcoat, assisted by Parker, and at once advanced toward the fire, rubbing his hands together, then reaching for the poker.

"Gracious, child, what brings you all this way on a

day like this? Doesn't Anthony Ayrton know how to look after his female relations?"

"I think you'd better listen to her story, Stephen. There are some disturbing features about it. The young lady has been through rather a lot."

Melrose finished stirring the fire. He put the poker back in its rack and turned to face me.

"I daresay."

I thought his eyes scrutinized me very closely, as though I were an unreliable witness on whose testimony he was being forced to depend.

"It won't take long, will it? I'm up to my eyes in probates for that woman."

"Not very long, sir," Parker said, giving me a meaningful look.

Melrose looked doubtful.

"Well, well, let's get on with it." He looked at his watch, then at the clock. "But don't make a meal of it."

So I went through my narration again, coming to the point as quickly as I could. Parker butted in to explain what he had discovered about the forged letters. Melrose asked to see them, glanced at one or two pages, and tossed them aside. By the end, his face looked grave.

"Well, my dear," he muttered, "you've given me a great deal to think about. A great deal. But"—he fiddled with his watch chain—"it is my opinion that you may be jumping to rash conclusions. I've known Anthony Ayrton and his sister since they were children. I was engaged by their father before them. Good people, all of them. Upright. They're not churchgoers, I'll grant you; but they're as full of Christian virtue as many who are. I think you may be making a foolish mistake. And from what you've told me of your own circumstances, an expensive one."

I shook my head firmly.

"No, sir, I don't think I am mistaken."

"Well, suit yourself. All the same, wouldn't it be best to have a word with Sir Anthony? Give him a chance to explain some of these . . . anomalies. That's only fair, isn't it?"

"Sir, I'd rather you said nothing to my cousin. I've made up my mind to be done with him. There are things I have not mentioned to you. Things not fit to mention. Please don't bring him here."

Parker came behind me and patted me reassuringly on the shoulder.

"Stephen," he said, "I think the girl is right. If nothing else, it's evident she's been frightened by something. Let's not bring Ayrton in at the moment. At least not until we've had an opportunity to ask a few questions ourselves. And I think Miss Metcalf deserves a chance to get clear of this district if she wants. Ayrton has no legal hold over her, has he? He's not her guardian or anything like that?"

Melrose seemed on the point of saying something, but appeared to change his mind. He shook his head.

"Very well," he said. "We'll do as you ask, miss." He paused. "You'll not be traveling on tonight, however, will you, Miss Metcalf?"

I shook my head.

"Have you got a place to stay?"

I explained about the Queen's Head and how Petrarch was stabled there.

"But I have no ready money," I went on. "I was meaning"—I thought quickly—"to sell some things of my mother's."

My hand was poised to open the purse, in which the jewelry was kept, but Parker grasped it firmly.

"There's no need for that, I'm sure. Stephen, I'm

sure your client would not begrudge a small sum to his niece? Even under these circumstances."

Melrose nodded.

"No, I'm sure he wouldn't. He must be quite distraught as it is, thinking what may become of her. Take what you can find in petty cash, John. We'll see about something more substantial when the bank opens tomorrow. Don't worry, I'll take full responsibility."

When I had been advanced the princely sum of three pounds sterling—and quite a lot it was in those days—Parker helped me on with my cape and offered to see me to my hotel. It was growing dark, and he was concerned lest I lose my way in the town. I said good-bye to Melrose, and we set off.

As we entered the hotel Parker turned to me.

"Come to us first thing tomorrow. We'll see to the money old Melrose promised and then talk about getting you to Newcastle. If that's still what you want."

"There's no coach tonight, is there?"

He shook his head violently.

"No, and you shouldn't even be thinking of it. You need to get some rest. I'll see they give you the best room in the place. Be sure to go straight to bed as soon as you've taken supper."

He went over to the desk and, after a brief conversation with the clerk, assured me that he had arranged everything.

He was on the point of leaving when he stepped up close to me.

"Miss Metcalf, if you don't mind, I would like to ask you something."

"Yes?"

"It's about what you told me earlier. About . . . Caroline Ayrton. You said . . . you heard her crying in another room. Surely . . . Miss Metcalf, I don't wish to seem impertinent, but surely you do not expect me to believe that."

I looked at him very calmly. I could see he was troubled.

"Good night, Mr. Parker. I'll see you tomorrow."

"No, wait. I have to know."

"Would it destroy your faith in me if I said I did believe it?"

He hesitated.

"I might—" He halted.

"You might doubt all the other things I've told you if you thought I'd been hearing voices. Well, you're entitled to think what you will, Mr. Parker. But I heard Caroline Ayrton. And saw her. And heard and saw more than that. I know what there is at Barras Hall. If you don't believe me, go and stay there yourself."

He looked at me for a long time, as though trying to make up his mind. I had come off the street into his office with a story too fantastic for words. He would not have been human if he had not had doubts.

"Well, Miss Metcalf," he said at last. "I don't know what to make of you or your story. You'd best get a good night's sleep. I'll see you in the morning."

Wrapping his scarf around his face, he went back out into the cold.

I was starving by now and asked if I could be served an early supper. One was brought to me in the dining room. It was still too early for the other guests to dine, so I ate alone. With warmth and food, I felt quite tired. I headed straight for my room, intending to go straight to bed, as I had been advised. The mere thought of sleeping somewhere where I would not be disturbed by strange sights or sounds was like a sleeping draft.

But when it came to it, I could not sleep. Thoughts of Arthur raced through my brain, giving me neither peace nor comfort. And I thought . . . Frankly I scarcely know what I thought. That Arthur was dead and buried in a grave behind James Ayrton's tomb. That a man who had died over a hundred years ago was waiting for me if I should ever return to Barras Hall. A man in black and something else, something that Caroline Ayrton had seen at night in the garden, creeping nearer and nearer to the house, something I myself had seen moving in the shadows near the fountain. The more I lay there, the more terrified I became. Even here, beyond the boundaries of my cousins' estate, the evil I had touched was reaching out for me again.

I could no longer bear to lie there in the dark. Getting out of bed, I turned the light on full. It was only a few minutes past eight. I went to the window and looked out: the snow had stopped falling, but the street below was white and glistening in the soft glow of two gas lamps. Each lamp had its own tiny world. Beyond their circles of light, the cold and darkness gathered.

For a little while now a name had been running through my head. Manners. Mrs. Manners. I racked my brain, but could not remember who she was or why her name kept nagging at me.

As I watched, the lights in the street seemed to dim a little. There was a flickering behind me as my own lamp dipped and surged again. Fluctuations in gas pressure were perfectly normal. But I was nervous all the same.

At that moment I realized who and what Mrs. Manners was. Her name had been mentioned by Caroline in her diary. The day she and Antonia went into Morpeth for the fitting at Madame Doubtfire's, Antonia had gone to visit her. She was a medium, and she lived in Copper Chase.

I felt a strange excitement take hold of me. A medium. Someone who could communicate with the dead. I looked down at the quiet street, at the footprints on the snow. Would Mrs. Manners be able to find Arthur for me? Speak to him? Receive a message from him? I shivered at the thought. But I had reason to believe the dead could speak. Arthur could lead me to the evidence I sought.

I put the thought out of my head and continued looking at the lamps and the pools of light they cast on the snow. I noticed that one set of footprints seemed strangely blurred, as though it was there and yet not there, a trick of shadows, a betrayal by my tired eyes. When I looked again, there was nothing there.

I made my mind up. I would visit Mrs. Manners. I would tell her what I knew. And she would set my mind at rest.

CHAPTER 28

"Isn't it a bit late to be going out, miss?"

It was the large woman, the one I had taken for the manageress. She was behind the desk, looking across at me with a concerned expression on her face. There was no one else around.

"It's only eight o'clock," I said.

"I'm sure I don't want to interfere, miss. But it is a terrible night outside. I'd stay indoors if I were you."

"There's someone I have to find. It's very important."

She frowned.

"Would it be Mr. Parker, miss? I can have someone fetch him here, if you like."

"No," I said. "It doesn't concern him."

"Can't it wait till tomorrow?"

I shook my head.

"I said I'd be there tonight," I lied. "She's expecting me."

"Are you planning to go far?"

"Not far. Just to Copper Chase."

She nodded, a little reassured.

"Well, you can be there in five minutes." She paused, coming out from behind the desk. "Do you know the way?"

"No. I thought perhaps you could give me directions."

"Of course, my dear. But I'm still concerned that a young thing like yourself should be setting out alone on a night like this. Look, you wait here and I'll fetch Ted. He'll see you 'round there safely, and if you tell him what time you're thinking of leaving, it'll be nothing to him to fetch you back again."

"No . . ." I began, but she had already gone. She was back half a minute later with Ted in tow. He was the hall porter, a tall man in his fifties with an enormous ginger-colored mustache. Smiling, he bent down to me.

"Well, miss, I understand you're determined to go visiting tonight."

I nodded.

"Who is it you have to see?"

I hesitated.

"M-Mrs. Manners," I stammered. "She lives in . . ."

He straightened, the smile slipping from his face.

"I know well enough, miss." He looked around at the manageress, who had come back out with him. They exchanged glances, then she turned to me.

"What business can you have with her, miss?"

"She's . . . my aunt," I lied. "I promised my mother I'd visit her when I got here."

She looked hard at me, then back at Ted.

"Well, there's no help for it, then, if she's the lass's

aunt. See she finds her way there safely, Ted. And be sure to set a time to fetch her safe back again."

Outside, it was bitterly cold. The pavements were treacherous, and Ted took me by the arm, helping me through the half-frozen snow. Our breath got tangled in the occasional light of the gas lamps on the main street, disappearing a moment afterward in the dark. The wind was as hard and cutting as ever.

"She's not really your aunt, is she, miss?" he asked me as we turned a corner out of the wind.

"How . . . ?"

"You're not a natural liar, miss, if you don't mind my saying so. And I've heard it said that Mrs. Manners has no living relatives. Not that that would matter to her, I suppose."

I stared ahead and kept walking.

"Is it someone close to you?"

"Someone?"

"That you want to speak to. They say she speaks with the dead."

There was a long silence between us, and only the snow falling.

"My brother," I said. "My brother Arthur."

"I see. Has he been dead long?"

"I . . . I don't know," I mumbled. "It's what I need to find out. Perhaps he isn't dead at all. I don't know."

We had turned another corner. Picked out by a street lamp, the name of the street we had entered was visible: Copper Chase. The snow and the silence, and Ted the only living creature anywhere within sight or hearing.

"Number nine, miss. Part of St. James's Terrace."

It was a shabby-respectable street of two-story

houses along one side. On the other, the dark shape of St. James's Church rose into the night like a cliff, hard against the winter sky.

"You know the house?"

"Most Morpeth knows the house, miss. And most stays well away. It doesn't do to meddle with the dead."

"I shan't be meddling."

He hesitated, glancing around at me.

"No," he said. "I don't suppose you will."

We stopped outside a house that seemed a little better kept than the rest.

"This is it," said Ted. "I'll leave you here and make my way back. Do you think you'll be finished by nine o'clock?"

Finished? It was as though I was visiting the dentist's or the dressmaker's. What I meant to begin that night would never be finished.

"Yes," I said. "I'm sure nine o'clock will be fine."

He touched his cap and made to leave, then, turning back, eyed me narrowly in the little light that came from a lamp on the other side of the street.

"Be sure to wait for me, miss, whatever happens. I wouldn't want you to have to walk back to the hotel in the dark."

Touching his cap a second time, he set off the way we had come, his footsteps deadened by the crisp snow. I saw his dark figure pass the first streetlight, then he turned the corner and I was alone.

There was a light above the door. I stood for a long time, hesitating in spite of the cold and my fear of the darkness around me. Finally I plucked up the courage to reach for the bellpull.

A bell jangled in the distance, at the end of a long passage, it seemed. Minutes passed. Behind me the wind sounded, plaintive and restless. I shivered and pulled my collar about my neck. There was a sound of footsteps and the door opened to reveal a middle-aged woman in a maid's uniform.

"Yes, miss? Can I help you?"

"I'm looking for . . . Mrs. Manners. Is this her house?"

"Yes, miss. But I'm afraid Mrs. Manners is not seeing anyone tonight. Are you interested in a communication?"

"Comm—no, I . . . That is, I need to see her urgently."

"Come back tomorrow, miss. There's a gathering at eight o'clock. You'll be most welcome. But not tonight."

"It's essential I see her. Tell her . . ." I thought desperately of what to say, of how to get past this obstacle. "Tell her a friend of Caroline Ayrton's is here. That I need to see her tonight. That I am in very grave trouble."

The maid seemed to hesitate.

"Wait here, miss. What name did you say again?"

"Caroline Ayrton. Say I am a friend of Miss Ayrton's."

She closed the door. Time passed, and I began to fear that I was truly unwelcome and that Mrs. Manners had told the maid to leave me on the doorstep until the cold drove me away. But the door finally opened again and I was ushered into the hall.

I had been expecting something fairly dramatic, though I cannot remember exactly what—thick velvet curtains, marble statuettes, paintings of Oriental deities, perhaps. But the hall was quite plain, an ordinary hallway in an ordinary English house. It was brightly lit and quite airy.

The maid led me into a parlor on the left. A woman was waiting for me in an armchair to the left of the fire. She stood as I came in.

"Mrs. Manners, this is the young lady who asked to see you."

"Very good, Florence. You can go back to the kitchen. If I need you again, I'll ring."

She returned her attention to me.

"Please," she said, "take a seat."

I noticed that she had not asked me to remove my coat. She was an even greater surprise than her house had been. A small woman in her early fifties, I guessed, petite, soberly dressed without being drab, her hair fixed in quite a modern style. She must have caught me staring.

"Not what you expected?"

"I . . ." I shook my head, reddening.

"I'm not what most people expect."

She sat down facing me and remained with her eyes fixed on my face for a minute or more.

"I know no one called Caroline Ayrton," she said at last.

"I think . . ." I hesitated.

"Yes?"

"I think you may have known her mother, Antonia Ayrton."

There was a brief silence.

"I rather thought you might say something like that. Antonia Ayrton. Yes, I know her. But I have not seen her in a good many years."

"Caroline was her daughter."

"Yes. So you said. You say you were a friend of this Caroline."

"I am Antonia's cousin," I said. "I have come today from Barras Hall."

She frowned. I saw her take a sharp breath. When she spoke, her voice had altered.

"I see. You live there?"

"Not any longer. But I have been there for about two months."

"Yes. I begin to understand why you have come to me. Well, I think you have told me enough. Please don't think me rude, but I must ask you to leave. There is nothing I can do for you. I'm sorry, but that is the truth."

"Please, I can't leave. You haven't let me tell you why I've come. You're the only person who can help me. My brother is dead. I believe he was murdered. You have to help me speak with him."

"No!" Her voice was suddenly high-pitched. She took several breaths quickly and seemed to grow calm. "I'm sorry. But that would not be . . . advisable."

"You're frightened," I said. "What is it? What are you frightened of?"

"Of you," she said. She hesitated. "Of the Ayrtons. Of Barras Hall. I will have nothing to do with that family. Or that place."

"Then you know something about what goes on there."

"You really should go."

"I can't go," I said. "I have no one else to turn to."

"Miss Ayrton . . ."

"My name is Metcalf. Charlotte Metcalf."

"Very well, Miss Metcalf. You must try to understand. I am a very ordinary woman with . . . curious gifts. I did not set myself up here as a medium by choice. When my late husband died, I was barely thirty years of age. I was stricken by grief, for we had only been married a few years and I loved him very much. I . . . attempted to speak with him. And he answered me. After that, I began to find myself . . . open to certain impressions. I am not wealthy, but I have a private income from my husband's estate. For over twenty years now I have opened my house for visits from the bereaved. I take no payment, I benefit in no material fashion from my work.

"Very ordinary people come to me. There is a séance once a week, on two other evenings I am available for private callers, and from time to time I see people by special appointment. They come from quite far away: Newcastle, Gateshead, even Sunderland. There are many from Berwick and the border country.

"What I deal with here is ordinary death. The spirits who come to this house are benign. They leave no startling messages, just words of comfort for those whom they have left behind. Do you understand me? This is no place for the disturbed. Whatever you have seen or heard at Barras Hall, I wish to make it no business of mine."

"They killed my brother," I said. "I am certain they killed Caroline. And before her, others, many others. And I know they mean to do away with me."

I was at that moment quite truly at my wit's end. My nerves, already ragged, seemed to snap. Everything crowded in on me at once, and I burst into tears, dark, stinging tears of hopelessness.

The next thing I remember was Mrs. Manners cradling me in her arms, hushing me, telling me to calm myself. I think she had witnessed her share of tears in that little parlor. By weeping, I had suddenly become part of her normal world, and she was able to respond to me as to any of her visitors.

When I had calmed down a little, she brought me a glass of brandy and made me take a sip.

"I think you'd better tell me a little more about yourself," she said.

"You'll help me?"

She frowned.

"I'll see what I can do."

The room in which the séances were held was at the rear of the house. Mrs. Manners led me there. She seemed a little nervous, as though uncertain of what she might be tampering with. I think she knew a great deal about Barras Hall, much more than I myself had guessed. Antonia must have given a lot away, either in conversation or indirectly in the course of the mediumistic sessions they had had together. And if there was ever talk about ghosts in Morpeth or the surrounding district, it was certain to find its way to the ears of Mrs. Manners.

She told her woman to see that we were not disturbed.

"Please," she said, "make yourself comfortable in that chair."

I sat down in a soft chair with a high back. The room was very plain and almost unfurnished. It had none of the heavy drapery or sickly ornamentation our modern minds associate so readily with the parlors of late Victorian or Edwardian mediums. There was nowhere to hide a bell or a plaster hand or a bag of ectoplasm. Gaslights on wall brackets gave the only illumination. A single plaque on one wall served for the only decoration: *Thou, God, Seest Me,* it read. A large circular table without a cloth was the focus for the week's communal séance. A freshly lit fire burned in the grate.

Mrs. Manners sat down quietly beside me.

"Charlotte," she said, "before we start, let me explain what will happen. I shall sit facing you with your hands in mine. You will be the channel through which I hope to make contact with your brother. I do not make use of spirit guides or other fancy devices you may have read or heard about. What takes place happens as a result of my sensitivity. It, in turn, is charged by your love and need. Do you understand me? You are to concentrate with all your strength of mind on your brother. On his face, his voice, his little ways. Is he still clear enough in your mind for you to do that?"

I did not hesitate.

"Oh, yes," I said. "It's as if I last saw him only yesterday."

"Good. Very good. But remember that he may have changed considerably since you last met. His experiences on this earth will have altered him beyond a doubt. And his death will have produced even greater changes."

"Do you mean I may not recognize him?"

She shook her head.

"No, not that. If he comes, you will know him, have no fear of that. He may try to speak to you, using my voice. You may possibly feel him touching you. And he may—though I stress that this is most unlikely—he may try to reveal himself to you. In a sort of physical image. You must not expect this to happen, but consider it a bonus if it does. Do not expect an appearance to take the form of a popular phantom. He will not wear a winding-sheet or carry chains. You may see just his face or his face and shoulders, or, just possibly, his entire body as it was last in life."

She paused and took one of my hands.

"Are you frightened?"

I nodded.

"That is only natural. But if your brother does come, you must know that there is nothing to be frightened of."

"Will I be able to speak to him?"

"Yes. He may not answer all your questions. The dead keep their own counsel, and I believe they are subject to higher powers that permit them to lift the veil only slightly. There are things about the next world that we are not permitted to know on this plane. If your brother seems reticent, you must not press him. Otherwise he may be snatched away, and it will prove impossible after that to bring him back."

"What about my mother and father? Will Arthur be with them?"

She nodded.

"Very likely. But let us concentrate on him for the moment."

She halted. I noticed that she bit her lower lip, like someone having second thoughts about an undertaking they are about to embark on.

"Charlotte, I have tried to explain to you what it is you are about to face. But it would be most unfair of me if I did not also tell you that there may be very great danger in this enterprise for both of us. The dead themselves are not a cause for any alarm. They bring us peace, not fear. But . . . sometimes things are stirred up that were better left alone. Hatreds. Resentments. A need for revenge. What we are about to do may touch upon all that. You have already had a glimpse of the darker side. If it shows any sign at all of invading our circle tonight, you must let me break the circle. Do you understand? I will not put either one of us in jeopardy. Is that clear?"

I nodded slowly. The room was still chilly. It had not been expecting us.

"Are you ready?"

"Yes."

"Then give me your hands. And think of Arthur."

CHAPTER 29

Now my life is almost over. I have come a long, long way from that place and that time. But not a day has ever passed without my seeing and hearing the events of that night. Some things never leave us. But if God were good, He would have taken those memories from me long ago, I would not have cared how or what price He exacted. For even now I fear my death, knowing, as I do now, as I have known for most of my life, that death is not a release. There is life after death, but such a life. . . . And there is no peace anywhere, for anyone.

The very touch of Mrs. Manners's hands was unlike that of any other person's I had ever known. There was a force in it, an energy; almost, I would have said, an intelligence. I closed my eyes.

"Concentrate," she whispered. "Let your breathing become slow. Feel your heart beating and feel it slackening."

I followed her directions. As time passed I felt myself relax. My breathing and my heartbeat did indeed grow calmer. I began to experience flashes of Arthur's face on my mind's eye. In time these flashes steadied and I could see him for increasingly longer spells. I could hear nothing but the hissing of the gas burner, the occasional crackling of the fire, and the regular breathing of Mrs. Manners a few feet away. The room grew warmer. I began to find it more difficult to breathe.

I opened my eyes. Mrs. Manners was still sitting facing me. Her head was slumped forward on her chest, which was rising and falling with great effort. Beads of sweat stood out on her forehead. Her grip on my hands was growing tighter. I continued to concentrate on Arthur.

It started almost without my knowing. The first thing I noticed was that the room was growing cold, although the fire still blazed as brightly as ever. It was the same unwholesome chill I had experienced at Barras Hall. Mrs. Manners started to breathe very heavily indeed. And then, over the sound of her breathing, I heard something else. Not Arthur's voice, which is what I had been expecting, but a sound like dry leaves rustling in the wind. I could not identify it at first. Then it began to rise in volume and I realized with a thrill of deep unease that it was the sound of several voices whispering. They were coming from nowhere and everywhere all at once.

As they grew louder I tried to make out what they were saying, but nothing seemed to make any sense, as though they were speaking in a foreign language or in a variety of different tongues. I heard my name repeated several times, *"Charlotte, Charlotte,"* in different voices, each time with great intimacy, as though a close friend were summoning me. Then, behind the whispers, a man's voice, rough and angry, the words still unintelligible.

Suddenly the voices faded and were replaced by a child's voice singing.

> Swift to its close ebbs out life's little day;
> Earth's joys grow dim, its glories pass away;
> Change and decay in all around I see;
> O Thou, Who changest not, abide with me!

Suddenly the voice was broken off. The room was utterly silent, except for sounds of labored breathing from Mrs. Manners. I could feel my hair rising. I knew something was about to happen.

Without warning, the flames in the two gas burners sank very low, almost to the point of extinction. The fire died down as though someone had thrown water on the coals. The room was almost dark now and growing colder every moment. Mrs. Manners began to moan and toss her head from side to side, though she did not once let go of my hands.

At that moment I heard a sound that made my flesh creep. Footsteps in the passage outside the room. Just like those I had heard outside my bedroom at Barras Hall. They approached the door. "Please," I prayed desperately, "let it be Florence." But I knew these were not Florence's footsteps. Something rattled the door handle. Mrs. Manners gave a loud cry and jerked her head back violently.

The next instant a tremendous force hurled the door open, sending it crashing against the wall. The doorway remained empty, utterly empty. But I could feel it now, that same dark presence I had known at Barras Hall. At first, there was silence, and then I heard something: a rustling sound, the same sound I had heard in my bedroom in the dark. It was in the room with us.

Suddenly Mrs. Manners opened her eyes. The rustling grew louder.

"Charlotte! Help me, Charlotte, help me!"

It was a girl's voice. With horror, I realized that it had come from Mrs. Manners's throat, but it was not her voice.

"Charlotte, they're hurting me! Oh, God, help me!"

Mrs. Manners's mouth opened and closed without real relation to the words, like the mouth of a ventriloquist's dummy.

"They want you back, Charlotte. You have to go to them. He won't stop hurting me until you go back."

"Who are you?" I asked in desperation.

"Caroline. My name is Caroline. You have to come back to us. He says he will hurt Arthur, he will hurt him if you don't come back."

"Where is Arthur? I want to see him."

"It isn't possible. Not here. At Barras Hall, but not here. Please, you have to come."

I tore my eyes away suddenly, for I had become aware of something else in the room. In the corner farthest from me, I saw someone—or something—standing and . . . standing and moving, except that its movements were so unnatural, so distorted they were not like movements at all, but displacements of the shadows that surrounded it.

At that moment Caroline screamed, a scream of such fantastic pain and horror that it still echoes in my head today. Mrs. Manners arched her back, pulling her hands from mine, and crashed back into her chair as though hurled there. I made to reach for her, but she shook her head violently.

"Get out of here!" she hissed. Her voice was weak, almost inaudible. "For God's sake leave."

I made a grab for her, intending to pull her from the chair and drag her with me from the room, but as I did so she summoned up what strength remained to her and sent me hurtling in the direction of the door.

"Leave!" she shouted.

I picked myself up and staggered out into the passage. I was truly terrified now and could think of nothing but getting out of the house and into the street. My legs were numb, they would scarcely hold me upright. I threw open the front door and stumbled through it. There was a small flight of stone steps leading to ground level. Gripping the handrail with all my strength, I climbed down to the pavement. My breath was jerking rapidly in and out, white and frosted against the light of a street lamp. I had left my cape and gloves behind, and in the sudden cold of the night air I felt myself shivering. But nothing would induce me to turn back into that house.

My mind was a blur. I could scarcely remember in which direction I had come. I looked up and down the street: surely the hotel was that way. I took a couple of steps, then stopped as I heard something.

On my right, slipping out from shadows into the narrow pool of light shed by the lamp, a horse-drawn carriage came into sight. The horses' feet rang out sharply against the stillness. I looked up at the driver. It was Hutton. Behind him sat Anthony and Antonia. They were watching me with unconcealed interest.

Anthony stepped down from the victoria. In a few paces he was by my side. He took my arm in a strong grip against which I knew it was useless to struggle.

"It's time to go home, Charlotte. Come with us and nothing will be said about what has happened today."

I pulled once, but he only tightened his grip.

"We only want what is best for you, my dear. We have always wanted what is best. Come now, we have a long drive home."

I said nothing. What was there to say? Still shaking, I mounted the little steps into the open carriage. Antonia bent over and helped me onto the seat beside her. She smiled and kissed me affectionately on the cheek. Anthony got in and sat facing us.

"Let's go home, Hutton," he said.

As the carriage started forward I looked around. Standing by the street lamp, watching us leave, were the two lawyers, Stephen Melrose and John Parker. I understood then how I had been betrayed.

CHAPTER **30**

WE DROVE BACK TO BARRAS HALL ALONG ROADS DEEP IN snow. A cold moon rose over the fields to stare down on us all the way, very white and pitiless. On either side of us, trees seemed to hurtle past. Their branches were frosted. They were tall and unevenly spaced. Hutton thrashed the horse into drifts in which I was sure he would get stuck, but somehow we managed to pull through and clamber on toward our destination. I was given a blanket in which to wrap myself, but left otherwise uncomforted.

For most of that journey we rode in a grim, angry silence. From time to time, passing through some treeless hollow bathed in moonlight or a rise among moorland, my cousin Anthony would fix on me a steady, unfriendly gaze.

The silence was only broken as we passed through the lodge gates and onto the drive leading to the hall. It was Anthony who spoke. I could not see him very well, for the moonlight was much obstructed here by high trees. But his voice came to me clearly across the crisp, shivering air.

"We are almost home, Charlotte. Perhaps this is the proper moment for me to address a few words to you. Neither my sister, Antonia, nor I can guess what your motives were in running away from us so precipitately. We have treated you well. Taken you in as one of our own family. Lavished kindnesses on you that you had neither reason nor title to expect. Opened our home and our hearts to you. All of that you have thrown back in our faces in an act of open ingratitude. We are bitterly disappointed.

"Mr. Melrose has told me some of the wild accusations you have been leveling against us. I do not have to tell you how shocking they are to us. But most shocking of all is the revelation that you have been snooping in my study and poking your nose into my private papers. More, that you went so far as to steal some of those papers in order to build up some elaborate fantasy about Antonia and myself. I cannot say how it hurt and grieved me to learn of that. In your favor, I can only conclude that your years in the workhouse coarsened whatever sense you may have had of virtue and morality."

He paused, expecting possibly some plea on my part, a denial of what he was saying. I remained silent, and he continued.

"For that reason, we are willing to regard the whole matter as closed. What is done is done. We have spoken with Parker and Melrose, and received their solemn assurance that nothing more will ever be said on the subject. Nevertheless you must expect that certain changes will be made. In return for our indulgence, much will be expected from you. There will be alterations in your behavior.

"Charlotte, you have to understand that ours is an old family, much older than Barras Hall. We have survived, we have flourished even in adversity because we have remained faithful to our traditions, traditions of which you, sadly, are wholly ignorant. But ignorance is no excuse. Very soon you will be educated. We shall make it our sacred charge to see that you understand. Too much is at stake to let you run about the countryside with tales and fables. You will learn the truth. You will see it with your own eyes."

He fell silent. We drew up to the front of the house. The moon was hidden behind the roof. There were only shadows here. As Anthony opened the door of the carriage Antonia leaned toward me.

"You have two days, Charlotte. Until your birthday. If you have not learned all you need to know by then, you will regret it bitterly."

She said no more. Stepping down, she held out her hand to help me to the ground. Leaving the blanket in the victoria, I followed her into the house. It was cold, but my body had gone beyond shivering. Nothing had changed. It was as though I had fallen asleep and found myself reliving a nightmare from which I had only temporarily awakened.

In the drawing room, I was told to sit down while Antonia rang for Mrs. Johnson. Anthony busied himself with a newspaper. Antonia turned her attention to me.

"We understand you dined at the Queen's Head, Charlotte, so you will not be in need of food. Nevertheless you must be both tired and overexcited by your exertions. That is a bad combination for the nerves. You will have to sleep tonight, otherwise I fear greatly for your health. I have asked Mrs. Johnson to prepare a draft to help you sleep. There is nothing noxious in it: she makes it from simples collected from the garden."

There was a knock at the door. Mrs. Johnson entered, carrying a tray on which stood a tall glass containing a pale green liquid. She placed it on a low table in front of me, curtsied, and left.

"I won't drink anything," I said.

"Come now. You aren't going to be difficult, are you, Charlotte? This is only warm milk with a few herbs. A little valerian, some motherwort, chamomile, some grains of pulsatilla. All gifts from God's garden."

I shook my head.

"You killed my brother Arthur," I said. "And now you want to kill me."

"Charlotte, you must stop this at once. No one has killed Arthur. He is still alive. Do you understand me? You comprehend absolutely nothing about what has been happening, whether to Arthur or yourself. You are in no position to judge our actions or those of anyone else. Now, behave sensibly and take your drink."

I shook my head.

Anthony looked up from the paper in which he had seemed to be engrossed.

"Charlotte," he said. His voice was low and imbued with a menace I had not detected in it before. "I said to you in the carriage that I anticipated changes in your behavior. I did not expect stubbornness. My sister has already spelled out to you the general consequences of further refractoriness. I shall make her generalities more specific. If you do not drink every drop of your medicine, I shall be forced to beat you. Perhaps you were beaten in the workhouse and think you are hardened. I assure you, they could not inflict on you a tenth of the beating I will administer. And if you still persist, I will beat you again. I will beat you until you bend your will to mine. If necessary, I will whip every inch of skin from your body if that is what it takes."

I had no more strength in me to defy him, for all that my fears were not of bodily pain. My only hope now, and such a faint one, was that the Reverend Watkins should have my letter very soon, perhaps tomorrow, and that knowing what he did, he would come to me at once. Anthony had said he was now attached to the cathedral at Durham. Surely not even the Ayrtons could defy the church, however old and steeped in tradition they might be.

With my eyes closed, I put the glass to my lips and drank the concoction. It tasted foul, but I forced myself to swallow it down.

"I'd like to go to my room now, please."

"Certainly, my dear. Let me take you."

Antonia rose and helped me to my feet. She kissed her brother good night and, taking my arm tightly in her hand, steered me to the door.

"Say good night to your cousin Anthony," she said.

"Good night, Anthony," I parroted.

"Good night, Charlotte. Sleep well."

We were just climbing the stairs to the first floor when I felt a wave of nausea come over me, followed by the most terrible giddiness.

"You've . . . poisoned . . . me," I said.

"Nonsense, Charlotte. It's just to help you sleep. You'll see."

I could see Antonia bending over me, her face wavering in the light of the candle she carried. My legs felt weak, and suddenly I felt them give way, toppling me to the floor. Desperate to stay conscious as long as possible, I fought to keep my eyes open. I saw Antonia leaning down and heard her voice as though from a very long way away, booming at me. Then I twisted as a tight pain gripped my stomach. I turned, looking up to the top of the stairs. The last thing I saw before losing consciousness was a figure standing at the top of the staircase. The tall figure of an old man dressed in black and wearing a long black veil that stretched from his head almost to his feet.

CHAPTER31

IT WAS THE AFTERNOON OF THE NEXT DAY WHEN I WOKE. MY limbs felt sore and heavy, and for a long time I could not clear my head. Sitting on the edge of my bed, I had difficulty finding my balance. Each time I tried to open my eyes, the light stung them so intolerably that I was forced to press them shut again. My head pounded with a dull ache. I had fleeting memories of terrible dreams, as though I had just spent days in a nightmare.

At last I began to come to. The pounding in my head subsided to a lower level. I was able to move my arms and legs more easily. I opened my eyes tentatively, then looked around.

I was not in my old bedroom. For a moment I could not say where I was, except that it was not there. But then I saw the bars on the window and realized where I had been taken.

I staggered to the door only to find it firmly locked. In desperation, I cast my eyes around the room. The only furnishing was the old truckle bed on which I had been sleeping, covered with a couple of thin blankets. There was no fire, no chair, no mirror. The only ornamentation was the bars.

Returning to the door, I hammered on it loudly, shouting for attention. Eventually my hands grew sore and my voice tired, and I sank down against the wall with my head in my hands, weeping. Time passed. My tears subsided, leaving me drained and frightened. I was conscious of hunger pangs and, more urgently, a growing need to use the toilet. Searching beneath the bed, I found a chamber pot. When I had used it, I covered it with one of the blankets from the bed and put it to one side.

Going to the window, I had to stand on tiptoe in order to see out. Below me was a drab yard backed by outhouses, the whole covered in a thick pall of white. It was still snowing heavily. If this kept up, Barras Hall would be quite cut off. I felt quite panicky at the thought, for it might prevent the Reverend Watkins from getting here in time.

"In time." For some reason, I had fixed on my birthday as the most critical juncture. Something was planned for that date, and I was increasingly certain that it involved my death, just as the same day ten years earlier had involved Caroline's.

I went back to the bed and sat down, utterly miserable and dispirited. I had tried my best to escape, and it had come to this. Whatever happened now, it was no longer in my hands to influence events.

I froze as footsteps sounded in the passage outside. There was a rattling of a key in the lock, then Mrs. Johnson appeared, carrying a tray. On it were a covered dish, a carafe of water, and a glass. She closed the door without a word, set the tray down on the floor, and came to the bed.

"Have you used the chamber, Miss Charlotte?"

"Yes."

She found it and, removing the blanket, covered it with a thick cloth she had brought over her arm.

"Your food's on the tray," she said. "You'll have no more until tomorrow, so make the most of it."

"Mrs. Johnson, why are you helping them keep me a prisoner? I thought you were my friend. You came to me in the graveyard that time. I thought you wanted to help me."

She seemed about to speak, then thought better of it, and turned away. As she reached the door she said, "I'll bring the chamber back when I come for the tray. Eat your food quickly, before it gets cold." When she left, I heard the key turn in the lock.

The meal was substantial enough: evidently they were not going to starve me. I was suspicious of it, remembering what they had given me the night before, but my hunger got the better of me in the end, and I gulped it down. My only item of cutlery was a spoon. Did they fear I might use a knife or fork to attempt another escape? Or that I might attempt violence on myself?

Mrs. Johnson returned about half an hour afterward. I tried again to engage her in conversation, but she ignored me pointedly and hurried out. This time she did not lock the door. A few moments after she had left, it was opened again.

Anthony entered, smiling gently, and shut the door hard behind him. He was dressed in his riding clothes and seemed to have come straight in from outdoors. His face was flushed with cold and he was a little out of breath. He stood before me for a while, saying nothing.

When he did finally speak, it was in a quiet, gently teasing voice.

"Well, miss, how do you like your new quarters? I venture you wish now you'd stayed put where you were. Well, you're not the first, you may take some comfort in that. You may very well meet some of the others before long. Mind you speak politely to them: some don't like to be angered."

He stepped around the bed and crossed to the window.

"The nights are still drawing in," he said. "Midwinter's day is not so very far away. A pity you will not see it. They won't wait, you see. I entreat them, but they won't wait. They are hungry. Hungrier each time. But I shall keep them till your birthday, that things may be done properly. Propriety is important. There are traditions to be preserved."

"What have I done," I asked, "to be treated like this?"

"Done?" He turned. "You have done nothing. It was never your destiny to do anything."

"My destiny? What destiny?"

"You shall see very soon."

He strode toward the door, and then, just as he reached it, as though by some afterthought, he reached inside his pocket and drew something from it. A piece of paper. He tossed it carelessly onto the floor.

"This is yours, I think."

With that, he passed through the door, locking it behind him. I bent down and picked up the paper he had thrown at me. It was my letter to the vicar of Kirkwhelpington, crumpled and soiled, and still containing my appeal to his predecessor, torn into tiny shreds.

* * *

There was no drug in my food. And that night sleep did not come, for all that I would have given anything to find it. Sleep or unconsciousness or even death. As the light faded, so the room began to fill with uneasy shadows. Darkness gave only momentary respite. I lay in my bed, huddled in my blankets, and heard the shadows coming to life all around me. In desperation, I tried clasping my hands over my ears, but that was almost worse, for what I could not hear I imagined.

She started weeping soon after it grew dark. I knew she was there, near me, crouching on the floor unseen. Sometimes her crying would stop, and when it did, the rustling started. More than ever I found it ugly and unsettling. Several times footsteps passed by outside my door. On each occasion the weeping would subside into a terrified whimpering.

Somewhere about the middle of that long night, all the noises stopped. The room became very quiet. And I could hear, very faintly in the distance, a soft, slithering sound, very slow and muffled and unpleasant, as though something shapeless and very old was fumbling its way through the house. The noise continued for a long time, but finally it faded away into the distance until I could hear it no more.

When it ended, there was a blissful silence for a while, then voices in the corridor not far from my room, as though several people were arguing. I did not recognize any of them. Certainly neither Anthony nor Antonia appeared to be among them.

Light reached my window very slowly and very late. I remained on my bed, watching the darkness melt and become a patchwork of shadows. At first, I could discern nothing out of the ordinary. But at a certain point, as the light gained in strength and individual features could be discerned, I noticed a gray shape crouching by the door. I could not take my eyes off it. As the light grew I saw that it was a girl my age, wearing a gray dress. Her skin was unnaturally pale, and her eyes were bright red as though she had been crying. She was sitting, just sitting, staring at me.

"Caroline?" I whispered. "Are you Caroline?"

She did not respond. The light continued to strengthen, but she did not move, as though she were an image from a magic lantern cast against the wall.

"Caroline," I pleaded with her. "You know what's happening. Won't you help me? Won't you tell me what they're going to do?"

At first, I thought she would not answer. Then, slowly, as though painfully, she unbuttoned the left sleeve of her dress and began to roll it up her arm. When it was a little above her elbow, she turned her arm and showed it to me. The front of her forearm was lined with deep, bloodless gashes from wrist to elbow.

I think I must have fainted. When I came to again, Mrs. Johnson was in the room, and there was no sign of Caroline anywhere.

CHAPTER 32

MRS. JOHNSON BROUGHT WITH HER A NEW DRESS, A BRIGHT RED dress that had been made specially for me, she said.

"It's for tonight, Miss Charlotte. For your birthday evening. I'll come back later to help you put it on. Miss Antonia wants you to look your best."

"But I haven't got a mirror," I said. "There isn't even a basin for me to wash in."

"I'll bring those later," she said. "And you'll need to have your hair done up. Miss Antonia wants you pretty as a picture."

"Was Caroline pretty?"

She looked startled.

"I asked if Caroline was pretty."

"I don't know who you mean, miss." She had recovered a little of her composure.

"Antonia's daughter," I said bluntly. "She died here ten years ago. You know exactly who I mean."

She backed away, fumbling with the cloth covering the chamber pot.

"I don't know what you're talking about, miss. I'm sure there's never been anyone here by that name."

"I saw her this morning, Johnson. You've seen her here yourself, haven't you. Why is she so pale? What did they do to her? What did Anthony and Antonia do?"

She made no further attempt to answer me. I watched her go, knowing she had the key to the truth, that she could tell me everything if she wanted to. What was she afraid of? Precisely how were my cousins controlling her?

I was left alone until early evening, when it began to grow dark. Mrs. Johnson returned with the things she had promised: a basin and a jug of hot water, together with a towel, some soap, a comb and brush, and a small ivory mirror. She seemed particularly awkward.

"Miss Antonia will visit you later," she said. "Just to see you're all right. Take your dress off, and I'll give you a hand with your hair."

I slipped my dress over my head and laid it on the bed beside the new one. Mrs. Johnson half filled the basin and, while I bent over it, wet my hair thoroughly before rubbing in plenty of soap.

"Miss Charlotte," she said. "I shouldn't be saying this, but you've been good to me, and I can't leave you without a kind word. You . . . you've got to be brave tonight. Whatever you do, don't let them see you're frightened: it will only serve to make things worse. Sir Anthony will come for you very late. You're to be taken down to the old temple in the woods. That's where it always happens. Do you understand?"

She started rinsing my hair, pouring water slowly from the jug.

"I'll leave a candle with you. It's as well for you not to be in the dark tonight."

"Can't you do anything? If I could get out of here, I'd be able to escape."

"No, miss, there's nothing I can do. I tried to help Miss Caroline, and I lost my own boy as a result. Don't think of trying to get away: they'll be sure to find you, and they'll make it worse for you if you put them to any trouble. Just try to be brave." She hesitated. "Have you still got that cross I gave you?"

I nodded.

"Keep it by you, miss. It may be some comfort."

She dried and combed my hair, then helped me into the red dress.

"I have to go," she said. "They'll get suspicious if I stay too long. Finish yourself off. I'll take these things with me later."

She turned and took me in her arms. There were tears in her eyes.

"God bless you, miss. I wish there was something I could do. I really do."

I thanked her. She took my old dress and left without another word, locking the door behind her.

It was dark by now, and with the candle lit the room seemed full of other darknesses. The house was still, expectant, as silent as James Ayrton's tomb on the other side of the woods. The only thing moving was time: I imagined it somewhere, personified, solid, a huge clock ticking my life away. A condemned woman knows what is waiting for her on the other side of the prison door. She pictures a rope and a long drop. I knew nothing at all.

I set the candle on the narrow mantelpiece and washed my face and neck and hands in its light. My shoes were the same old pair I had been wearing since I arrived at the hall: skirts were so long in those days, women never bothered much about their footwear. With the help of the mirror, I combed my hair into shape again, wishing I had a brush to give it more body.

I settled down to wait for Anthony. Mrs. Johnson's words, far from comforting me, had set me on edge. The silence seemed more than ever full of menace. Then, faintly echoing somewhere behind the silence, I could hear the sound of voices again. Not arguing this time, but murmuring ceaselessly. And among them I could just distinguish isolated voices singing. There was music somewhere, too, quiet music played on a harp or a harpsichord. I strained my ears, wondering where the sounds could be coming from, but it was useless, they were too faint and too far away.

It must have been about an hour after that that the door opened and Antonia came into the room. She looked flushed and unhappy, as though under a great strain. Her face had been powdered and rouged, but the makeup did not conceal her own high color or the unhealthy brightness in her eyes. She closed the door and told me to stand.

"Turn around, turn around. I want to see how you look."

I twisted awkwardly. She tutted with dissatisfaction and began to fuss about my dress and hair. Pulling and nipping me, she straightened a seam here and a lock there.

"What is to happen, Antonia? I'm frightened. I want to know."

"Better you don't, child. You needn't worry, it won't take long."

"I'm to be killed, aren't I? Like Caroline and Arthur, that's what happens, isn't it?"

"Killed? If it were only that simple, my dear. If it were only that easy."

"What are all the voices? And I can hear music."

"Music?"

She paused, listening. The tinny echoes of the harp-sichord could still be heard from somewhere almost out of earshot.

"It's your birthday in a couple of hours, Charlotte. They're gathering for your party. You'll meet them soon."

"Meet them? Who are they?"

"Don't ask questions, Charlotte. You'll know soon enough."

She stood back and examined me.

"You'll do," she said. I noticed that she had been biting her nails. Her movements were jittery. She was like someone who barely manages to remain sane while all the time teetering on the edge of madness.

I ran toward her, thinking she must relent, thinking I must be able to reach her. My hands clutched at her dress, I tried to throw my arms about her neck.

"For God's sake, Antonia, don't leave me here like this. You're my cousin, you're my friend. Why don't you help me get out of here?"

She looked at me as though her heart were break-ing. I think she saw not me, but her own daughter, Caro-line.

"Oh, if only I could, if only I could. But it's out of my hands, can't you see that?"

She pulled herself away, pressing my hands aside. Stumbling to the door, she opened it and ran out, locking it hard behind her. I heard her footsteps clatter down the stairs then fade along the passage.

After a while I began to brush my hair again. Moving the looking glass to one side, I started. Behind me, bathed in the light of the candle, was a second face.

Caroline's face, white, with black eyes that stared hard at me. I turned, but there were only shadows.

"Caroline? I saw you watching me. I'm not afraid of you. I want to speak to you. Please. Please don't be frightened. I came back as you asked. I've read your diary, I know all that happened."

This time she answered. Her voice seemed very close, yet coming from nowhere in particular. I was certain of one thing, that it was not inside my head.

"Listen to me, Charlotte," she said. "Listen carefully. I want to help you, but I don't know how. The others are near me, very near."

"Others? What others?"

"You'll meet them soon. Some of them are very old. They've been here for centuries. Even before this house was built. They want you, just as they wanted me. It's how they keep their strength, how they stop the loneliness and the pain of age. They need company, our company. Don't you see? Don't you understand, Charlotte? That's what this is all about. They always need more, they're never satisfied. And the older they become, the more they need. They won't leave the living in peace until they are given what they want. And then again and again It never ends. Never."

I could see her now. She was quite plain, a dull gray figure seated on the bed, watching me with sad, sad eyes. I remembered Annie's eyes, that haunted look in them, the recurrent pain and humiliation of her father's abuse. Caroline's eyes held something worse again. Something more sordid, more deeply violated.

"What did you see on the lawn?" I asked, for I was desperate to know everything, to be prepared for whatever it was I had to face. "What was it?"

She drew violently away from me, shaking her head

backward and forward, her eyes glittering with refusal.

"You must tell me," I insisted. "I have to know."

She stopped and slowly sank to the floor. It was the posture I had seen her in before, defeated, withdrawn. I crossed the room, no longer afraid of the poor creature, and kneeled down in front of her. Tentatively I stretched out my hand to touch her, but my fingers passed through air. No, not quite air, but a coldness that was more than air.

"Please," I said.

She looked at me softly.

"I want you to be my friend," she said.

I nodded.

"Yes," I said.

"James Ayrton dabbled in forbidden things." Her voice was a whisper from very far away. "He wanted power. Eternal life. He was willing to risk damnation for it. But he . . . called up something he should not have. Not a spirit. There are other things. He was already very old, and it destroyed him. And then it took possession of his tomb. He feeds it when he can."

"Feeds?"

She shook her head.

"Not flesh. I don't mean that—or not quite that. I'm not exactly sure. It—" She stopped. "No more, please. I've seen it. I don't want to talk about it."

It was as far as she got. At that moment the temperature in the room dropped at an alarming rate, as though dry ice had been poured into it. Caroline looked up. I saw her draw back, shaking her head. Snatching up the candle, I stepped toward her as though I could protect her bodily from whatever it was that threatened her. The next moment she was gone. I heard a rustling sound, then the room was full of silence. A hateful, angry silence.

CHAPTER 33

ANTHONY CAME FOR ME AS PROMISED ABOUT HALF AN HOUR before midnight. Unlike his sister, he was perfectly calm and self-possessed. He looked me up and down with an appraising air, like a show judge examining a heifer. It was the first time in my life I had ever experienced that close scrutiny of a man's eyes, that attentiveness to my body. Even now I am not sure whether there was anything sexual in his gaze. If there was, it was well enough masked, muffled by a different sort of hunger. Anthony Ayrton wanted peace at any cost, and I was just the latest coin in the ongoing payment he made to his tormentors.

"Exquisite," he murmured. He ran a hand through my long hair. "He will be so pleased. They will all be pleased."

" 'He'?" I asked. "Who is 'he'?"

"You haven't guessed? I thought you cleverer than that. My ancestor James, of course, James Ayrton."

"I've seen him," I said.

"Yes," he said. "I know you have. We have all seen him."

"Why does he wear a veil? Why does he want to hide his face?"

He looked troubled, then shook his head.

"Too many questions. You'll find out everything in the end. I promise. Now, Charlotte, it's time to go. We mustn't keep them waiting."

He took me by the left arm, with a very firm grip, and opened the door. The passage at the foot of the stairs was lit up brilliantly. Candle holders of one kind or another had been placed every few yards: flambeaux, stubby candelabras on *torchères,* girandoles attached to the wall, sconces on either side of each window, all blazing with tall white candles.

"This is all for you," said Anthony. "In celebration of your coming of age."

"I shall only be fifteen," I said.

"Tonight you come of age. It is your destiny."

He led me down the passage and through the house, shining everywhere with light. The voices and the music had fallen silent. The only sounds were our footsteps passing from carpet to stone and from stone back to carpet.

Anthony had a fur-lined cape ready for me at the door. He himself put on a thick black coat and a fur hat.

"Where is Antonia?" I asked.

"She will stay here until I return," he said. "She sends her apologies."

He took his watch from his pocket and tutted.

"Come. It's almost midnight."

Outside, it was bitterly cold. We hurried into the woods, taking the familiar path that I knew led to the folly. Anthony carried a storm lantern in his left hand while keeping his grip on me with the other. The light revealed his profile every time I turned, heavy and angular, his lips set hard, like a man going into battle. I was his trophy, I supposed, or his oriflamme.

I had expected—no, I am not sure now what possibilities had passed through my mind. But lights, certainly, a brightness comparable to that now filling the house; and noises, singing perhaps, the dead gathering in shrouds to meet me. Instead the woods were silent and dreadful, without light anywhere. I caught sight of the folly once by chance, etched against the skyline as we came up to it from a hollow. It was just a dark mass of stone. The next moment it disappeared again behind a screen of trees.

Minutes later we turned at a bend in the narrow pathway and the temple was in front of us. I now saw that two small lights were burning in front of it, one on either side of the door. Otherwise it was in darkness. The door was lying wide open.

The very sight of that open door filled me with terror. I pulled back, forcing Anthony to halt.

"No," I said, "I won't go."

"Damn it, you'll go where I say you'll go."

"Not in there!"

He said nothing further, but yanked my arm and continued pulling me down the path. He was strong, I could not possibly resist him.

We reached the door. Inside, the folly was in blackness. I could already smell it from where I stood, a dark, stale odor that made me gag. Anthony pulled me in. Near the door a chain had been fixed to the wall, ending in a sort of manacle. He fastened this around my wrist without saying a word, and left me.

I heard the doors being closed. Then Anthony lit a candle. It burned dully in the heavy air, revealing nothing but his shadowed form. I heard him sigh as though he was in pain, or like someone who, having known pain, senses its return. He now began to light candles, thick flax-colored candles arranged in groups on top of tall *torchères* placed at regular intervals around the sides of the folly.

The light grew slowly, wakening shadows from their profound slumber. And not only shadows, but whispers, as though these too had been secreted in the blackness. Out of the shadows, something else emerged. I had expected some sort of emptiness, a tall, abandoned room flanked by stone walls. This was vastly different. From the ceiling hung vast clouds of spiderwebs, thicknesses of them, intricate, dark and matted with a century and a half of filth. The walls were encrusted with them. The air was weighed down by their heaviness.

In the gaps between the *torchères* stood cold pillars of black marble. Atop each one was set a bronze figure or head, rather like the busts that graced the marble pedestals in the entrance to the hall. But these figures were not the likenesses of Greek athletes or Roman emperors. Those that I could see from where I stood were grotesque: black angels with the wings of bats, demons with the horns of rams or goats, griffins with claws like scythes. The heads were leering, demoniac, threatening. Everything was folded and tangled in swaths of cobwebs, among which dark shapes climbed or hung suspended.

All about the floor were scattered gilded chairs, old chairs, their velvet seats long rotted, their wood crumbling, coated in dust and yet more webs. The walls were hung with huge golden mirrors, now tarnished and cracked and smeared with dust, in whose faces were reflected every so often the lost glimmer of a candle flame. There were ragged tapestries, and beside them paintings, moldy, threadbare with age, in which dim figures of men in strange garments, like priests or hangmen, could be discerned.

Light fell upon light. Anthony had almost completed his circuit. The whispering had become a steady drone. And now for the first time I was able to see that the far end of the folly was not empty, that the shadows that gathered there were alive and moving.

I almost fainted. The smell, the fetid air, the moving figures up there in the darkness, the sense of greedy expectation—all bewildered and dizzied me. Closing my eyes, I bent my head and breathed in deeply in an attempt to steady myself. As I opened my eyes again I noticed something on the floor beside me, next to the door. It was red and colorful, and out of curiosity I bent down as far as I could to pick it up. It was a toy soldier, a painted lead soldier in a red coat and bearskin hat, identical in every respect to the one I had given Arthur two Christmases previously. The longer I looked at it, the more certain I became that it was the very same soldier, not a duplicate.

Anthony returned.

"I'm sorry I have had to chain you like this," he said. "But if you tried to run . . . There would be trouble. Do you understand me? It would anger him."

I held up the soldier.

"You told me Arthur never came here. You pretended to search for him. Why? Why did you lie to me?"

He reached out his hand and took the soldier from me, turning it around and around between finger and thumb, like a collector examining an item of great rarity and value.

"He must have dropped this," he said. "I'm surprised I didn't notice it."

"Then you admit he was here?"

He handed the soldier back to me.

"Of course. He has been here all along. He is still here."

"Here?"

"In the folly. Where he has been almost from the day he arrived. We had to wait, of course. We knew he would draw you here, like a bee to honey. Sir James insisted nothing be done with him until tonight."

"You kept Arthur here? In this stinking place?"

"Please calm yourself, Charlotte. He has been well looked after. Not as well as you, perhaps, but Sir James wanted it that way."

"Take me to him. I want to see him. Please. I don't care what happens, I want to see Arthur."

He looked down at me, as though weighing pros and cons, then nodded.

"So you shall. Yes, indeed, so you shall."

Unlocking the manacle, he released my arm and as quickly seized me by the other.

"You must not run, little Charlotte," he whispered. "For there is nowhere to hide. He will find you wherever you go. He is your ancestor as well as mine. You have him in your blood. He is part of us both."

His touch felt loathsome, his breath and his voice, everything about him. I tried to pull away, but he had me fast. We walked together slowly toward the center of the folly. I could see them flitting in and out among the shadows, the figures of children, all about my age, white-faced, staring-eyed, huddled together for cold comfort. And I realized with the deepest revulsion that I was soon to join them here, that it would go on forever. The excitement I had felt on first hearing that Arthur was alive had wholly drained away, for what did being alive matter? What did anything matter—being brother and sister, being reunited, being young and pretty and good?

Arthur lay on a low truckle bed, on top of a pile of dirty blankets. He was dressed in his old clothes, the clothes he had entered the workhouse in and which he had now outgrown. He seemed at first unaware of us, as though he slept. I could see only his back, for he was turned away from us and curled up almost in a ball, like a young child afraid of the darkness in which it is forced to sleep.

Then, as though startled into wakefulness, he gave a jump, straightening on the bed and, for a long moment, lying there quite still, listening to our approach, or so it seemed. I wanted to call to him, seeing him thus, quite past belief, alive and breathing as I had so long hoped; yet I feared to startle him, and so stood alongside Anthony, waiting for Arthur to turn. It was then that I noticed his left leg was chained to a heavy bolt set in the floor.

He did not move, other than to raise himself a little on his left arm. I glanced at Anthony, but his face was impassive, and I could take no instruction from it. What was wrong? I started to move closer, but Anthony laid a hand softly yet firmly on my arm, restraining me.

"Speak very quietly," he whispered. "You must not startle him."

I took a slow breath.

"Arthur," I said, "don't be afraid. It's me, Charlotte. Your sister Charlotte."

I saw his thin body stiffen. But he did not turn at

once, as I had expected him to do. Instead he raised himself further and turned his face sideways, as though trying to locate my voice among the shadows.

I called his name a second time, very low.

"Please, Arthur, I'm not a ghost. I'm not dead. It's really me." I hesitated, then lied. "I've come to take you away. We're going home."

He turned. Dear God, how I wish he had not. But he turned and I saw a little of what my cousin had done to him.

Even as I cried out and covered my eyes with my free hand, Anthony was drawing me into his embrace, whispering frantically in my ear.

"Charlotte, Charlotte, you must believe I did it for his sake, truly for his own sake. To stop him seeing. A blindfold would not have been enough. He might have torn it off, or one of them found a way to dislodge it. Believe me, I gave him laudanum."

But with or without laudanum, he had torn out my brother's lovely eyes, and the bloody sockets that stared back at me had broken my heart as surely as confirmation of his death would have done. Without another word, I tore myself out of Anthony's weakening grasp and dashed the last few feet to Arthur's side.

He stiffened as I sat on the bed beside him, throwing my arms around him, embracing and kissing him as I had done for so long in my imagination. But then, as I continued thus, alternately weeping and crooning his name, I felt him go limp and almost drift from my arms. He endured my kisses, as he might have endured a stranger's caresses or blows, with frank indifference. I spoke to him, I whispered his name, I pressed the toy soldier into his hands, I told him who I was, and all he could do was slump in my arms like a rag doll.

Whether it was the effect of overmuch laudanum, or a surfeit of fear, or an utter, despairing inner change, I realized that the creature I held in my arms was no longer the brother I had known, but a shell, a gutted carapace from which the spirit had long since departed. His eyes apart, this thing had Arthur's face, the same features grown older, thinner, and paler than I remembered. But it was not my brother. Not really. Not any longer. Not in any way that mattered.

I turned in a rage to Anthony.

"How long?" I screamed. "How long has he been like this?"

He looked about him awkwardly, half-expectantly.

"Not long," he said. "A few weeks. That is why you were kept in the house. To prolong your endurance. You would have broken more quickly. Sir James wanted you here, but we defied him."

"You've destroyed him," I shouted. "Don't you see? Don't you see what has become of him?"

Anthony shook his head.

"It doesn't matter, Charlotte dear. Only one thing matters here, and that is the feeding of the hunger."

"Tell him to go to hell," I cried. "None of this is necessary, none of it. Can't you see?"

He shook his head again, sadly.

"He is in hell," he whispered. "They are all in hell. That is all there is, Charlotte. All there has ever been."

"I don't believe that. I can't believe it."

That was when he appeared. Shadowed. Pearled by the little light. More silent than the tomb his body lay in. He was dressed in his black veil; it hung from his head almost to his feet, covering the whole body. Behind the thin fabric, I could see a little of his features, white and insubstantial, the lineaments of age. There was a stench, a grave-stench, that had not been there before. He took a step toward us. His feet made no sound, no sound at all.

CHAPTER 34

IT WAS ARTHUR WHO REACTED FIRST, TWISTING BACK FROM ME and scrambling across his bed as far from James Ayrton as the chain around his ankle would permit. He could not see him, yet the terror wrapped about his face was unmistakable. A low, penetrating moan escaped from his lips. I reached for him, but Anthony snatched my wrist and pulled me roughly off the bed, hissing at me to behave myself. As if behavior mattered there.

Arthur's moans subsided into a fearful whimpering. Ayrton reached out a hand toward him, and he flinched back from it, for all the world like someone who could see.

"He can see him," I said. "Blinding him made no difference. Did it?"

Anthony did not answer, but I knew I had hit on the truth. That James Ayrton was visible, not to the naked eye, but to whatever inner sight it is we all possess. Or, now that I have had these many years to ponder the matter, not visible so much as inwardly present, as though imprinted, fused, united in the most intimate fashion with my brother's spirit. For all that he had tried, my cousin Anthony had failed to blind Arthur's inner sight. Until James Ayrton came in his tattered veil and charnel-house stench to cast a final darkness over whatever little light remained flickering there.

With a thin hand, Ayrton tugged at the veil, drawing it slowly up over his wasted head and draping it over his arm. His face seemed made of clay, white clay, dragged and squeezed into the hollows and ridges of his endless suffering.

"My congratulations," he whispered, his speech a graveyard speech, half-articulate, as though it traveled, dislocated, through clay or centuries. "I hope we celebrate your birthday with the solemnity that is your due."

I could not tear my eyes away. Horror, true horror. His face, his white face, his slippery face had begun to flutter, as though it had no true shape, as though the folds of skin were flapping like a handkerchief crumpled in a man's hand.

"It was never meant to be like this," the flapping mouth said. I saw little teeth appear and disappear in the black cavity, like seeds in rotten fruit. "This was a temple of light; I wanted to fill it with eternal jubilation. Eternal life, not . . . this. You would have been a princess here, I would have set a crown of roses on your pretty head. But it came from outside. An error. A mistake, a matter of words, a mere stumbling over formulae. But there is no forgiveness here, not in this world we inhabit."

The eyes rolled like guttering flames in candle wax, their light struggling against the surrounding whiteness.

"When he has finished with you both, it will be my turn. I am grown very thin, I am almost bone again."

He stopped, as though listening for something. I heard, in the shadows, a slithering sound. Ayrton looked at me, then around at Arthur, still cowering on the bed and whimpering gently. The slithering grew louder. At that moment, there was a sound of heavy knocking on the door. Anthony gripped my arm tightly, startled and afraid. The banging came again. I looked around, thinking some impossible salvation had come, and in that instant made up my mind. With a sudden effort, I broke away, tearing myself with all my strength from Anthony's grasp, stumbling back into the shadows toward the entrance. Taken unawares, Anthony was several seconds in recovering, then I heard his feet pounding behind me.

As I reached it the door burst open. I screamed, not knowing what lay in front of me. Moments later I felt Anthony's hand on my arm again, his fingers clutching me like steel. And then, abruptly, everything changed. There was a voice from the darkness in the doorway. Hutton's voice, on the verge of panic.

"Sir Anthony, you've got to come."

"What the hell do you mean?"

"It's your sister, sir. She's gone mad. She's set light to the hall, it's out of control. We tried to stop her, but it was no use. You've got to come, sir."

There was a sound behind us. A rustling louder than any I had heard before.

Anthony hesitated only for a moment, then he pulled my arm and began to drag me through the doorway.

"You can't leave Arthur behind!" I shouted. "You can't leave him there."

But he ignored me. With Hutton following, we ran, hand in hand, down the long, tangled path, away from the folly. As we came up from the river, we topped a rise, and there before us, bright against the night sky, was the southwest corner of the hall, burning like a torch. We plowed on, picking our way in the darkness, through trees and undergrowth.

At last we broke free of the woods and came out into the open by the side of the house. The fire was taking hold rapidly now. Antonia must have run from one room to the next, laying flame to curtains or bedding or whatever else would easily ignite.

We pressed around to the front of the building. A small group of figures was gathered on the drive outside. A police sergeant was sitting on the front steps, his helmet beside him, his head down between his knees, coughing furiously, while a constable stood beside him, trying to help. Mrs. Johnson and Hepple were standing a little way off, looking on helplessly.

Anthony thrust me into Hutton's hands, telling him to keep tight hold of me, and ran toward the house. He had scarcely gone half a dozen paces when someone dashed out from the shadows and seized him. There was a rush of light from behind, and I recognized the stranger as the solicitor, John Parker. Anthony struggled to free himself of his grip, shouting wildly.

"For God's sake, let me go! I have to help her! Get your hands off me, damn you!"

He was too strong or too mad for Parker to restrain for long. Tearing himself free, Anthony bolted up the steps and into the house. For a moment the solicitor made as if to go after him, then, seeing me struggling with Hutton, ran toward us instead.

"Let her go," he snapped. Hutton, having already seen the police, shrugged and let my arm drop. Instead of joining Johnson and Hepple, he stalked off alone, no doubt thinking to see to the stables.

"Miss Metcalf! Are you all right? I was worried sick in case you were inside as well."

"What's happened? Where's Antonia?" I shouted.

"She's still inside. There's no telling where she is. Nobody can get to her now. If she doesn't make it out on her own, she's done for."

I looked up at the house, then back at him. We were standing far back now; the flames had taken hold on the ground floor and were spreading more and more rapidly.

"Why did you come?" I asked.

He must have heard the bitterness in my voice.

"I'm sorry," he said. "I tried to get here sooner, but the roads were blocked until a few hours ago."

"You handed me back to them," I said. "I trusted you, and you just stood there and let them take me."

"There was nothing I could do then, believe me. That scoundrel Melrose told Sir Anthony everything. Your cousins arrived at his house that evening, guessing you had gone to Morpeth. I pleaded your case, but they wouldn't listen to reason. I've told Melrose he can find another partner. But thank God you're safe."

At that moment there was a crashing sound. Glass came flying out of one of the upper windows and landed tinkling on the gravel of the drive. We all looked up. Antonia was standing at a window on the second floor, her long hair streaming around her shoulders, outlined by fire. She had changed into her wedding dress. In one hand, she held a lighted candle that lit up a face contorted by fear and grief and madness.

"I've beaten you!" she screamed. Her voice was unsteady, distorted by the roaring of the flames. "Beaten you all!"

She started laughing and then as suddenly broke off. For a moment—but perhaps it was only shadows—

for a moment I thought I saw a second figure appear in the window beside her, looking down on us. A young woman in a gray dress. A young woman with long blonde hair. I thought she looked sadly at me. The next instant a rush of fire swept from the interior of the room and engulfed Antonia. The old wedding dress, its frills and lacework, ignited instantly. Like a torch, she turned to flame and was lost from sight.

I turned to Parker.

"My brother," I said. "He was here all the time. He's chained up in the folly."

He stared at me.

"I've just seen him," I said. "Please, you've got to hurry. I don't know what's happening."

"It's all right," he said. "He'll be safe now."

"No, you don't understand. He's not safe. He's in terrible danger."

"But surely there's no one there. . . ."

I think he saw it in my eyes, as though the things I had just seen were imprinted on my pupils. The next moment he turned to the constable and told him to follow him.

"Which way?" he asked.

"I'll come with you."

He shook his head.

"No, you stay here with the sergeant. Does she know?" He pointed at Mrs. Johnson.

"Yes," I said.

They forced her to lead them to the folly, much against her will. I stayed behind with the sergeant, who was slowly recovering his breath, sitting with him on a stone pedestal far back from the house. Hepple remained standing, staring transfixed at the flames. The house burned and burned. There were no other sounds, only those of the flames, the cracking timbers, the explosions of breaking windows. We sat and watched and waited.

A long time later John Parker and the constable returned alone. They were visibly shaken, but neither would say a word about what they had seen. I asked about Arthur, but John would only say that they had found no one. The bed had still been there, and the chain, but Arthur was gone.

"It would be a waste of time to look for him tonight," he said. "I'm sorry, but that's the truth. We'll come back at first light with more men and conduct a proper search. And now I think we should get you back to town."

They went back to Barras Hall the next morning as promised, half a dozen of them, all bound by the strongest of oaths to absolute secrecy. For John had guessed that what they might discover would not be fit for public knowledge, and the others agreed.

They found Arthur, not that day, but some time later, following a suggestion of mine. His body had been left in James Ayrton's tomb. They identified him by parts of his clothing and the lead soldier they found in one of his pockets. I still have it. It is on the desk in front of me even now, as I write. John never told me what had been done to him. But I was not allowed to see the body, and whenever I spoke of it, John would tell me it was better I did not know.

I never saw Antonia or Anthony again. By the time the flames died down, there was no trace left of them. Their remains were never recovered. I was gone by then, taken back to Morpeth by John Parker. By the time he went back to search in James Ayrton's tomb, nothing was left of Barras Hall but blackened walls. I was not sorry, not even for its lost beauty. I had no intention of going back again.

No one ever learned what became of Mrs. Johnson, Hutton, or Hepple. They must all have vanished on the night of the fire, slipping into the darkness, bearing their memories with them. Such memories.

Years later, when all the legalities had finally been completed, I became the heir to Barras Hall and all its lands. John was my husband by then; he married me when I was eighteen, and we lived together happily until his death in 1945. He is the only one to have known any of this before you, Doctor.

I never returned to that place, though I took pains to see it cleansed. I met the Reverend Watkins at last and told him all I knew, and it was he who did what had to be done at Barras Hall. The folly and the graves are still there, the woods have grown wild, it has become a wilderness. You may go there if you wish, but you will find nothing.

I have seen Arthur twice since then. He appeared once on the birth of my first daughter, once on that of my grandson. They are the scions of the Ayrton line, though I have told them nothing of their inheritance. They are happy enough. It is best they do not know.

Sometimes over the years I have caught sight of something out of the corner of my eye, something there and then not there, a shadow possibly, no more. And once or twice I think I have seen James Ayrton. On a street corner or ahead of me on a path or watching from a window. Tricks of the light, perhaps. But I saw him last week. That was not a trick of the light. He was waiting. They are all waiting. Still waiting for me, after all these years.

The Vicarage
Kirkharle
near Kirkwhelpington
Northumberland

10 October 1992

Dr. John Simpkins
St. Botolph's College
Elvet Place
University of Durham
Durham City

Dear John,

Thank you. Well, perhaps not that exactly. I haven't slept for nights, thanks to your Mrs. Parker. Or should I say, Charlotte Metcalf? But you were quite right, it did interest me. Very much indeed.

You must be wondering why I haven't replied until now. Well, I wanted to check a few things. Her story fits in very well with some rumors I've heard from time to time from older parishioners. Most of that generation have gone now, of course, but in my first days in the parish I met quite a few of them. And buried them before long.

I managed to dig up some papers belonging to the Reverend Watkins—the one young Charlotte tried to write to and later met. He ended up a prebendary at Durham Cathedral and died in 1942 at the age of eighty. The cathedral archives still have his letters and things, and they let me hunt through them a few weeks ago. I didn't visit you while I was there, I knew you'd only want to talk if I did, and I preferred to go through some of this stuff first.

There's one letter in particular which would interest you. I don't think it should have been in the file where I found it—it seems to have got in by accident. He wrote it to the bishop back in 1905. I've made a note of the important parts. This is a sample:

My Lord Bishop,

I remain for the time being in Kirkwhelping-ton, where Michael Collins has received me most hospitably. He is most assiduous to his duties, and the parish is flourishing in his care. We talked with great seriousness on my first evening, after which we spent above two hours in the church, asking divine assistance for the task ahead of us. Mrs.

Parker had been most specific in her communications, and my own experiences with the child Caroline Ayrton had prepared me somewhat. Nevertheless I will not conceal my apprehension during that night or the following morning.

Collins and I set off early for Barras Hall. The house is no longer standing, as you know, and in the three years since the fire the grounds have been much overgrown. We had some difficulty finding our way to the old folly, which was our first objective. I had only seen it once before, and this time found it much deteriorated. Weeds have grown on the roof, part of which has fallen in. There is thick moss on the walls, outside and inside. And yet it was not only standing, but unchanged in that other sense of which you and I have spoken.

I noticed it the moment I came in sight of the building: a sense of wickedness so overpowering I could scarcely breathe. My Lord, I am at a loss to say what can have happened in that place to have left such a foul impression. Collins felt it, too.

We performed the ceremony as instructed. I will tell you more of it when we are face-to-face. There are certain things it would not be proper to commit to writing. I feel greatly shaken in spirit and in need of your counsel. I need you for my friend as much as for my bishop.

The graves we consecrated, but I am not easy in my mind about them. Mr. Parker tells me that they found the bones of several children there, when they dug here two years ago. I think it might be best to consider having the remains moved to properly consecrated ground.

The exorcism of Ayrton's tomb was harder than that of the folly, and I am not confident of success. It may need a further visit, possibly by yourself. But even then . . . My Lord, I am no longer certain that the power of the church is unconquerable. Even speaking in His name, I felt vulnerable. There is a darkness there that not even the light of the Gospel may dispel. I know this verges on heresy, and I am troubled by it; but if you had seen what I have seen . . .

Collins is in bed. He has a fever and is badly depressed. I am afraid for him, and heartily sorry for ever taking him to that place. I cannot leave for the present, but once he is on the road to recovery, I ask your permission to return to Durham. We must talk. I hear things at night. I hear voices, my lord. I pray God they do not follow me when I leave here.

I think that's enough, John, don't you? I was able to get hold of the diocesan records about the Reverend Michael Collins. He was aged thirty-four when Watkins wrote that letter. It seems he stayed on at Kirkwhelpington for a few years longer, then left the church and went into teaching. There's a note in his file that says he committed suicide when he was thirty-nine. He was found—believe me, John, I'm not making any of this up—at the gate to Barras Hall. He'd blown his brains out with a shotgun.

John, I visited the graveyard myself yesterday. It's badly overgrown, but it fit Charlotte Metcalf's description. The mounds she wrote about are all still there, and I have a feeling no one ever did get around to moving the bones that had been buried in them. Ayrton's tomb is still standing. It still has the hole in the side: I stayed well clear.

I have something to tell you when we meet. About the sounds I heard near the folly. It was only for a moment, I could have been mistaken. But I will swear before my God that I heard something. I think it was children's voices. They were singing. I could not make out the words.

John, there's something you should know. Your woman had a grandson: she mentions him at the end of her account. A boy called Roger. He was born in 1936, so he's—what?—fifty-six now. Anyhow, it turns out that Roger Parker inherited the Ayrton estate when his mother died, a couple of years ago. Roger is a builder, quite a big name around Newcastle. Maybe you've seen his lorries with *Parker Construction* on the side.

It seems that Roger thinks the Barras Hall estate will make an ideal building site. He wants to raze what's left of the old hall and put up a replica. The plan is to turn it into a country-house hotel. He'll have golf and shooting and fishing in the grounds. Little chalets somewhere. I saw him a few days ago. He showed me the drawings he's had made. The folly is going to be a "feature." Even the old graveyard. He's thinking of having the old Ayrton family motto carved over the gates: *They shall inherit it forever.* I tried to tell him what I knew, but he only laughed at me. I'd like you to come down and have a word with him. To make him understand the real nature of what he has inherited. But I don't think he will listen.

I'll see you in a few days, John. In the meantime please do something for me. Keep your bed-room door locked at night. Tightly.

> Yours,
> Norman

Jonathan Aycliffe is a pseudonym for Daniel Easterman, the bestselling author of BROTHERHOOD OF THE TOMB, THE NINTH BUDDHA, and NIGHT OF THE SEVENTH DARKNESS. He was born in Ireland in 1949 and studied English, Persian, and Arabic at the universities of Dublin, Edinburgh, and Cambridge. For several years he was a professor at Newcastle University. He currently lives in England with his wife.

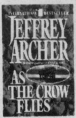

OUTER BANKS
Anne Rivers Siddons

Four sorority sisters bound by friendship spent two idyllic spring breaks at Nag's Head, North Carolina. Now, thirty years later, they are coming back to recapture the magic of those early years and confront the betrayal that shaped four young girls into women and set them all adrift on the Outer Banks.

"A wonderful saga." — *Cosmopolitan*

MAGIC HOUR
Susan Isaacs

A witty mixture of murder, satire, and romance set in the fashionable Hamptons, Long Island's beach resort of choice. Movie producer Sy Spencer has been shot dead beside his pool. Topping the list of suspects is Sy's ex-wife, Bonnie. But it isn't before long that Detective Steve Brady is ignoring all the rules and evidence to save her.

"Vintage Susan Isaacs."
— *The New York Times Book Review*

ANY WOMAN'S BLUES
Erica Jong

Leila Sand's life has left her feeling betrayed and empty. Her efforts to change result in a sensual and spiritual odyssey that takes her from Alcoholics Anonymous meetings to glittering parties to a liaison with a millionaire antiques merchant. Along the way, she learns the rules of love and the secret of happiness.

"A very timely and important book...Jong's greatest heroine." — *Elle*